Stuart Kaminsky

RETRIBUTION

A Lew Fonesca Novel

A TOM DOHERTY ASSOCIATES BOOK
NEW YORK

RETRIBUTION: A LEW FONESCA NOVEL

Copyright © 2001 by Double Tiger Productions, Inc.

All rights reserved, including the right to reproduce this book, or portions thereof, in any form.

A Forge Book
Published by Tom Doherty Associates, LLC
175 Fifth Avenue
New York, NY 10010

www.tor.com

Forge® is a registered trademark of Tom Doherty Associates, LLC.

ISBN: 0-812-54036-0
Library of Congress Catalog Card Number: 2001040483

First edition: December 2001
First mass market edition: December 2002

Printed in the United States of America

0 9 8 7 6 5 4 3 2 1

To Enid,
who fills my days with life
and touches my nights with her smile

With thanks to Stephen King
for suggesting that I tackle
this story idea

BY STUART M. KAMINSKY

Lew Fonesca Mysteries
Vengeance*
Retribution*

Abe Lieberman Mysteries
Lieberman's Folly
Lieberman's Choice
Lieberman's Day
Lieberman's Thief
Lieberman's Law*
The Big Silence*
Not Quite Kosher*†

Toby Peters Mysteries
Bullet for a Star
Murder on the Yellow Brick
   Road
You Bet Your Life
The Howard Hughes Affair
Never Cross a Vampire
High Midnight
Catch a Falling Clown
He Done Her Wrong
The Fala Factor
Down for the Count
The Man Who Shot Lewis
   Vance
Smart Moves
Think Fast, Mr. Peters
Buried Caesars
Poor Butterfly
The Melting Clock
The Devil Met a Lady
Tomorrow Is Another Day
Dancing in the Dark
A Fatal Glass of Beer

Porfiry Rostnikov Novels
Death of a Dissident
Black Knight in Red
   Square
Red Chameleon
A Cold, Red Sunrise
A Fine Red Rain
Rostnikov's Vacation
The Man Who Walked
   Like a Bear
Death of a Russian Priest
Hard Currency
Blood and Rubles
Tarnished Icons
The Dog Who Bit a
   Policeman

Nonseries Novels
When the Dark Man Calls
Exercise in Terror

Biographies
Don Siegel: Director
Clint Eastwood
John Huston, Maker of
   Magic
Coop: The Life and Legend
   of Gary Cooper

Other Nonfiction
American Film Genres
American Television Genres
   (with Jeffrey Mahan)
Basic Filmmaking
   (with Dana Hodgdon)
Writing for Television
   (with Mark Walker)

*denotes a Forge book
† forthcoming

Terror in the house does roar,
But Pity stands before the door.

—William Blake,
"Morning"

PROLOGUE

IN ABOUT FIFTY THOUSAND years, give or take a few centuries, the state of Florida will be gone. The Gulf of Mexico and the Atlantic Ocean will cover the peninsula that rests just above sea level. Geologists tell us it has happened before and they know about when it will happen again.

This information does not keep the tourists, retirees, winter residents from the North who Floridians call snowbirds, and the less than savory drifters and always hopeful dreamers from adding each year to the population. They are attracted by the weather, beaches, opportunities for theft and mayhem, or the hope of a last frontier or a final resting place.

The west coast of Florida faces the Gulf of Mexico. On the white sand shore a little over fifty miles south of Tampa lies Sarasota.

Money magazine ranks the city as one of the fifteen most livable communities in the United States. *Southern Living* magazine recently named Sarasota County "the nation's per capita arts capital." The wealthy residents sponsor and support five live equity theaters, world-class museums, an opera company and opera house, a ballet company, a performing arts center, a circus tradition, and lots of film festivals.

One can spend a day, a week, or a lifetime avoiding the mean streets, the dark corners, and the violence that occurs daily, at least until they become a victim or witness it on television.

Sarasota is a beautiful bright orange blanket over a layer of darkness. Most people who come here don't look under the blanket.

And then the newspaper or television news on Channel 40 lifts it to safely reveal a woman murdered in front of her infant triplets, a cabdriver staggering into the lazy Sarasota-Bradenton Airport bleeding from two bullet wounds in the chest, the rape and murder of a woman in her bed in a safe and expensive condominium community.

For every high-rise there is a trailer park.

For every theater there are six crack houses.

For every festival there are a dozen bank robberies.

For every millionaire there are a hundred desperate souls who would kill for twenty dollars.

For every new upscale mall there's a Circle K waiting to be robbed. The night clerk working is often a single mother with a child or two, her eyes questioning each customer who enters after dark.

And for me, two men had died in the past two days and a woman had died twenty-two years before them.

Nothing really held their deaths particularly together but me. The first death hadn't even made it to television. Each of the other two turned out to be big stories for almost a week until a teenage girl and her boyfriend murdered the girl's mother. That was news because the dead woman and the girl were white and the boyfriend black.

Our murders are frequent, black, white, and red, colorful, the stuff our natural, morbid curiosity draws us to, and then we move away to work, eat, watch television, or go out to the movies.

I want nothing but to be left alone. I don't want corpses, problems, weeping women, doomed children. I don't want them but they make their way to me. I had come to Florida, to Sarasota, to escape from memories of the dead.

I had fled from such visions, from the helpless who asked for help, from the dead who needed no help, and from those who were haunted by ghosts who were as real to them as my ghosts are to me.

The world intrudes on my seclusion because I need to eat, to have some place to live, and to keep my clothes reasonably clean. I work as little as I can and live in isolation as much as I can.

The Cincinnati Reds have spring training here and we have a minor league team, the SaraSox. I've never gone to a game, the opera, the ballet, or one of the five live theaters.

I take my pleasures in small guilty doses.

Until the very end, I took no pleasure in what I had just been through.

It had begun with pain and ended with promise. I'll tell you about it.

1

THE LEFT SIDE OF my face hurt.

A woman named Roberta Dreemer, affectionately known to her few friends and many enemies as Bubbles, had filled the doorway of her rusting trailer in the mobile home park just across from the Pines Nursing Home seconds after I knocked. Bubbles Dreemer was a very big woman.

She had been easy to find. She had a phone and it was listed in the Sarasota phone directory. It seemed like a quick, easy job for Richard Tycinker, attorney-at-law in the firm of Tycinker, Oliver and Schwartz with offices on Palm Avenue who needed Big Bubbles's testimony in an assault case.

I handed Bubbles the folded sheet. She looked at it for a beat and hit me. Then she slammed her door.

It was a Thursday. Still morning. I was sitting by myself in a booth at the back of the Crisp Dollar Bill, almost directly across from my office/home on Washington Street, better known as 301. I was doing my best to forget Bubbles Dreemer. I'm not good at forgetting. That is one reason I see Ann Horowitz, the shrink treating me for depression.

I had bicycled to the trailer park and back to save the cost of a car rental. From where I lived and worked I could bike or walk to almost anything I needed or wanted in Sarasota. Before I went into the Crisp Dollar Bill I had stopped at the Main Street Book Store, the largest remaindered bookstore in Florida, gone up to the third floor, and bought a two-videotape 1940 serial of *The Shadow* starring Victor Jory. It took six dollars of my fifty. I was using some of what was left on a beer and a Philly steak sandwich that, thanks to Bubbles, was a little painful to eat.

My name is Lew Fonesca. When people look at me, they see a five-foot-seven, thin, balding man, a little over forty years old with a distinctly Italian, distinctly sad face. That's what I see when I look in the mirror, which I do my best to avoid.

I came to Florida five years ago from Chicago after my wife died in a hit-and-run accident on Lake Shore Drive. I was headed for Key West. My wife, whose name I've spoken only twice since she died, was a lawyer. I was an investigator in the office of the state's attorney of Cook County. My specialty was finding people. I'm not a cop. I'm not a lawyer. I'm not a private investigator. I'm not even an accountant.

My car had died in the parking lot of the Dairy Queen that I could see from the booth in which I was sitting at the Crisp Dollar Bill if I leaned to my right and looked through the amber window. Thirty feet from where my car died, there had been a "FOR LET" sign on the run-down two-floor office building at the back of the DQ parking lot. I had rented a small two-room office on the second floor, converted the small reception room into an underfurnished office and the equally small office behind it into the place I slept, read, watched television and videotapes, and thought about the past.

My goal in life was simple. To be left alone. To make enough to keep me in breakfast, burgers, videotapes, an occasional movie, and payments to my shrink.

Almost all my meals were eaten within a few hundred yards of where I lived, worked, and watched old movies on tape. There was Gwen's Diner at the junction of 41 and 301 where a big photograph of young Elvis in white smiled out in black and white with a proud sign under it that said, "Elvis Presley ate here in 1959." There was the DQ owned by a sun-weathered man named Dave who spent most of his time alone in his small boat in the Gulf of Mexico. And there was the Crisp Dollar Bill where the bartender and owner Billy Hopsman played an endless series of tapes and CDs he loved that seemed to have nothing in common. There was Mel Torme, Verdi operas, the Pointer Sisters, Linda Ronstadt, Ruben Blades, B. B. King, Blue Grass, Dinah Washington, Sinatra, and odd German stuff that sounded like Kurt Weill gone into a depression not far from my own. You never knew who you might hear from the Bose speakers when you entered the Crisp Dollar Bill. Right now it was Joe Williams singing "Don't Be Mad at Me." Billy had been a hippie, a cabdriver, and for a brief time a minor league catcher with a very minor league Detroit Tigers farm team. Best of all, Billy was not a talker. He wasn't much of a listener either except for his large collection of tapes.

The door of the Crisp Dollar Bill opened and in walked Marvin Uliaks. Actually, you couldn't call Marvin's mode of transportation "walking." It was much closer to a shuffle. In this case, a nervous shuffle.

Marvin had brought an unwelcome blast of sun behind him reminding me that there were hours to go before I could call it a day.

"Close the door," Billy said automatically without looking up from the copy of the Sarasota *Herald-Tribune* laid out on the bar in front of him.

Marvin shifted the weight of the oversized book under his arm, pulled himself together, and closed the door. Then he squinted, blinked, and tried to adjust his eyes to the amber darkness.

Marvin's nose was pushed to one side as if his face were permanently pressed against a store window. His large popping eyes made him look amazed at even the most inconsequential contact with other human beings. Marvin was short, had an unkempt mess of brown hair beginning to show gray at the temples, and was so thin that you wondered how well he could stand up against an evening breeze off the Gulf. I imagined Marvin in a hurricane, arms out, hair blowing as he went spinning in the air, a startled look on his face as he passed the same cow Dorothy had seen on her way to Oz.

Marvin had the kind of face that made people say, "He'll never win a beauty contest." As I was soon to discover, people were once again wrong. The great "they," the ones we mean when we say "they say," were often wrong but completely protected by being someone other than you and me.

Marvin's eyes adjusted quickly and he headed straight for my booth. He dropped the huge book in front of me and sat facing me across the table. The pockets of his well-weathered denim jacket were as bulged out as his eyes. He folded his hands in front of him on the table and looked at me.

"Look at it," Marvin said.

He was harmless and quiet, two levels below minimally bright. I pushed my *Shadow* videos aside and opened what was clearly an album of photographs and newspaper clippings. The first item was a newspaper clipping that said Marvin Uliaks, age three, had won the annual cutest child contest at the county fair in Ocala in 1957. The article, wiltingly Scotch-taped in the album like every other item, had a photograph of a smiling blond kid with curly hair wearing a sailor suit. The kid was pointing at the camera and beaming. Flanking the little boy were a thin, sober-looking man with a baby in his arms and a pretty brunette who was holding Marvin's free hand. The woman wore a little hat and held her free hand up to shield out the sun. The man and woman were identified as the proud parents of Marvin.

"That's me all right," Marvin said, tapping a finger on the newspaper clipping. "My mother, my father, and my baby sister.

"My sister, Vera Lynn. She was named for a singer."

" 'Till We Meet Again.' " I said.

"Don't know where, don't know when," Marvin sang.

Vera Lynn, the British singer during World War II, was a
favorite of my father's who made it through the war with
all his organs and body parts except his right eye.

"Look at the next one," Marvin said with excitement.

In the photograph, Marvin's father was holding the little
blond boy upside down by the ankles. The father had a
little smile. The boy was grinning.

"Turn the album upside down," Marvin said, turning the
album. "See, now I look right side up and my father looks
upside down."

"You're right," I said, turning the album around again.
"Marvin, what . . . ?"

"Keep looking, Mr. Fonseca. Keep looking," he urged,
turning the page.

"Fonesca," I corrected.

"Yeah, oh, sorry. My name's Uliaks."

"I know," I said, looking at several pages of photographs
that meant nothing to me.

"I went to your office," Marvin said. "You weren't there.
I went to Gwen's. You weren't there either. I went . . ."

"You found me," I said.

"Yes," he said, shaking his head once with pride.

"Why?" I reached for my beer.

"I want you to find Vera Lynn."

"You want me to find your sister," I said, putting the
beer down. "I'm a process server. I find people to give them
orders to appear at court or in a lawyer's office for a deposition, or to produce documents. I'm not a private investigator."

"You find people," Marvin said. "I heard. Old guy at
Gwen's told me."

"A few times," I said. "A few times I found some people."

"There, there she is," he said, tapping on a photograph
on the page I had just turned to. He was tapping on the
color photograph of a very pretty and very well sculptured
blonde in a blue dress. The girl was smiling. Her teeth
looked white and perfect. I guessed she was no more than
eighteen. Another girl about the same age stood next to the

blonde. She was pretty, thin, wearing a red dress and no smile.

"Who's the other one?"

Marvin craned his neck awkwardly to get a better view at the photograph with a look of amazement as if he were seeing it for the first time.

"Sarah," he said. "She's been dead a long time. I need to find Vera Lynn."

He was looking at me and rocking back and forth.

"When was the last time you saw Vera Lynn?" I asked.

He bit his lower lip considering the question.

"Twenty, twenty-five years maybe. I got a letter."

He reached over and turned the album pages quickly past yellowed notes, withering photographs, cracking postcards, matchbooks, and some candy wrappers.

"Here," he said, triumphantly slapping the page he was looking for with the palm of his hand.

I was looking down at an envelope.

I had come to the Crisp Dollar Bill to have a sandwich, a beer, and to feel sorry for myself, not for Marvin Uliaks. I removed the letter from the envelope.

Marvin fidgeted around and leaned forward getting nearly on top of me.

"Letter's from Vera Lynn," he said, pointing to the neatly scripted name in the corner of the envelope I had laid aside. "She's not in Ocala no more. She's not in Dayton no more. I called, asked. Long time ago. I looked for her couple of times. Took the bus or a car out of Ocala after the wedding."

I was tempted to ask Marvin about Dayton and whatever wedding he was talking about. I didn't. Instead, I said, "This letter's almost twenty-five years old."

"I know. I know. I just want you to find her. Tell me where she is, is all."

"Why?"

"Family business," he whispered as he rocked. "Important family business. All I can say about it. Family business is all I can say."

"Why now after all this time?" I asked.

"Somethin's come up. Family business. I don't want to

talk about it. Please just find Vera Lynn. Let me talk to her, like just a minute. Converse."

"Fresh beer?" Billy called from the bar.

"No, thanks," I said.

"On me, Mr. Fonesca," Marvin said. "On me."

"You want privacy, Mr. F.," Billy said from behind the bar. "I've got a job out back Marvin can do, cleaning out the cabinets."

Marvin shook his head "no."

"No, thanks," I told Billy. "Marvin and I are old friends."

Actually, I had known Marvin for a couple of years, but we weren't friends. He did odd jobs in the three-block stretch of stores on 301 from Main Street to the Tamiami intersection, basically my neighborhood. Marvin washed windows, ran errands, swept up in exchange for food from the restaurants, an old pair of shoes or pants from a shoe or clothing store, a dollar from other businesses, and a place to sleep behind the sagging Angela's Tarot and Palm Reading shop down the street from where I worked and lived.

I was now engaged in the longest conversation I had ever had with my friend Marvin.

"I got a confession, Mr. Fonesca. I got drunk. Just a little. To get up the nerve to come find you. Then I was ashamed of being drunk so I sobered. So now my head is hurting fierce."

I gulped the last of my beer, patted Marvin on the shoulder, slid out of the booth, and got up.

"She's gone, Marvin," I said. "Get some sleep."

"I've got money," he said, digging into the pockets of his old denim jacket. Crumpled singles, fives, and tens appeared in his gnarled fists. He dropped them on top of the open album and kept digging into his pockets.

"See, I can pay."

Like a kid doing magic tricks Marvin continued to produce bills from his pants pockets, shirt pocket, the cuffs of his socks.

Lincoln and Washington looked up at me from the top of the heap of bills.

"We got a discrepancy there?" Billy called.

Marvin was hyperventilating now, his large eyes fixed

on my face waiting for the answer to all his prayers.

"Almost all my life's savings," he said, his face pressing against an imaginary window of expected failure. "Just about all I've got. I'm not asking for favors here. Oh, no. I'm hiring you just like any other Joe. You too busy now? Okay, but I'm a . . . a . . ."

Marvin wasn't sure of what he was and I wasn't going to tell him.

"Billy," I called. "You have a paper bag?"

Billy looked over at the pile of bills.

"For that?"

"Yes."

"Paper or plastic?"

"Paper," I said.

Billy pulled a paper bag from under the bar, came around, and handed it to me. I shoved Marvin's money into it and handed Marvin the bag. He pushed it back at me.

"I'm saying 'please,' " Marvin said. He looked as if he were going to cry.

"Twenty dollars a day," I said with a sigh. "If I don't find Vera Lynn in five days, I give it up and you promise to give it up. Deal?"

Marvin went stone still.

"Give me forty in advance for two days," I said. "Most it can cost you is a hundred. I'll need the album and the letter."

He nodded and smiled.

"That's business," he said, holding out his hand. We shook and he dipped into the paper bag to pull out four tens. He handed them to me. "All's you got to do is find her, tell me where she is. I'll do the rest. It's important."

"I'm closing up for an early lunch, Mr. F.," called Billy, closing the newspaper. "Meeting some people at Longhorn. Place's like a morgue this morning anyway."

I assumed both Marvin and I were prime contributors to the funereal atmosphere.

I closed the album, tucked it under my arm, went to the bar, and handed Billy one of the four tens Marvin had put in my hand. Billy nodded and Marvin followed me into the street.

Traffic was moving slowly, but there was a lot of it. I wanted to cross the street, go to my room, and watch *The Shadow*, but I knew I'd be looking at Marvin Uliaks's album.

"Anything else you can tell me about her?" I asked.

"All in the book," he said, tapping the album. "All the answers I got. Like the Bible. Got the answers. You just have to figure out what they mean. I never could, not in the album, not in the Bible, not in any book pretty much even when I was a kid. But you know how to find me. Right now I'm going to Lupe's Resale to do some work unless you want me to come with you."

"Go to Lupe's," I said. "I'll find you if I need you."

He stood on the sidewalk while I waited for a break in traffic and jogged across the street, past the DQ, through the parking lot, and up the stairs to my office. When I turned around, Marvin was standing where I had left him looking up at me. I motioned for him to go to Lupe's. I pointed in the right direction. He shook his head in understanding and walked to his right while I entered my office.

Home. The day was cool. A little over seventy degrees. Typical winter in Sarasota. I didn't need the air-conditioning, which was good because I don't have any. The ancient air conditioner that came with the office had given out. Ames McKinney had kept it alive for more than a year. We had buried the window unit in the Dumpster at the DQ with Dave's permission.

I opened the windows, pulled the chains on the venetian blinds, flipped on the fluorescent light, and listened to it crackle as I sat down at my desk with Marvin's album in front of me.

There wasn't much in the office to distract me. There was a single chair across the desk. A wastepaper basket with a Tampa Bucs logo under the desk and facing me on the wall was a poster, the only decoration in the room, an original *Mildred Pierce*. Joan Crawford looked across at me feeling my pain and Mildred's. Tomorrow was Friday. I'd watch my tape of the movie tomorrow night in the next room where I had my cot, television, and VCR. Tonight I was watching *The Shadow*.

The beer and Marvin's appearance had taken a little of the sting from my cheek. Not enough, just a little.

Except for a possible call from a lawyer with papers to serve and dinner that night with Sally Porovsky and her kids at the Bangkok, Marvin Uliaks's album was the only obligation on my schedule for the week. It was more than I would have wanted, except for Sally and the Bangkok, but I had taken the forty from Marvin. I touched the cover of the album and glanced at my answering machine.

I got the answering machine from a pawnshop on Main Street. It was so old it would probably be worth taking to the Antiques Road Show in another few years. But it worked. I didn't want to talk to people, not to old friends and acquaintances in Chicago, not to my own relatives, certainly not to the Friends of the Firefighters or someone claiming they could save me money on my phone bills. So, I never answered my phone, even when I was in my office or my room. If I was there and I was willing to talk to the person who started to leave a message, I would pick up. My answering machine message to callers was eloquent in its simplicity: "Lew Fonesca. Leave a message."

I put a tentative finger on my cheek where Bubbles had slapped me. My cheek didn't appreciate the touch. There were two messages on the machine.

Message one: "This is Richard Tycinker's assistant Janine. Mr. Tycinker has an order for appearance at a deposition for you to serve, maybe two if I get the paperwork and court date set this afternoon."

Message two: "Lew? Flo here. Give me a call. Adele's . . . It's about Adele."

Tycinker could wait. I didn't like the way Flo sounded.

I had known Flo Zink for about three years. She was loud, vulgar, sixty-eight years old, in love with country and western music, and very rich. Flo lived in a big house on the coast with a great view of Sarasota Bay. When her husband Gus had died two years earlier, Flo, who had developed a friendship with gin decades earlier, made it a love affair. Adele Hanford was an orphan who had been through more hell in her sixteen years of life than most families would experience in five generations.

Adele had run away from her mother to join her father in Sarasota. Her father had not only sexually abused her but turned her over to a cheap pimp on the North Trail who had in turn sold her to a middle-time slug named John Pirannes. Adele was an orphan because her father had murdered her mother who had tried to protect Adele. Adele had shot Pirannes and her father was killed by . . . but that story's over. With the help of family therapist and friend Sally Porovsky, I had managed to have Adele taken in by Flo as a foster child. Adele had gone straight. Adele was doing well at Sarasota High School, even won a few prizes for poetry and stories, one of which was published in *Sarasota City Tempo* magazine. Adele's story was about an abused girl who runs away from her family and finds salvation and respect as a waitress. I liked the story. I didn't like the message from Flo. Flo had given up her love affair with alcohol for the chance to take in Adele. I didn't know with certainty how tempting the memory of the comfort of gin might be and Flo's voice was a toss-up between tipsy and distraught. Adele wasn't easy. Before I called Flo, I opened Marvin Uliaks's album.

Marvin's album contained eighty photographs and a few postcards and newspaper clippings. Under each photograph Marvin had neatly printed in pencil the name of the person or persons or things in the photographs. No dates. I went through photographs of parents, aunts, uncles, people I supposed were friends, pictures of people clipped from magazines and newspapers including Mario Van Peebles, Al Unser, Bette Midler, Lionel Hampton, the Marlboro Man, Lainie Kazan, Bruce Cabot, and Douglas MacArthur. There were a few dozen of Marvin as he aged from golden childhood to gradual nearly blank homeliness. In each photograph, Marvin was smiling or grinning. He looked better smiling. There were also six photographs of Vera Lynn. In the most recent one she looked about eighteen, a pretty girl in a white Sunday dress with a big white bow in her short blond hair. Marvin's little sister would be in her mid-forties now.

I read the one letter in the album, the one Marvin had shown me. It didn't help much. It was postmarked Dayton,

Ohio. It was in pencil, short, written simply in block letters for a slow-witted brother or by a slow-minded sister.

DEAR MARVIN,
CHARLES AND I ARE MARRIED. WE ARE GO-
ING TO MOVE. FORGIVE ME. I'LL WRITE
AGAIN.

YOUR SISTER,
VERA LYNN

Vera Lynn's printing was clear. Finding her might be easy or impossible. If I ran into emptiness, I could simply give Marvin his album back. I wouldn't insult him by trying to return the forty dollars.

I decided to call Richard Tycinker's office first. I got his secretary Janine who told me the papers were ready for me to pick up for delivery.

"Bubbles Dreemer slapped me in the face when I slapped her with the papers," I said.

"Part of the job, Lewis," she said.

Janine was black, in her late thirties, raising two kids alone and managing to look like a model. Sympathy was not part of her job description.

"I was telling you so you could make a note in her file for the next person who served her papers," I explained.

"If it happens," she said, "it will probably be you."

"I'll deliver it in a hockey mask," I said.

"Summons delivered by Michael Myers," said Janine.

"Might stun her long enough for me to get away."

"Might," she agreed. "It would work on me."

"Is Harvey in?" I asked.

Harvey was the official file coordinator for the firm of Tycinker, Oliver and Schwartz. His real job was unofficial computer hacker. Schwartz had offered me a retainer. I had turned down the retainer and agreed to a flat fee for each legal paper I delivered to the unwilling and often unsuspecting. Instead of the retainer, I got the use of Harvey's talents when I needed them. Harvey had once been a successful businessman in love with alcohol, computers, and a series of three wives, all of whom eventually left him alone with his computers and the bottle. Lately he had cut out the alcohol and was spending more time on the computer, Diet Pepsi, and women. There was enough unravaged in the forty-nine-year-old Harvey to attract some very attractive women.

Harvey had a very well equipped room down a corridor near the washrooms where the lawyers and secretaries could drop by and check on whether Harvey was drinking Diet Pepsi or something stronger.

Some of what Harvey did bordered on the illegal. The firm knew it, counted on it and the signed document by Harvey that he would never engage in any illegal activity on the Internet.

Janine connected me with Harvey, who answered, "Yes?"

"It's Lew," I said. "Got your pen?"

"Always."

"Vera Lynn Uliaks. Born, I think, in Ocala. Lived there till about 1970, somewhere in there. Moved to Dayton, Ohio, maybe. Probably got married there. Don't know to who, someone named Charlie. Brother here in town, Marvin Uliaks."

"That's it?"

"That's it," I said.

"Are we in a hurry? I've got a few company projects."

"No big hurry," I said.

"Should have it for you by tomorrow," said Harvey. "You want to call me?"

"Yeah," I said.

"Having a bad day, Lew?" he asked.

"They're all bad days," I said.

"I've been there," Harvey answered. "Back to work."

He hung up. So did I.

Flo Zink was next on my short list. The phone rang once. Actually, it was only half a ring when she picked it up.

"Lew?" she asked.

There was a lot in that question. Panic with a dash of fear and maybe, just maybe, a shot of Jack Daniel's.

"How are you, Flo?"

"How am I? How am I? How the fuck do I sound?"

"Charming," I said.

"How fast can you get here?" she asked.

"On my bike? Half an hour."

"Rent a car. I'll pay."

"Flo, what . . . ?"

"Adele's gone. I'm not going to spill my soul on this goddamn telephone. Get here."

She hung up. I checked my watch. I had an appointment with Ann Horowitz in two hours. I don't have a shower. I don't have a sink or a toilet. I usually shower after my morning workout at the YMCA downtown, which is a ten-minute walk from my place. But there is a building restroom outside my office and four doors down. It is not on the top ten list of facilities in Sarasota County, but it had a mirror and I had an electric razor, the same one my father had used for ten years before he died and my mother gave it to me in a box of his things. It worked well enough to get me through the day.

The thin guy in the mirror looked at me and shook his head as we shaved. I normally didn't take a good or even passing look at the man in the mirror. His cheek was Bubbles Dreemer pink. I didn't like meeting his sad spaniel look. I washed, brushed my teeth, combed back my remaining hair, and felt no more ready to meet the world than I had when I got up that morning.

The EZ Economy Car Rental Agency was six doors down on my side of 301. It had once been a Texaco gas station. The two guys who owned and ran the place were Alan and the older Fred. They looked like rotund cousins. They thought they had a sense of humor.

"Ah, Mr. Lewis Fonesca. How can we be of service to you today?" asked the older, pink-cheeked Fred.

Fred had a paper cup of coffee in his hand. Alan was nowhere in sight.

"Where's Alan?" I asked.

"Home. Got Le Grippe, the flu, the bug."

"Sorry."

"Hey, he's home losing weight, watching Judge Judy, drinking green tea, and chewing on Advil. He should be happy. How can I make you happy?"

"What've you got?"

"Personality," said Fred who stood up from his desk and saluted me with his coffee. He was wearing navy slacks and a short-sleeved pullover with "EZ Economy" embossed in white on the single pocket. "And coffee. It's bad but it's strong. Put three packets of Equal in it and it's tolerable."

"Tempting," I said, "but I'm thinking more of a deal on something small and cheap."

Fred took a sip of coffee and nodded to indicate he knew just what I wanted. I knew he did. He just wanted to bicker for a while.

"Got a '99 GEO, tracker, runs smooth, fifteen thousand plus miles. How long you need it?"

"I don't know. A day, maybe two."

"One hundred a day, everything covered including insurance. Is that a bargain or is that a bargain?"

"That's a bargain," I agreed. "Give me a better one."

Fred shrugged and drank some coffee. He looked deeply into the cup, maybe reading the grounds and my future.

"How cheap we going here? You got a homeless client or something?"

"Something," I agreed.

"The '88 Cutlass, the white one with ninety-four thousand miles. Looks good. Runs. I'll sell it to you for five hundred."

"I'll rent it for twenty-five a day," I said.

"You're no fun today, Fonesca," he said, going to the wall and taking a set of keys off one of the little hooks.

"I didn't know I was fun any day," I said as he looked at me and tossed the keys.

He was about to come back with something Fred clever but the telephone was ringing.

"Car's where it always is. I think it has some gas. I'll keep a tab. Quick question."

The phone kept ringing.

"Okay."

"Who gave you that cheek?"

"Woman named Roberta Dreemer," I said.

"Bubbles," said Fred. "She's living hell."

"I've got the mark of the devil," I said, thinking it was true in more ways than one.

Fred picked up the phone and waved good-bye to me.

"Glaucoma?" he said to whoever was on the other end of the phone.

I didn't stay to hear the rest. I headed for the white Cutlass.

2

IT WASN'T FAR to Flo's place. I took Fruitville to the Trail, then down to Siesta Drive, made a right, crossed Osprey, and then took a left into Flo Zink's driveway just before the bridge to Siesta Key. I would have preferred to keep going to the beach and just sit on a bench watching the gulls and pelicans.

There was a small black Toyota in the circular driveway. The white minivan wasn't there. Flo had lost her license twice in Florida for DUI violations. She hadn't hurt anyone, but that wasn't the point and she knew it. Flo had her license back but seldom drove even when ice-clear sober and when she did drive it was the white minivan.

The door was opened before I had a chance to knock.

Flo stood there, denim skirt, blue and red checkerboard shirt, and a glass in her hand. Her hair was white, cut short, and looking frizzy. Flo reminded me of Thelma Ritter, even looked a little like the actress. I told her that once. Her answer had been, "Gus always said I looked like Greer Garson."

Behind Flo I could hear her stereo blasting from the

speakers throughout the house. All she played was country and western music, most of it from decades ago. She liked Roy Acuff, Roy Rogers, and The Sons of the Pioneers. Patsy Cline was, however, her favorite and it was Patsy in the background wailing, "If you loved me half as much as I love you . . ."

"Let's get it out of the way before you come in," she said. "I've been drinking. I plan to stop again when you find Adele and bring her home."

"Can I come in?"

She stepped back and lifted her arm. I stepped in.

Patsy sang, ". . . you wouldn't do half the things you do."

"Can we turn the music down?"

"Why not?" Flo said, leading me into the large living room and heading for the stereo against the wall. She turned a knob and Patsy faded into the background.

"Adele worked this out," she said. "Set up this Internet music thing, found a radio station in Fort Worth that plays my music, and figured out how to pipe it through the stereo. Adele is smart."

Flo took a drink and pressed her lips together.

Flo's home, a large sprawling one-story building with no exterior beauty but a great view of Sarasota Bay, was decorated in early Clint Eastwood. The furniture was ranch western and lots of Stickney. There were Navajo rugs on the wood floors and Hopi blankets on the sofas and chairs. Aside from the rugs and blankets, Flo's house was dark wood and simple furniture. On the table in the center of the room between a sofa and two chairs sat a genuine Remington of a cowboy on a rearing horse. A stag head with massive antlers looked down at us from one wall.

I sat in one of the chairs. Flo sat on the sofa, one arm draped over the back, the other holding the drink that she looked at from time to time to be sure it existed.

"You want a drink?" she asked.

"I've already had a beer this morning," I said.

Her eyebrows went up.

"Careful there, sad eyes," she said. "Beer can lead to all sorts of things. Let's get to it. Adele's gone, took the van. She's . . . what happened to your face?"

"Someone hit me," I said with a small smile to suggest that such things happen.

"Why?"

"I served her papers."

"Slap the messenger," she said with an understanding tilt of her head. "You hit her back?"

I didn't answer.

"Give me her name and I'll go kick her ass for you," she said.

"She's big," I said. "And kicking her ass won't make me feel better. Flo, why am I here?"

"To find Adele," she said. "I told you."

"Are you sure she ran away?"

"Drove, been gone three days. Took the van. Left a note. Here."

She reached into the pocket of her flannel shirt, pulled out a sheet of paper, and handed it to me. It was double folded. I opened it and read: "Flo, I don't know if I'm coming back. I'll pay you for the van when I have the money or I'll return it. There's something I've got to do. I'll call. You know I love you." It was signed "Adios, Adele."

"Why?"

"Maybe she couldn't take me acting like a mother. I don't think so. She seemed to like it. Maybe she ran away with Mickey what's-his-name, works at the Burger King right over there on the Trail. She's been seeing him. But I'm betting on Conrad Lonsberg."

"The writer?" I asked.

"Not many other people around here named Conrad Lonsberg, are there?" she said, working on her drink. "Yes, the great Conrad Lonsberg."

She held up her glass to drink to the name. There wasn't much left to drink.

I knew Lonsberg had a place in Sarasota. He was seldom seen and never attended any literary parties or gave talks or went to the Sarasota Reading Festival. Once in a long while his photograph would appear in a big magazine, *People, Vanity Fair*, places like that. But there was never much text.

I had read his classic *Fool's Love* when I was about seventeen. I guess almost everyone had read it. It was now over forty years old and still selling along with his two collections of short stories, mostly reprints from the series he did for *The New Yorker*, and his second novel, *Plugged Nickels*, which had stayed on the *New York Times* bestseller list for one hundred twenty weeks. *Plugged Nickels* came out in 1978. That was the year his wife died. And that was it. I seemed to remember that Lonsberg had moved from someplace east, I think Connecticut, to Sarasota. He had two children, a son and daughter. He gave no interviews, allowed no photographs of his children. Seemed to have no friends and made it clear he wanted minimal contact with the world. Lonsberg was a Sarasota legend. People reported Lonsberg sightings along with Stephen King, Monica Selles, and Jerry Springer glimpses.

I sympathized, empathized, sometimes envied Lonsberg's decision. I didn't remember *Fool's Love* very well. It was a short novel about a teenage girl from a small town who leaves home and heads across the country to live with her aunt who has a supposedly wild lifestyle. The girl meets all kinds of people on the way and when she finally gets to her aunt finds that the aunt is basically no different from the mother she left behind.

"Lonsberg?" I prompted Flo who was looking up at the stag head.

"Remember when Adele got that story published?" she asked. "First prize, right in *City Tempo*. Her picture in the newspaper."

"I remember," I said.

The story had basically been autobiographical, loose ends tied together by fiction and the names of all the characters changed. I was in the story, sort of. There was a detective hired by the girl's mother to find her. The detective's name was Milo Loomis. He was big, tough, and had a sense of humor. No one would recognize me in Milo, but it wasn't hard to spot her central character, Joan, as Adele. The story was honest. Joan wasn't spared her responsibility for the things that had happened to her.

"Lonsberg read the story," said Flo. "A few days after

the magazine came out, he called, gave me his name, asked if I was Adele's mother. Tell you the truth, I didn't know who the hell Conrad Lonsberg was, but Adele did. She's been great, Lew. These months . . . her grades went up. She pretty much stayed home though she worked on the school paper. She started going with this Mickey kid. Seemed okay. Friendly. Things were going great. Then this Lonsberg calls. I sort of remembered the name, I think. He asked if he could talk to Adele. Adele was shaking when she took the phone. Anyway, Lonsberg told Adele that he had read her story and would like to meet her. She stood there holding the phone waiting for me to give her permission."

"And you did?"

"Adele's picture had been in the paper, remember? She had been interviewed by Channel 40. Adele is one beautiful sixteen-year-old. But then again I seemed to remember Lonsberg was an old guy, older than yours truly Florence Ornstein Zink."

She drank to that too.

"So," she went on, "seemed okay to me and I figured from the look she had that she would probably see him even if I said 'no,' but thanks for asking, I thought.

"They set up a time the next day after school," Flo went on. "He gave his address on Casey Key, north end. I drove her down, a thick folder full of her stories and poems in her lap. You know that big stone wall on the north end of the Casey?"

"Which one?"

"The one out toward the water. White stone walls maybe nine feet high?"

"I think I know the place. That's where Lonsberg lives?"

"That's where," she said, looking at her now-empty glass. "Adele rang a bell. Few minutes later the gate was opened and she went in."

"And you?"

"Wasn't invited," she said, getting up with a sigh. "Sat in the van reading something. I can't remember what. Sat for about an hour. I was thinking of ringing the bell when she came out, all excited. Lonsberg wanted to work with her, wanted her to come every Saturday morning. So, that's what we did. She told me he was a nice old man. I know about nice old men. Old men are still men. So, every Saturday we drove to Casey Key and I sat in the car reading. Son of a bitch never invited me in, never so much as came over to the car and introduced himself. I kept asking Adele if he tried to get in her pants or touch her. She said he didn't. Went on like this for five or six months, then six weeks ago Saturday she came out, got in the car, and said, 'Let's get away from here.' We got away. She was mad as a cougar with an arrow in his ass and she was shaking. Adele's been through a lot we both know about, and she can handle herself. She wasn't handling herself after that visit. She wouldn't talk about it. And she never went back to Lonsberg's place. A couple of days later she started going out with this kid Mickey, the one from Burger King, almost every night. I saw some of the old Adele coming back. Smart-ass talk, schoolwork just barely getting done. She stopped writing and I think she was making it with this Mickey."

"So something happened at Lonsberg's that day and she's run away with Mickey," I summarized as Flo went to the wooden liquor cabinet to pour herself another drink.

"Lonsberg called last week," she said, bottle in hand closing the cabinet door. "Adele talked to him for maybe thirty seconds, mostly she listened and then at the end said 'yes' and slammed down the phone."

Flo brought her bottle to the sofa and poured herself another drink, putting the bottle on the table in front of the Remington horse.

"She tell you what the call was about?"

"Nope," said Flo, taking a drink. "Not a word. Then, like a fast fart from a buffalo, she leaves a note and takes off."

"I'll find her," I said.

"Good," Flo said, toasting.

"Does Sally know?"

Flo shook her head "no."

Sally Porovsky was a social worker with Children's Services of Sarasota. Adele was one of her cases. I was also seeing Sally and her two kids from time to time. In a way, Adele had brought us together.

"I'll let her know," I said.

"She'll call in the cops," said Flo. "They'll find her, put her someplace. They won't let her come back here. I'm one tough old bitch, Fonesca, but I need that girl back here and I think she needs me."

"I'll be careful," I said.

"I'll write you a check," she said, putting down her glass and starting to rise.

"No," I said.

She looked at me, closed her eyes, and shook her head in understanding.

"But I do want two things."

"Name 'em," she said.

"I want to look at Adele's room and I want you to stop drinking."

"My drinking is none of your fuckin' business," she said, now standing over me.

"Back on the wagon or I tell Sally this isn't the place for her."

"You little pope-loving wop son of a bitch," she said.

"I'm immune to flattery, and besides, I'm Episcopalian," I said. "Flo, the wagon's making its rounds. Climb in."

"God's truth," said Flo, sagging, "I don't know if I can."

"You can," I said. "You want Adele back?"

"Oh, shit," she said, putting down the half-full glass in her hand. "How about beer? Two a day, no more."

"Deal," I said, getting up and holding out my hand. She took it and held on.

"I'm sorry what I said," she said softly. "I was wrong to call you . . ."

"I can live with it," I said, still holding her hand.

"Find her for me, Lew," she said.

Now there were definitely tears.

"I'll find her, Flo. Let's take a look at her room."

Flo led me down a corridor, past closed doors to an open one. It was clearly a girl's room. Brightly colored. Flowered comforter. Stereo in the corner. A few stuffed animals. A desk and bookcase and posters on the walls, four of them, three of recent rock idols with blaring colors and one small one in black and white of a woman from another time and place.

"Who's that?"

"The woman? Willa Cather. Adele says she was a great writer, wanted to be like her."

"Anything missing?" I asked, moving to the clean, clear desk.

"A stuffed penguin is all I'm sure of," Flo said, looking around. "And clothes. She took clothes."

One of Lonsberg's books was on the shelf along with a collection of classics we all claim to have read in school but never did or don't really remember. The Lonsberg book, a paperback, was a bit battered from frequent readings. I opened it to the title page. In a scrawl I had trouble reading was a note in ink: "Adele, you have the talent. Don't lose it. Don't compromise." It was signed. I couldn't read the name but I could make out the "C" and the "L" at the beginning of each name. It was an autographed first paperback edition.

"Mind if I take this?"

"Take what you need," Flo said. "I don't read that stuff. Louis L'Amour and a few others, Frank Roderus, that's what I read. Lew, I kept hoping she'd just come back but . . ."

There was no diary, no journal, no short stories or notes by Adele in her desk, drawers, bookshelf, or closet. Flo walked me back through the house giving me directions to Lonsberg's house.

"You have Lonsberg's phone number?" I asked.

"No," she said. "Come to think of it I don't think Adele did either. She never called him. He always called her."

I touched her shoulder at the door. She gave me a weak smile of courage and out I went. Before I reached the Cutlass, the voice of Tex Ritter blasted through the Zinc house singing of lost dogies.

When I got in the car, I reached for *Fool's Love* and flipped it open. Every page was covered with thick black Magic Marker lines. Adele had put in a lot of work making this book unreadable.

I drove away with twenty minutes to make it 'til my

appointment with Ann Horowitz. I found a two-hour parking spot across from Sarasota News & Books. A new crowded upscale Italian restaurant had just opened across the street from the bookstore at the corner of Main and Palm. Parking didn't come easy and two-hour parking meant two-hour parking or a ticket.

I found a pay phone and called Harvey the computer.

"Haven't had time yet," he said.

"I'm not calling about Vera Lynn Uliaks," I said. "I need an unlisted phone number."

"When?"

"Now," I said, holding my hand over my ear to blur the sound of a couple in their fifties doing battle as they headed in the general direction of the library.

"Okay," said Harvey.

"Don't put me on hold," I said. "I can't take the music."

"Name?"

"Conrad Lonsberg," I said.

"He doesn't have a phone," said Harvey. "That's an easy one. Tycinker wanted to reach him a few months back about some case. No phone. I can give you an address."

"I've got one. Harve, what do you think about AA?"

Pause and then. "They can help," he said. "It's like a religion if it works. I tried it, needed too much support, went cold on my own. So far so good. Why are you asking?"

"I've got a friend," I said.

"Good luck. Talk to you tomorrow."

He hung up and I checked my watch. I had five minutes, just enough time to stop at Sarasota News & Books, pick up two coffees and a biscotti. I paid Ann Horowitz twenty dollars a visit when I could afford it, ten when I couldn't, and always brought her coffee and a chocolate biscotti.

She was just around the corner on Gulf Stream, a small office with a small waiting room. Ann had no secretary and a select few patients. At the age of eighty-one and with her annuity from Stanford University plus investments she had mentioned from time to time plus the money her husband Melvin still brought in as a successful sculptor, Ann could have retired two decades earlier. But therapy was what she did and enjoyed in addition to conversation, history, odd facts, coffee, biscotti, and opera. Ann and Melvin had chosen Sarasota because their only son lived here with his wife and two grown daughters.

Ann's inner door was open. I could hear her talking. From the pauses, I figured she was on the phone so I moved to the doorway where she motioned for me to take my usual seat across from her.

Ann is a small woman with a tolerant smile. She likes bright dresses. Her hair is gray, straight, and short enough to show off her colorful earrings.

"No," she told the person on the phone, "I'll see you at four . . . no, you will not kill yourself . . . I understand . . . four. Did you read the book? . . . I gave you a book, *Lost Horizon* . . . No, I did not want you to rent the movie. I wanted you to read the book . . . You've got a few hours. Start reading."

She hung up the phone and accepted the coffee and biscotti from me, placing both on the desk to her right, and looked at me.

I knew what she was looking at.

"I got slapped by a woman I was serving papers," I explained as she examined the side of my face.

"And what did you do?"

"Do?"

"In response to being slapped. What did you do?"

"I got on my bike and left."

Ann shook her head.

"What should I have done?" I asked.

"Getting on your bicycle is one thing. Getting angry is another. Saying something to the woman."

"I wasn't angry," I said.

"You should have been. You should let yourself feel, but don't worry. I'm not commanding you to feel. It doesn't work that way. Here, take this with you," she said, handing me a copy of *Smithsonian* magazine. "Article in there about gargoyles. Fascinating."

I took the magazine. There was a grinning stone gargoyle on the cover, just the right gift for a depressed client. Ann took the lid off the cup of black coffee and dipped the biscotti.

"Can you do it today?" she asked, looking at me as she lifted the saturated biscotti to her mouth.

"Not today," I said.

She wanted me to speak the name of my wife. I had done it only twice since she had died, once to Sally and two weeks ago when I managed to say it to Ann. Saying her name aloud had brought back images, memories, pain, the empty feeling in my stomach, the sound of my heart madly pulsing blood through my veins, my neck, my head.

"Feel better?" Ann asked when I had said my wife's name.

"No," I answered. "Worse. Much worse."

"Of course," she said. "This is therapy, not magic."

I had gone through this opening session ritual four times since then with Ann asking me to speak the name aloud. I had managed it only that one session.

"Can you do it?" Ann asked, biscotti in hand.

I took a deep breath, felt the beat of my heart, closed my eyes, and softly uttered, "Catherine."

"And you feel how?" Ann asked, redipping her biscotti.

"Sorry I said it," I said, reaching for my own coffee, which unlike my therapist's was strongly fortified with half and half and two packets of Equal.

"Of course you are. You are still in love with your depression and self-pity. You've held it around you like a child's comfort blanket since your wife died. If you give it up, what are you left with?"

"We've been through this," I said.

"And each week we become different people," she said. "Sometimes different people with different answers. This time you said her name."

"Without my depression," I said. "The few times anxiety takes over. I shake. I can't do anything. I walk till I'm exhausted. Even *Mildred Pierce* doesn't help. I think . . . you know all this."

"You would rather be depressed than anxious," she said, continuing to work on my burnt offering.

"Is that a question or an observation?"

"Your choice."

"Yes, I would rather be depressed," I said.

"You owe it to Catherine to live depressed and guilty. You want to hide, not feel and slowly die, a hermit, a saint who does not deserve life."

"I know."

"I'm just recapitulating," she said. "Do they have flavors other than chocolate?"

"Yes."

"Next time if you remember, bring almond or something," she said.

"I'll do that."

"Change is good, small stimulation from small changes. I just segued from my own taste to a metaphoric reference to your state of mind."

"I noticed," I said.

"You were meant to. You wouldn't be one of my favorite clients if you couldn't follow what I say."

"I thought I was your favorite," I said.

"You are part of an elite group."

"Am I making progress?" I asked.

"Do you want to make progress?" she asked in return. Good question.

"I don't know."

"You still seeing Sally?"

"Yes, tonight. Why?"

"You can turn in your blanket of depression for something else," she said. "Like coming back to life with a real person."

"I'm not giving up my wife," I said.

"You said her name," Ann said with a smile, pointing her finger at me. "Progress. I'm not asking you to give her up. I'm asking you to place her gently inside you where she belongs and go on with your life."

I shook my head and said, "We keep saying the same things."

"But in different ways and . . . tell me, Lewis, are you starting to feel different?"

"Yes," I said.

"And it makes you anxious?"

"Angry."

"At who? Who are you angry with?"

"You."

"Say something about her," Ann said, leaning back.

"What?"

"Your wife. Did she do anything that annoyed you?"

I closed my eyes, and shook my head "no."

"She was perfect," Ann said. "Nobody's perfect. Remember the last line of *Some Like It Hot*? When Joe B. Brown finds out Jack Lemmon isn't a woman? 'Nobody's perfect,' he says."

"She left doors and drawers open," I said. "Medicine cabinet, kitchen cabinets, dresser drawers. All the time."

"And what did you do?" Ann prompted.

"I closed them."

"Never got irritated?"

"For a while. Then . . ."

"You liked her having little faults?"

"I guess," I said. "I think I can remember everything in those cabinets and drawers."

"Do you want to remember them?"

"No . . . yes. This isn't fun."

"It's not supposed to be fun. You don't know how to have fun yet."

Ann stood up and jogged in place a few seconds.

"Knee tightens," she said, sitting again. "You showed me her photograph. She was pretty."

I nodded, seriously considering never coming back here again.

"Lewis, you are not pretty."

"I know. We . . . she picked me. We had . . ."

"Fun?"

"A lot in common," I said. "Movies, books. We found the same things funny. Monty Python, Thin Man movies, Rocky and Bullwinkle."

"Moose and squirrel," Ann said in a terrible imitation of either Natasha or Boris. "What?"

Something must have broken through. I bit my lower lip.

"Sometimes she called me Rocky," I said. "If I was being

particularly dense, she called me Bullwinkle. I . . . I called
her . . . No more."

Ann clapped her hands and rocked forward once.

"Perfect. Are you still going to the beach?"

"When I can."

"And the gulls, do you still hear them speak?"

"Gulls don't speak," I said. "Sometimes their squawk . . .
I've told you this . . . Sometimes their talk sounds like
they're saying, 'It's me.' "

"You like the gulls?"

"Yes."

"And the pelicans?"

"And the pelicans who dive like clumsy-winged oafs into
the Gulf literally going blind from the constant collision
with the water in search of food."

"You are getting very literary, very poetic," said Ann.

"As my friend Flo would say, 'Bullshit.' "

"You are the gull crying, 'It's me.' You are the pelican
going blind while it dives for food."

"I'm literary. You're cryptic."

We went on like that for a while. I glanced at the clock
on the wall over her desk. Five more minutes.

"You ever read Conrad Lonsberg?" I asked.

"Yes," she said. "Compelling, disturbing, elevating. Isn't
that what the reviews said? All true but there was a true
despair behind those poems and stories. I met him once,
briefly, here in Sarasota. I recognized him from the old
photograph on the jacket of *Fool's Love*. He was more than
forty years older than the man in the photograph leaning
against a tree with his hands in his pockets. But the eyes
were the same. I remember. Our eyes met. It was at De-
mitrio's on the Trail. Melvin and I were there. Lonsberg
was with a young woman. Our eyes met for an instant and
he knew I recognized him. I think I smiled to let him know
his secret was safe and I would not bother him. I wonder
if he has had any therapy. Judging from his books, I would
say it would be a good idea as long as he didn't go to one
of the quacks with shingles. Why the interest in Conrad
Lonsberg?"

"Remember Adele?"

"Vividly," said Ann. "There is a connection between this evocation of Conrad Lonsberg and Adele? It is not a simple stream of consciousness, a seeming non sequitur?"

"No."

"You want to tell me what you are talking about or, rather, what you want to ask me?"

"Too long to tell the whole story," I said, looking at the clock on the wall. "Our time is just about up and I hear your next client coming through the outer door."

"Give me the question," Ann said. "In your eyes, you have a question."

"Why would Adele, who Lonsberg has been working with, deface her copy of one of his books and not just tear it up or throw it away?"

"You want a two-minute answer, which is the time we have left?"

"What I want and what I get are almost never the same," I said.

"She is angry with him, very angry, feels betrayed, but can't bring herself to throw away the book. Something is unfinished. Something went very wrong. In that which we call reality. In the reality of Adele's mind. Lewis, I would need more information. Ideally, I would need Lonsberg and Adele together in this room. I think that unlikely. Meanwhile, I'll end with a question. Why did you leap the chasm of thought from being angry with me and identifying with seagulls to Adele and Lonsberg?"

"I don't know."

"Next time," she said, rising. "Think about it. Come with an answer."

"I'll try."

"It's an assignment," she said. "Like college. You fail to answer, you get an F and I make you do it again."

I fished out two tens, Marvin Uliaks's tens, and handed them to her.

"You should read *Fool's Love*," she said as I moved toward the door.

"I did."

"When?"

"A long time ago," I said.

"You read it as a boy. Read it as a man. You think it's hot in here?"

"Maybe, a little."

"Monday?"

"Monday, same time?"

"Yes," she said, moving to the thermostat.

In the small reception office, a woman—slim, long blond hair, well dressed, eyes down and covered with thick sunglasses—looked down. I walked past her and out into the sunshine.

3

STOPPED AT BRANT'S Book Shop on Brown Street, a short street with Bee Ridge on the north end and the shopping mall with Barnes & Noble on the south. Brant's is a one-story used-book institution that looks as if a good wind would blow off the roof or an NFL lineman would step through the creaking wooden floor. But there wasn't much you couldn't find there.

I picked up a copy of *Fool's Love* for a dollar and a quarter and walked over to Rico's, great prices, good food, terrific calamari, nearly perfect lasagna, just like my mother didn't make. I had a Gorgonzola sandwich on a roll with a diet Coke and watched a court show on the big-screen television. A stern-looking wizened woman in a black robe was calling a stupidly grinning teenager a liar. He seemed like a liar to me too. She ruled against him. I don't know what he did, kicked a dog, stole a CD player. The girl he had to pay a hundred thirty-four dollars to looked about Adele's age—thin, dark, pretty, a ring through her eyebrow. I figured she had done some lying too before I started watching. Almost everybody lies. Everybody lies. Everybody dies.

"I read that," said the young woman who waited on me, pointing at *Fool's Love*. She was dark, looked a little like my cousin's daughter Angela, and smiled.

I didn't know her name but I had seen her in Rico's before. At this hour of the afternoon, business was slow. I was the only customer.

"You like it?" she asked, nodding at the book.

"Read it a long time ago," I said. "I'm thinking of reading it again. You like it?"

"Great book," she said. "I don't read books, and that one, they made us read that one in school, Mr. Gliddings at Riverview. You know Pee Wee Herman went to Riverview?"

"I heard," I said.

"Only book they made me read that I liked, you know?"

"Must be good. You know he lives here?"

"Who?"

"Conrad Lonsberg, the guy who wrote the book," I said.

She stood up straight and her smile broadened.

"He'd have to be a couple hundred years old," she said.

"No, it's true. He's alive. He's here."

"I believe you," she said. "That's interesting. Want another diet Coke?"

I declined, paid my bill, left her a twenty-percent tip, and got back in the white Cutlass. The drive down Tamiami Trail to Blackburn Point Road took me less than fifteen minutes. I turned right on Blackburn Point, crossed the small bridge over Little Sarasota Bay, turned right again, and kept going on Casey Key Road past houses great and small, many hidden by trees and bushes.

Flo's directions had been perfect. The walled-in fortress of Conrad Lonsberg was down a paved cul-de-sac. There was a gate. I parked just past it and walked back. There was no name on the door, not even an address, but there was a bell semihidden in the stone wall on my left. I pushed it, heard nothing, and waited. Nothing. I pushed it again. Nothing. Then I saw the camera. It was on the right at the top of the wall, its lens pointing straight down at me, camouflaged by a plant with big leaves.

I wasn't sure if I could be heard but I said, "My name is Lew Fonesca. I'm a friend of Adele Hanford's. Could I talk to you for a few minutes?"

I don't know why but I held up my copy of *Fool's Love* for the camera.

Nothing happened. I stepped back and noted that the camera lens didn't follow me. I got in the car, turned around, and parked where I could watch the gate. The Gulf was behind me. I turned off the engine, opened the windows, and listened to the surf. A few gulls drifted by, most of them made their squawking sound. A few said, "It's me."

I opened *Fool's Love* and began to read:

By the time Sherry Stephens hit State Highway 71 at Weaver's Texaco station, she had become Laura Ordette. She shifted her full duffel bag, the green one her brother George had given her when he got back from Korea, into her left hand.

Laura Ordette didn't look back. Laura Ordette was not the kind of woman to look back. Sherry Stephens would probably be crying now walking along the roadside of Martin's Lagoon Street, probably be looking back, thinking about what she was leaving. Sherry Stephens would be thinking about the small room she shared with her sister. Sherry Stephens would be thinking about her sister and her mother. Her mother was at work now answering calls at Rowlinson's Real Estate. Sherry's mother had a good telephone voice, deep and friendly. Those who actually met Grace Stephens were often surprised to see a small, serious woman in no-nonsense suits. Sherry's father? Was he worth thinking about? Not by Laura Ordette. He was a red-faced, red-necked slab of beef who drove trucks across six states. Sherry would be worrying about missing school. Not Laura Ordette. Sherry was fifteen. Laura was eighteen and had three hundred dollars in her pocket. Sherry had saved it working after school at Pine's Drug Store. Well, she had worked for most of it. About half she had taken from the cigar box in the bottom drawer of her father's dresser.

A car passed going in her direction. It stopped. "Want a ride?" the man asked. He was as old as her father. He smiled like he meant it but she knew he didn't. He might be harmless. He might be hoping. Sherry would have said "no" and kept walking without looking at him. Laura looked, appraisingly, sighed, and said, "What kind of car is that?"

"Buick."

"I don't ride in Buicks," Laura said. "My parents died in one."

The old guy drove on mumbling something.

Laura Ordette knew many things besides the fact that the duffel bag was heavy. She knew that all adults were liars. She knew that most kids were liars. She knew Reverend Scools, the pastor at her church, was a liar and stupid. The only people who didn't lie, who didn't have to, were the smart ones with money and power. They didn't have to lie though maybe they did it for fun. She knew that she would grow old and die. She knew that when she died she was not going to go to heaven or hell. You just died. That was it. The rest was shit. She knew that men and boys who were old enough looked at her thinking what it would be like to have her tits pressed against their naked chests, their tongues in her mouth, their wang tall and hard inside her. Yucch. Laura Ordette was above that. If people were all animals, and that's what she believed, the ones who were worth breathing were the ones who stayed above being breeding animals distracting themselves while they waited to get old and die.

Laura Ordette was going to New York. She knew the bus schedule. She had called to be sure there would be a seat. Laura Ordette was going to New York, the daughter of a wealthy Concord family who disdained their money and pleas and walked out to make it on her own. She would become a writer, a Broadway ticket seller, a greeter at some big art gallery on Fifth Avenue. She would go for that job in her one good dress, all made-up, tell them how she was going to New York University at night, and get the job. She was going to get her own room. She was going to meet rich, smart people, see a real play, speak in a voice nothing like that of Sherry whose name she was already forgetting as she had forgotten what her father had done to her, what her mother had said. No, not her father. That Sherry's father, that weak, whining Sherry's father and mother. Laura Ordette's parents were upstanding, supportive, there for her if she wanted to go back.

When she hit State 70 she put the duffel bag down. It had D. Stephens stenciled on it in black. Laura would get rid of it when she got to her home in New York. About two blocks down she could see the sign for the bus station. She lifted the duffel bag again and waited till the traffic let her cross.

She was happy. She was on her way. Then why was she crying?

Two hours had passed and I was almost finished with the book. I stopped after the scene in which Laura dumps the fully clothed drunken high school English teacher into his bath of cold water.

No one had come in or out of the Lonsberg fort. I headed for the nearest pay phone. That took me all the way back to a gas station on the Trail. I called the Texas Bar and Grille on Second Street. Big Ed Fairing answered the phone.

"Ed, is Ames there?"

"He's here. I'll call him."

I heard Ed bellow for Ames above the late-afternoon beer and burger crowd.

"He's coming," said Ed. "You know they're creeping up on me, Fonesca?"

"Who?"

"Developers," he said. "This used to be a perfectly respectable run-down street with some character. Now, art galleries, Swedish tearooms, antique shops. They're creeping up. The upscaling of downtown is taking away its character. We'll be looking like St. Armand's Circle in two years. People have no sense of history. You know what they're putting in next door? I mean, right next door where the cigar store was?"

"A tanning salon?" I guessed.

"No, Vietnamese fingernail place," he said. "That'll bring in a lot of business. Here's Ames."

"McKinney," Ames said in his deep and slightly raspy western Sam Elliott drawl.

Ames is tall, white-haired, grizzled, lean, brown, and almost seventy-five years old. Ames was not supposed to bear arms. It was a right he had lost after using an ancient Remington Model 1895 revolver to kill his ex-partner in a duel on the beach in the park at the far south end of Lido Key. Ames had hired me to find his ex-partner who had run away with all the money in the bank and everything he could sell from the company he and Ames owned, a company worth forty million dollars. Ames was ruined. The bank took the company. Ames with a few thousand dollars in his pocket had tracked the partner for more than a year on buses from Arizona to St. Louis and then to Sarasota. I had found the partner. I tried to stop the two old men from dueling. I failed but I was there when it happened and testified that the ex-partner had fired first. Ames got off with a few minor felony counts and two months in jail. He now believed that he owed me. He never got any money back but he felt that I had helped him regain his self-respect.

Ames had a job at the Texas Bar and Grille, a room in back, and a motor scooter. He also had access to Ed Fairing's considerable collection of old rifles and handguns that Ames kept in perfect working order.

Ames considered me his responsibility. He was probably also the closest thing I had to a friend.

"Ames, Adele is missing," I said.

"Run off?"

Ames was with me all through the ordeal with Adele and her parents. Ames had gotten along particularly well with Adele's mother Beryl. When Beryl died, Ames rode shotgun at my side, literally, when we got Adele back from her life on the North Trail. When Ames looked at Adele with disapproval, Adele's inventive foul language disappeared. There was something about the old man that made people want to earn his respect.

"I don't know," I said. "You know the Burger King on 301, near the Ringling School?"

"Know it," he said.

"Kid works there named Mickey. Don't know his last name. Must be about twenty. See if you can track him down, find out where he lives. Adele might be with him."

"If I find her?" he asked.

"Leave a message on my machine," I said. "You ever hear of a writer named Conrad Lonsberg?"

"I have."

"He lives out on Casey Key. He might know something about Adele. I'm waiting for him."

"Want help?"

Which meant, do you want me to come down there with a shotgun, break down the door, and threaten the noted man of letters.

"Not yet," I said. "You read any of his books?"

"Liked *Plugged Nickels*," said Ames. "Didn't read the poetry. The first one, *Fool's . . .* something."

"*Fool's Love*," I said.

"*Fool's Love*," he said. "Couldn't get through it. Too much feeling sorry for everybody."

"It's considered a classic," I said.

"Not by me," Ames said.

"Can't say I'm looking forward to finishing it," I said.

"Put it away. Try *Plugged Nickels* if you have to read him. I'll call you."

I hung up, got back into the Cutlass, and drove over the bridge. It was almost dark when I parked across from Lonsberg's gate. Across the Gulf of Mexico I could see the sun balanced big and yellow-red on the horizon line. A white heron flew in from the water and landed about a dozen feet from the car. It strutted, long-necked, gracefully, and then stood as still as a pink lawn flamingo. I was watching the sun beaming off the heron till the bird decided to look at me and fly back out over the water. I watched the sunset. A few seconds after it was down I heard the gate open.

It was on some kind of automatic device like a garage door. A battered blue Ford pickup rumbled out and the gates closed behind it. I had my lights off though it was dark enough to use them. I followed whoever was in the Ford down the road, off the Key, and over the bridge toward the mainland.

I stayed far enough behind that I hoped he wouldn't see me but close enough that I wouldn't lose him. He wasn't going fast. Since the windows of the pickup were tinted, I couldn't see who was driving but at least it was a human from the Lonsberg enclave. It was a start.

The pickup went north and turned into the mall just before Sarasota Square and parked near the Publix. I parked in the next aisle.

A lean, average-sized man with white hair, gray chinos, and a black short-sleeved polo shirt got out. The shirt wasn't tucked in. I knew Lonsberg was about seventy. This man walked like a man twenty years younger and in a hurry. I followed. He got a cart at Publix. So did I. I followed him around and got a few decent looks. The face was sun-darkened, lined, good teeth that looked real, a serious look. He selected grits, eggs, cheese, a wide variety of vegetables, meat, chicken, fresh grouper, and a big jar of Vita herring in sour cream. He added six gallons of bottled water and six half gallons of Diet Dr Pepper before deciding he had all he needed or wanted. His eyes met no one's and no one seemed to take note of him.

I got behind him in line with my four cans of albacore tuna.

While he emptied his cart, he looked back at me for an instant and in that instant he knew I recognized him. He turned his eyes back to his unpacking, his back to me.

While the clerk was putting his groceries in plastic bags, I paid for my tuna and followed him out to his pickup.

"Conrad Lonsberg," I said.

He said nothing, just piled his bags in the back of his pickup truck.

"Adele Hanford," I said as he opened the door of his pickup and started to get in. He stopped, turned his head, and looked at me. He knew how to stare someone down.

He had obviously had a lot of experience. We were a good match. I had a lifetime of patience and since he didn't close the door and drive away I was sure this contact was not over.

"You're Fonesca. Adele's description was nearly perfect," Lonsberg said, one hand on the trailer railing. "I thought she was engaging in a little creative hyperbole. Where is she?" he asked, his voice now low. I thought he was trying to keep himself in control, battling something. Rage, disappointment?

"That was my question," I said. "I'm looking for her."

"Why?"

"It looks like she ran away from her foster home," I said. "Her foster mother is a friend. Adele is . . . I'm sort of responsible for her."

"Flo Zink," said Lonsberg, now tapping his left hand on the truck's door. He kept looking at me and then made a decision. "Adele says you're a private investigator."

"I'm a process server."

"What do you do not for a living?" he asked.

"Brood, watch old movies, think too much about the past," I said.

He nodded in understanding. A fat woman with a full shopping cart wheeled noisily past us giving us both a glance. Lonsberg pressed his lips together, thought, looked away and then back at me.

"Follow me," Lonsberg said, getting into his pickup and closing the door.

I got into the Cutlass and followed him out of the parking lot and down the Trail. Seven minutes later I pulled behind him at his gate. He leaned out of his open window and waved for me to get out of my car. I did. The passenger side door of his pickup opened. I got in next to him. He looked at me, pushed a button on the dashboard, and watched as the gate swung open. We drove in. He pushed the button again and the gate closed behind us.

I don't know what I expected to see, probably one of the three-story ultra-modern white concrete designer houses with wide windows, decks, and nonnative palm trees.

We drove toward the only house on the three- or four-

acre property, a reasonably modest one-story wooden building with a covered porch hovering over a trio of white
wicker chairs and a wicker table. The house wasn't small,
but it wouldn't go for more than one hundred eighty-five
thousand in the current market in any other location. The
grounds were green, the road we went down unpaved and
narrow. To our left, however, was the Gulf of Mexico. The
view and the expanse of beachfront would put the property
in the two-million-dollar range. Along Lonsberg's beach,
birds strolled and waves rolled in. There were four plastic
beach chairs not far from the shoreline facing the water. A
sand pile about three feet high was in the process of giving
itself up to the tide.

Lonsberg parked in front of the house and got out.

"Don't worry about Jefferson," he said as I got out too.

"Jefferson?"

At that moment I learned who Jefferson was. A gigantic
dog of a dozen breeds looking like a hairy version of the
Baskerville hound bounded around the house heading toward us. No, amend that. He was heading for me and barking. Jefferson knew how to bark.

"No," Lonsberg commanded gently.

The dog hesitated, put his head down, and kept moving
toward me, slowly now, growling.

"Here," Lonsberg called a little louder. The dog ran to
him. Lonsberg put out his hand and the dog gave it a sloppy
lick. Lonsberg patted the dog's head. Jefferson closed his
eyes in ecstasy.

"He won't bother you," Lonsberg said, moving to the
back of the pickup and handing me a bag of groceries.

Lonsberg picked up the other bag and headed onto the
low porch. Jefferson still seemed particularly interested in
me. He stood there watching as we entered and followed
us inside after Lonsberg opened the door. I felt the big dog
nudge past me.

Jefferson might not bother me but he was a significant
distraction.

I followed Lonsberg through the hallway, past a room to
our left filled with books and bookshelves, a sofa, and two
very old overstuffed chairs, one with a matching hassock.

The sofa and chairs were a set. They looked as if they had been bought by someone's great-grandmother who had re-covered them a century ago with blue and red flowers against a background of what might have once been yellow but was now a worn-out off-white.

A glimpse of another room on the right as we moved to the sound of Jefferson's claws ticking against the wooden floor revealed an office with a desk, more bookcases, a row of file cabinets. The desk was clear except for a computer and a printer.

A few doors were closed. The kitchen was as big as the two rooms in which I lived and worked, which means it was an average-sized room with a wooden table in the mid-dle surrounded by four chairs. Lonsberg put his bag on the table. So did I. Jefferson moved quickly to sniff at both bags. I could now see that Jefferson had jowls and large teeth. I had known Jeffersons in the past. He was a drooler.

"Have a seat," Lonsberg said, putting his groceries into cabinets and the refrigerator.

I sat waiting. Jefferson decided to sit next to me and regard my face with his head tilted to one side.

"Do the police know you're looking for Adele?" he asked, stacking his cans in a cupboard.

"No."

He shook his head as if that were solid and solemn good news. Then he turned, wiped his hands on his pants, and sat across from me.

"What do you see, Fonesca?" he asked.

"See?"

"Me, what do you see?"

"A man, lean, healthy-looking, good head of hair, seri-ous, judging whether or not he's going to tell me some-thing."

"What do you know about me?" he asked.

"Famous writer, haven't published much. Man who likes his privacy."

"Have you read anything of mine?"

"*Fool's Love*, long time ago. I'm rereading it," I said.

Jefferson moved close to me and rested his head on my lap.

"What do you think of it? The book?" Lonsberg asked, hands folded on the table.

"It's a classic, great book," I said.

"What do you think of it?" he repeated.

"Does it matter?"

"Yes," he said.

"So far, it's not my kind of book. Maybe when I really get into it . . ."

"It was a fluke," Lonsberg said. "I was a kid who thought he could write. It was short, easy. I expected nothing to happen, except that I'd keep working in my father's drugstore in Rochester, marry Evelyn Steuben, have children, go to pharmacy school. The book happened to hit the right agent and the right publisher at the right time. Teenage girl rebels, sets off on her own, learns the truth about people, the good, the bad, grows up fast, gets swept up in the anti-Vietnam business, moves in with a cello player old enough to be her grandfather. Controversy on that one. Publicity. Big success. Fonesca, the book is second-rate. Too short. Too easy with answers. It's smart-ass wit and a few good observations."

"I think it's better than that," I said.

"So does most of the world," he said. "I don't."

I wondered why this famous recluse was giving me the thirty-second biography and interview he wouldn't have given to *The New York Times* or *Time*. I thought I knew.

"Adele," I reminded him.

"Adele," he said, turning his head toward the wall to his right. There was an eight-by-ten framed black-and-white photograph on his kitchen wall. Four people were lined up against a background of trees. The man was a young Lonsberg.

"My wife, Evelyn," he said, looking at the photograph. "My two kids, Laura and Brad. Both grown. Both with kids."

"Where are they?" I asked.

"Evelyn? She died more than twenty years ago. Laura and Brad live here, not in the house. Laura is in Venice. Martin's in Sarasota."

Jefferson drooled on my leg. I patted his head.

"Adele," I reminded him again.

"What about you?" he asked. "Your story?"

"My story?" I asked. "Why?"

"Your story," he repeated.

"Adele," I said again.

He looked at me and nodded.

"Your story first," he said.

I told him about my wife's death, a little about my family, less about what I did, a mention of my depression.

"What do you take for the depression?" he asked.

"Nothing, I see a psychologist."

"I take Chinese herbs," he said. "Acupuncture.

"They work on my blood pressure, my liver problems, but they can't penetrate, get inside whatever it really is that we call 'soul.'"

"Adele," I said.

"Come on," he said, getting up. I eased myself away from Jefferson and followed Lonsberg through a door. Jefferson followed. At the end of a short hall was a door, a particularly thick wooden door. Lonsberg opened it with a key and we stepped in.

It was a strange sight. Inside the room was a huge vault, the kind you might see in a bank. This vault door was open. I followed Lonsberg in.

"What do you see?" he asked.

"Empty shelves," I said. "Except for that box."

The wooden box sat closed about chest high in the middle of one of the dark metal shelves.

"Two days ago they weren't empty," he said. "They were filled with manuscripts, neatly bound, carefully placed in folders, everything I've written over the past thirty-five years."

It had been rumored that Lonsberg had written a few books since he went into hiding from the world, but these empty shelves represented more than a few books.

"Someone stole them?" I asked.

"Adele," he said.

"Why? How?"

"She knew about the vault," he said, surveying the empty shelves. "I showed it to her, let her read a few things."

"You didn't call the police?"

"I'm a recluse," Lonsberg said. "You know that. I started out just wanting to be away from the reporters, the fans, the scholars, and then it became a minor literary myth. I began to live it. It grew. The more I tried to protect my privacy, the more I was sought out by the determined. And the more reclusive I became. Now I like it that way. No, amend that. I've grown comfortable in my relative isolation. There've been rumors for years about my 'secret' writing. I was stupid enough in the last interview I gave I don't know how many years ago to a small magazine, stupid enough to say that I still write. I don't want the police. I don't want to be in newspapers and tabloids. I don't want television crews parked at my gate. I dread stepping into a courtroom, a press of reporters, a gaggle of fans."

"A press of reporters," I said. "A gaggle of fans. Like a pride of lions?"

"A literary critic has finally entered my house," he said flatly.

"No, I'm a man trying to find a missing girl. You think Adele took everything?"

"Yes, and I want it all back," Lonsberg said. "No questions asked. No charges filed. I'm told the manuscripts are worth millions of dollars. Be worth more when I die. Those books and stories are my legacy to my children and grandchildren."

"Why didn't you just have some of them published while you're alive?"

He looked at me intently.

"I write because I must," he said. "I don't want to be misunderstood by a world that will laud, speculate, read my stories and contort them into their stories, turn my work into movies or television miniseries. It happens to them all. If it can happen to Tolstoy, Melville, Dickens who are perfectly clear, it can and will happen to a minor quirk in the history of literature named Lonsberg. Let it happen when I'm dead. I write them to stay sane, to trap my demons on paper. I've got some money that still comes in from my books, but I'm not rich. And every year the fewer and fewer things written about my work have grown more obtuse and stupid. People should read novels and short stories instead of reading books about novels and short stories."

Jefferson was sniffing at the shelves. Lonsberg and I watched. And then Lonsberg spoke again.

"You know Adele," he said. "You're a process server. You know how to find people and you know how to keep quiet. Find her. Return my manuscripts. I'll give you five thousand dollars if you get my work back. Quietly."

"And Adele . . . ?" I asked.

"No questions," he said. "I get my manuscripts back and press no charges."

"I've got questions," I said.

He nodded.

"Why would she do this?" I said, looking around at the empty shelves in the vault.

"I don't know," he said.

I had a feeling he did, but there are right and wrong times and ways to deal with lies. It takes a feel for the person who is lying to me. I can call someone a liar, which results in grief, almost always mine. Or I can wait till I find the truth myself or the right time to ask the question again. I usually wait.

"Holding them for ransom?" I asked.

"No," he said.

"Why?"

Lonsberg moved to the wooden box, took it down, and brought it to me.

"Open it," he said.

I took the box and opened it. It was filled with cash. Fifties, twenties, hundreds, tens, fives.

"Forty-six thousand four hundred in that box. Adele knew it was there. There are other places in the house with a lot more money. I don't use banks. Adele knew where it all was. There's not a dollar missing."

He looked at me and took the box back.

"Makes no sense, does it?" he said.

"So she took them to hurt you," I pushed, knowing I could push only a little further, but I decided the moment was right. He looked just a bit bewildered by the emptiness of the vault. "Did you and Adele ever?"

"Sex?" he asked. "No. Would I have liked to? Yes, I'm old but I'm not dead. I also know what statutory rape is. I never touched her, never even kissed her. I have a grandson older than Adele. I turn seventy in two weeks. Letting my ancient libido go at the risk of losing Adele's talent would have been stupid. Do you think I'm stupid?"

"You're not stupid. Then . . . ?" I asked.

"You'll have to ask her," he said. "Well?"

"One short story," I said.

"What?"

"If I find her," I said, "and you get your manuscripts back, you give me one short story, any one."

"No. I'll give you the five thousand dollars," he said.

"One short story," I answered. "Full rights."

Lonsberg looked at me. So did Jefferson.

"I can't do that," he said.

"You keep any copies of those stolen manuscripts?" I asked.

"You know I didn't."

"Adele, or whoever took them, could be taking your name off now and sending them out under their name to agents, publishers, Internet sites."

"They'd be worth nothing," he said. "Or at least not very much. Their value has nothing to do with whatever quality they may have. Their value lies in the fact that they were written by Conrad Lonsberg. Find me some scribbles and stick figures, junk by Picasso on a sheet of paper, and I'll get you half a million dollars as long as it's signed and authenticated. No, it's more likely they could all be getting shredded or thrown into a bonfire right now," he said.

He shook his head.

"Okay, someone doesn't like you, Lonsberg," I said.

"And her name is Adele. Ten thousand dollars," he said. "I'll pay you ten thousand to get them back."

"What does money mean to you?" I asked.

"Food, shelter, paper, postage, a few clothes, security for my family," he said.

"What does your writing mean to you?"

"I get your point. You want me to give up something important to me," he said.

"Something that means something to you. Adele means something to me. Not money."

"You're a remarkable man, Fonesca," he said, smiling again. "You may also be a stupid one or you've read too many romantic novels."

"Movies," I said. "I got it from movies."

He looked at me for a long time and came to a decision. "And from life. All right. You can have the rights to a story if you get all my manuscripts back."

"Plus one thousand dollars for expenses, in advance."

"I pick the story," he said. "Adele said you're a good man. She thought I was a good man. She was wrong about me. Her judgment does not match her talent."

"One of her problems," I said. "We have a deal?"

"We do," said Lonsberg.

"Tell me again, how many people know about your vault and the manuscripts?"

"My son, daughter, Adele, me, and you," he said. "I bought the place because it was isolated and because it had the vault. The last owner was a drug dealer. He had to leave the country quickly."

"Your son or daughter may have told someone about your manuscripts," I said. "Maybe Adele mentioned it."

"Fonesca," he said evenly. "Whoever took them knew when I was going to be out. Whoever took them got past Jefferson who wouldn't let a stranger in. Both of my children know they get the manuscripts when I die. And they are quite aware that no one can sell or publish those stories, certainly not with my name on them, while I'm alive. My will is clear."

"Did your son and daughter meet Adele?"

"Yes."

"They get along?"

"With Adele or each other?" he asked.

"Both."

"I think they liked Adele," he said and then paused. "As for each other, it's on and off. And in anticipation of your next question, I think my children respect me. I think they don't like me. I'm not a tender man, Fonesca."

"I've noticed. I'll need their addresses and phone numbers," I said, turning and walking out of the vault. "Anyone else Adele might have met through you?"

"There is nobody else," he said, moving into the kitchen with the box of money in his arms. Jefferson ambling behind us. "Wait."

He put down the box, pulled a small, battered black notebook out of his back pocket and a click pen from a front pocket, tore out a page, and quickly wrote the names and addresses of his two children. Then he opened the wooden box and counted out a thousand dollars in bills of various denominations.

"I'll be in touch," I said, taking the cash and the small sheet and heading toward the front of the house. "You want a receipt?"

"You get nothing with my name signed and I want nothing with yours," he said behind me. "I have one last question."

"Go on," I said.

"Who slapped you?" he said, looking at my cheek. "And don't tell me you fell. I know what a slap looks like. I've had them. Good ones. Solid ones. Usually I deserved them."

"I served papers on a woman named Bubbles Dreemer this morning," I said. "She took exception."

"Great name, Bubbles Dreemer," he said.

"It doesn't belong to a great lady."

"Makes it even better," he said. "Mind if I use it?"

"It's not mine to give," I said.

I went out the door.

Jefferson's claws tapped behind me along with Lonsberg's soft footsteps.

Outside he said, "I have a button inside. When you get to the gate, I'll buzz you out."

I took a last look at Lonsberg with Jefferson at his side. Lonsberg had one hand in his pocket and the other on the dog's huge head. I walked down the dirt trail to the gate. I heard the gentle buzz, pushed at the door, went out, and watched the door close behind me with a metallic slap.

4

I WAS THIRSTY. Lonsberg hadn't asked me to stick around for lunch or have a glass of beer or a Coke. I headed for the Texas Bar and Grille on Second Street.

The late-afternoon crowd was just beginning to fill the place that was meant to look like an authentic Old West bar and eatery but looked more like a set from a John Ford western. Round wooden tables and simple wooden chairs. Wooden pillars of no distinction. A bar without stools. There was a buffalo head on one wall, authentic western weapons mounted all over the place. The prize displays were a carbine authenticated as the fifth ever made and a shotgun with a butt plate saying it was the official property of Buffalo Bill Cody. It was dated 1877. This had also been authenticated by Ed Fairing who served the best burgers in town, no competition. His specialty was a one-pounder with onions and mushrooms grilled inside the burger. His steaks were all served the same, rare in the middle, burnt on top, and his chili dared all but the most adventurous. The Texas was a success. It might well survive the onslaught of what passed for this year's Sarasota culture quickly surrounding it. My guess was that it would gradually change from a hangout for hard hats, nearby CPAs, and lawyers who wanted to sit back, eat food that would kill them, and swap stories. It would fill with tourists. It would become "the place you've just got to see." There was already some of that. Ed would even make money, but it wouldn't make him happy. He had moved south from an office job to become a western barkeep, not the proprietor of a chic luncheonette or a tourist attraction.

And so, Ed greeted me glumly as I moved to a space at the bar, which even sported a rail for the rare booted foot. Ed was big, heavy, with a head of bushy black hair with long sideburns, deep black eyes, and the face of a world-weary barkeep.

"Busy," I said.

"Yeah," he agreed. "Beer and chili?"

"Beer and burger, half pounder," I said.

"With the works?"

"With," I said. "Ames back?"

"In the kitchen," he said. "I'll tell him you're here."

Ed plopped a bottle of Miller heavy on the counter and moved toward the back of the bar. I took a drink and looked around. I picked up a little, a couple of guys in their thirties in suits, collars open, ties loose, loudly arguing about what the defection of Hardy Nickerson to the Jaguars had really meant to the Tampa Bay Bucs, a trio of paint-stained, T-shirted guys growing bellies and telling jokes with four-letter words, a man and woman in their fifties leaning across bowls of chili and whispering so that I caught only "there's no other way" plaintively from the man.

Then Ames appeared.

Tall, lean, shaved, serious. As he always did, he held out his hand. His grip was firm. We shook and he moved next to me. His gray pants were worn cotton. His shirt was long-sleeved and blue. I thought he had done some trimming of his brushed white hair.

"Wasn't there," he said, moving next to me. "Mickey at the Burger King. Hasn't been at work for two days. Full name's Michael Raymond Merrymen. Lives with his father in a development called Sherwood Forest out on McIntosh just off Bahia Vista."

"I know the place," I said. "You get an address and phone number?"

"Yes."

He reached into his shirt pocket and handed me an envelope. The front of the empty envelope told the recipient that he might already be the owner of a new house, a new Lexus, or ten thousand dollars. The back of the envelope told me in Ames's penciled hand where Mickey lived with his father.

"Thanks, Ames," I said. "Beer?"

"Coke," he said.

When Ed came back with my burger and a Coke for Ames, Ames and I moved to the table the quiet couple had just left. We pushed their dishes aside.

"Girl's in trouble?" Ames said.

"Looks that way," I said.

"What kind?"

I told him everything. He listened, drank slowly, nodded from time to time, and when I was finished said, "I don't hear the why of it."

"I don't either," I said. "Maybe we'll find out when we find Adele. Let's try Mickey the burger prince."

We put Ames's scooter into the trunk of the Cutlass. Ames was good at figuring out spaces, what would fit where. Also, the scooter was no vooming Harley.

I drove down Fruitville. Ames sat at my side and said nothing as I listened to two talk-show guys trade giggles and bad jokes much to their own amusement. We passed the Hollywood Twenty Cinemas parking lot, the Catholic Church with the Spanish welcome on its white sign, the Chinese Star buffet where you could get a decent lunch for five dollars, and made the turn to the right on McIntosh Road just past Cardinal Mooney High School. The Jewish Community Center was on our right. McIntosh Middle School was on our left and then on our left again was a sign that said, "Sherwood Forest, Deed Restricted."

We drove down a tree-lined street of well-maintained single-family houses, mostly the two- or three-bedroom variety, no two quite alike. A heavy old woman was walking a tiny white dog. She waved her pooper scooper at me and pointed the scooper at a sign that said, "Maximum Speed 19 MPH." To remind us of the seriousness of the statement we hit a yellow speed bump that felt as high as a low hurdle. The Cutlass scraped the ground when we hit and I slowed down.

We found the house of Mickey Merrymen at the end of a cul-de-sac between two other larger houses. There was a late-model blue Chevy in the driveway and the house's night lights were on.

Ames and I got out and went to the front door. There didn't seem to be a bell and there was no knocker. So I did it the old-fashioned way. I knocked.

The man who opened the door was somewhere in his forties, lean, with recently barbered dark hair. He wore a determined scowl, a red sweatshirt, and a pair of khaki pants. He was barefoot and had a baseball bat in his right hand.

"We're looking for Michael Merrymen," I said as Ames stepped forward.

"You found him," the man with the bat said. "I've been waiting for you for hours."

He stepped back to let us pass. When we were inside he walked ahead of us into a living room with one of those long gray couches that form an "L." A shorter matching couch faced it and a low coffee table covered with magazines and books sat in the middle of the brick-walled room.

"You're the Michael Merrymen from Burger King?" I asked as the man motioned for us to sit on the L-couch. Flo had described him as a kid. This was no kid. Flo's sense of youth might have been a bit warped.

I sat. Ames stood. The man with the bat paced.

"Yes," he said.

"You know why we're here?" I asked.

"It's about her," he said, stopping. "That little bitch."

"We're looking for her," I said, keeping my eyes on the bat that shifted from hand to hand.

"She's not hard to find," he said angrily, pointing in the general direction of his kitchen. "She's right next door."

"Right now?" I asked.

"Right now," he said. "You want to hear my side of this or are you just going to sit there?"

"Your side," I said.

He let out a deep sigh and stopped pacing to lean on the bat and look at me and Ames. Then he looked at Ames again and said, "You two are the best they could get. An old man and a little guy."

"Your side of the story," I repeated.

"Okay, it started when I moved in," he said. "I had my land surveyed. The neighbors on both sides were on my land. A few inches on one side. Almost a foot on the other. Hot tub right over the line on one side. Tangelo trees on the other."

I looked at Ames who folded his arms and waited to see where this was going.

"Okay, I thought. Live and let live, but no tangelo tree dropping fruit on my property and no lard ass dipping almost naked in her hot tub and spying on me. Are you following this?"

"Yes," I lied. "Go on."

"Okay, then came the mailbox," he said. "Deed restricted community. My mailbox didn't meet their rules. They turned me in. I was given a written order to move my mailbox back and get it repaired. But that's not what you want to hear."

"No," I agreed.

"You want to know about her," he said, tapping the bat on the floor. He reminded me a little of Fred Astaire tapping a black cane before he went into a dance.

"Yes," I said.

"Well, I got the dog," he said. "No restrictions on dogs. Only have to clean up after them, keep them leashed if you walk them. I got a dog. I got a pit bull. Staked him in the yard so he could reach the property line. He could go right up to that fucking hot tub. So she started the calls. Got a lawyer. Said the dog smelled up the neighborhood even though I cleaned up after him. They are out to get me and you have to stop them. I can get a lawyer too."

"What the hell are you talking about?" Ames asked.

"The bitch next door," Merrymen repeated. "I called to get her to shut up and that's why the fuck you're here for Chrissake."

"You're Michael Merrymen?" I asked.

"Yeah, funny," he said. "My son and me are the Merrymen of Sherwood Forest."

"Your son?" I asked. "He's Mickey?"

"Michael Junior," he said. "Works for me at the Burger King. I'm the manager. What the hell are you talking about? Did they make an Internet search for the two dumbest deputies in the county and come up with you?"

Ames looked at me. He had a low boiling point but he didn't show it. He looked calm. He always looked calm even when he was gun to gun with someone who might want to end his life. This time the someone had a baseball bat, but Ames didn't care. Loyalty and dignity were important to him above all things and I had the feeling though he was giving away about thirty years and a baseball bat, Michael Merrymen might be in trouble.

"We're not deputies," I said, pleading with my eyes for Ames to stay put. "We're looking for your son."

"My son? What the hell for? And who are you?"

"Your son is friendly with a girl named Adele Hanford," I said. "She's missing. Her foster parent doesn't want to call the police so she asked us to find her."

Merrymen laughed and shook his head.

"Mickey is among the missing," he said. "We don't get along that well. He goes for days at a time. Usually to his idiot grandfather."

"Your father?" I asked.

"My dead wife's father," he said. "I don't know who else he sees or what he does."

"Your father-in-law's name?" I asked.

"Corsello, Bernard. Why?"

"You've never met Adele?" I asked in return.

"No, and I don't give a shit about her or what Mickey is doing with her," he said.

"You'd best watch your mouth," Ames said evenly.

"I'd best . . . this is my fucking house," Merrymen answered, pointing the bat at Ames.

The fat end of the bat was inches from Ames's chest. Merrymen's chin jutted out.

"If you'll just let us look at your son's room, we'll go quietly," I said.

"No," he said, smiling at Ames who didn't smile back.

I got up to leave. Merrymen walked across the room to a door off the kitchen. He opened the door and the dog came running in. He was big for a pit bull though not as big as Jefferson, but this was a pit bull and Jefferson was just a dog.

The pit bull looked at Merrymen and Merrymen made the mistake of pointing the bat at Ames again. The dog knew what he was supposed to do, but so did Ames and Ames was smarter than the dog. He yanked the bat from Merrymen's hand and as the dog leaped toward him, Ames flipped the bat and took a full swing at the animal that was in the air flying toward his throat.

Ames connected. A line drive. The dog flew across the room, hit the wall with a yelp, and turned to attack again. Only now there was something distinctly wrong with his right front leg. He growled and limped forward. Ames readied the bat and then swung it once four feet in front of the dog who squealed, turned, and headed back for the door from which he had come.

Ames walked slowly over to the door and closed it.

"You son of a bitch," Merrymen said, reaching for the bat.

Ames held out his arm warning the hysterical man to stay back.

"You break in . . ."

"You invited us in," I reminded him.

"You attacked my dog. In my house. You bastards. She sent you, didn't she?"

Merrymen pointed toward the kitchen again.

"We're looking for your son," I reminded him. "We're looking for a girl named Adele."

"You're looking for jail time," he said. "I'm calling the police. What are your names?"

"Hal Jeffcoat and Glenn Beckert," I answered. "Now we're leaving."

I moved toward the front door. Ames backed away with me and dropped the bat on the tile floor. Merrymen took a step toward his fallen club.

"Best not," Ames said.

"Go, go report to the bitch that you almost killed my dog," Merrymen shouted. "I can get another dog. Two of them."

"Just be sure you clean up their manure and yours," said Ames.

We went through the door. Ames pushed it closed behind us.

"He might have a gun," I said.

"Might," Ames agreed.

We hurried to the Cutlass and got in. Merrymen's door didn't open. I made a circle in the cul-de-sac and headed away from the far side.

"You know how to swing a bat," I said.

"Played some," Ames said calmly.

"In high school?"

"Farm team. Pittsburgh Pirates. Didn't have the temper or talent for it," he said. "Long time ago."

I checked my watch. I still had an hour and a half before I met Sally and her kids for dinner.

"You've got some time?" I asked.

"Whatever the Lord if there is one is willing to give," he said.

I pulled over to the Walgreen drugstore at Tuttle and Fruitville. Walgreens drugstores seem to be about half a mile apart throughout Sarasota. The phone book was reasonably intact and I found a Bernard Corsello on North Orange. We drove, said nothing. I turned on the radio. A talk-show host I didn't recognize was on WFLA talking about serial killers. The NPR station had the market report. I switched back to AM and found WGUL, the oldies station.

A woman was singing, "Let me free."

" 'Let Me Go, Lover,' " Ames said. "First song written for a television drama. Don't know her name."

The woman on the radio was just singing, "If you'll just let me go" when we pulled in front of a one-story house just north of Sixth. The neighborhood was a couple of notches below middle class. The houses were small, in reasonable shape with neat green yards.

A half-moon and bright stars. A nice evening. On the cool side. Some kids on bicycles, two black, one white, the kids purposely came close to hitting us and zipped away jabbering to each other.

There was no driveway. The concrete walkway was narrow and cracked. There were lights on in curtained rooms on both sides of the door. I found the bell, pushed it, listened to it ring inside, and waited. No answer. I rang again. No answer.

I tried the door. It opened but not much, about three or four inches. It was hitting something.

"Mr. Corsello," I called through the crack.

No answer. I pushed the door again. It gave. A little. Ames pitched in. Whatever was blocking the door gave way enough for me to stick my head in. I saw what was blocking the door.

The body was facedown, head toward the door. There were two reasons to think he was dead. The floor in front of your front door is an unusual place to take a nap. I've known stranger ones, but the blotch of blood and the hole in his back took whatever hope I might have had.

"Dead man," I told Ames.

He nodded as if he were accustomed to finding dead men on a daily basis. I stood trying to decide which way to take this. I looked around the street. Nothing. No one. A small red car with a bad muffler zoomed down the street.

I thought about the missing Mickey and Adele and I motioned for Ames to help me push some more. When there was enough room, we slid through the door. I closed it behind us. There was a light on in the entryway. From where we stood we could see the entire place. Small living room with an old overstuffed chair placed about four feet away from a giant television screen where an old episode of *Jeopardy!* was going forward silently. It was an old show. Alex Trebek, with no gray hairs, played with the cards in his hand.

Beyond the living-room area was a kitchen with a table

and four chairs. To the left were three doors. Two were open. The closest one was a bedroom with a neatly made bed, a big dresser, and a giant Jesus on the cross over the dresser. The second open door was a bathroom. No light was on in there.

"Don't touch anything," I said, kneeling at the body for a number of reasons.

First, I wanted to confirm that he was really dead. He was. Completely. The body was cool. The dead man was wearing a robe. It was pulled high enough so I could see the only other thing he had on, a pair of underpants.

I guessed the dead man had been in his late sixties, maybe older. I guessed he was Bernard Corsello. I wondered about a lot of things.

"Quick look around," I said. "Touch nothing."

"What am I looking for?"

"Something that says this has something to do with Adele. Something I don't want to find."

Ames strode over the body and into the living room. I went for the open bedroom. On the table next to the bed was a flat and warm glass that seemed to have about two inches of some liquid in it. I smelled it. Cola. Next to the drink were two pens, a pad of paper, a telephone, a wallet, and some change. I picked up the wallet, opened it, and found sixty-two dollars. I rubbed off my prints with my shirt and put the wallet down. Nothing else in the room seemed interesting except for the hanging Jesus who looked down on me. I didn't say anything to him. I hadn't since I was a kid.

I went into the bathroom. Nothing of interest. The third room, the one with the closed door, I opened with my shirt as a mitt. The lights were off. I hit the wall switch and wiped away my print.

This was clearly Mickey Merrymen's home away from home. The drawers were open, and nearly empty except for a few T-shirts and a single pair of underpants with a hole in them. A CD player sat on the small dresser. The bed was a mess. There was a small bookcase next to the bed. There were only a few books in it, all horror stories, Straub, Koontz, King, Saul, McKimmon. What made it clearly

Mickey's room were the three photographs tacked to the wall above the bed. They were small. One was on an angle. Adele was in all of them. From the holes in the wall around the three photographs I guessed there had been more, lots more.

Adele was alone in two of the photographs, both outdoors. Adele from stomach to head. The other of her alone was also outdoors. In the first she was smiling. In the second, she pursed her lips with a pretend kiss for the camera. She looked like any other pretty sixteen-year-old. Her past didn't show. In the third photograph, Adele was leaning against a tall young man who reminded me of both Michael "the bat" Merrymen and a young Anthony Perkins. His arm was around Adele. He was grinning. I liked his white button-down shirt. I liked his smile. I didn't like having Adele's photographs on the wall. I took them down, dropped the tacks in an empty wastebasket, and pocketed the pictures. There was nothing else I could find to link Adele to the house. I doubted the police would go over every print in the place, but there was nothing I could do about it.

I found Ames in the kitchen looking at the refrigerator. There were magnets holding up three messages. Each magnet was a photograph, Einstein, Marlon Brando, and Hank Aaron. One message was a simple grocery list. The second message read: "Insurance due first Tuesday of the month." The third message was, "Remember to call for pizza for Mickey and the girl."

I pulled the pizza message from under Hank Aaron and said, "Anything?"

Ames shook his head "no" and we headed toward the corpse and the door.

"Didn't take his money, the television, CD player," I said.

We moved past the dead man and Ames stepped out of the door. I should have hurried after him but I looked one last time at the dead man and the thought came. That was the way I wanted to see the man who had run down my wife four years ago on Lake Shore Drive. He had left her bleeding, dying, barely alive. It took at least five minutes before someone went to help her. It was too late. The driver had gone on. What was that murderer doing now? Was he haunted by what he had done? Had he been a drunk who didn't remember the life he had taken? I looked back at Jesus in the next room expecting no answer or solace.

"Best be going," Ames said.

I looked back at Corsello one last time, wiped the door handle, went into the night, and wiped the outside handle.

"Now?" asked Ames.

I looked around. The street was almost empty. Half a block down to our left an old black woman was laboring under the weight of two heavy shopping bags. We got into the car and drove.

I dropped Ames and his scooter back at the Texas Bar and Grille.

"We're looking for Flo Zink's white minivan," I said as we maneuvered the scooter out of the trunk. "This kid," I said, pulling out the photograph of Mickey and Adele, "is probably with her."

"I'll ask around," Ames said.

Neither of us said what we were thinking. Adele had killed before. She had killed a man who deserved killing. Adele, in short, knew how to pull a trigger. If something had happened, something . . . I gave up.

"I'll call you tomorrow," I said.

Ames nodded, locked his scooter, and waved as I got into the Cutlass.

It had been a busy day. And it wasn't over.

I called the police from a pay phone on Main Street. If I leaned back I could have seen the downtown police headquarters. I hit 911.

"How can we help you?" a woman asked calmly.

I told her, with my best James Mason imitation, that a man was dead. I quickly gave the address and hung up before she could ask for my name.

When I got to the Bangkok, the place was packed. Sally saw me making my way through the crowd. She was seated at a booth with her two kids, Michael, fourteen, and Susan, eleven. Sally raised a hand and I moved to the booth.

Sally and Susan sat on one side of the table. I sat next to Michael on the other.

"Someone hit you," Susan said, pointing to my cheek.

"Yes."

"Why?"

"I brought her bad news."

"It happens," Sally said.

Sally is and will always be a year older than I am. She is solid, ample, and pretty with clear skin, short wavy hair, and a voice that always reminded me of Lauren Bacall.

"Ready to order now?" asked a beautiful Thai waitress in a yellow and white silk dress.

"You look terrible," Michael said, turning toward me.

Neither of Sally's kids disliked me. I think I puzzled them. I never made jokes, didn't work at making them like me. And I'm sure they wondered what their mother found in the soulful, balding man who reached for the tea and said, "You guys?"

"Crispy duck," said Sally.

"The same with a Thai iced tea," said Michael.

"Another one. Thai iced tea too."

"I'll have the tofu pad thai," I said.

The pretty waitress smiled and walked away.

"So," said Sally. "How was your day and how can you afford this?"

"New clients," I said. "Two of them."

"Your cheek?" she said.

"Someone slapped me."

"You deck him?" Michael asked.

"It was a woman," I said.

"Did you deck her?" asked Susan.

"She was a lot bigger than I am," I said.

"Most people are," said Susan. "That doesn't mean you should let them hit you."

"It's part of my job," I said. "I slap people with a summons. They slap me with their hands."

"It's more than that," Sally said, looking into my eyes.

Yes, I thought, I've just come from discovering a dead man, almost certainly murdered. I not only found him, I pounded his head three or four times when I tried to open his door.

"There's more," I said. "Later."

During dinner, Susan did most of the talking, mainly about a friend named Jackie who may have decided she no longer wanted to be friends with Susan. Jackie's transgressions were numerous. I know one was that Jackie had begun sitting at a different table at lunch. I don't remember the others. I don't remember eating. I sort of remember paying the check with some of the crumpled bills from Marvin Uliaks. I sort of remember Sally asking the waitress to pack up the pad thai and rice I hadn't touched and put it in a little white carton for me to take home.

I do remember being in the parking lot where Sally told the kids to go to her car and she walked me to my rental and handed me the brown bag of rice and pad thai.

"What is it?" she asked as we stood in the parking lot.

Some kids came running out yelling and laughing from the 7-Eleven at the end of the small mall. I looked at them and back at Sally.

I had been seeing Sally for a few months. We were friends. Well, maybe we were more than friends, but nothing intimate, not yet. I couldn't. I hadn't been able to find a safe place for the memory of my dead wife. I didn't know if I ever would even with Ann Horowitz's help.

And Sally had been a widow for more than four years, too busy for men, not interested in becoming involved, not really being pursued. We were friends. She was also a family therapist and at the Children's Services of Sarasota. Adele had been and officially still was one of her cases.

"Adele," I said.

I looked over at Michael and Susan quarreling over something in the backseat of her decade-old Honda.

"What happened?" Sally asked calmly.

"You know about her and Lonsberg?" I asked.

"What she told me. What Flo told me," she said.

"Adele's missing," I said. "It looks as if she ran away with a kid named Mickey Merrymen. You know the name?"

"No," she said. "What does this have to do with Lonsberg?"

"Adele and Mickey may have stolen a roomful of Lonsberg's unpublished manuscripts."

"Why?"

"I don't know," I said. "But it gets worse. I'm not sure you want to know the rest."

"I've got to find Adele," she said. "I need to know whatever there is to know."

"You don't have much free time to search for missing girls," I said. "Not with your caseload."

"I get a little help from the police when I need it," she said.

"And from your friends," I said. "Mickey Merrymen's grandfather is dead. Murdered, I think. Ames and I found his body about an hour before I came here."

"Which accounts for your lack of appetite."

"Which accounts for my lack of appetite," I agreed. "Can you forget this conversation for a few days while I look for Adele?"

"No," she said, glancing over at Michael and Susan who were now looking at us impatiently.

"They thought you were coming over for Trivial Pursuit," Sally said.

"Not tonight. Can you forget?"

"No," she said. "But I can lie and say we didn't have this conversation. I lie a lot. It's part of my job. Sometimes, too often, you have to lie to kids to give them a chance to survive. Call me. If you don't, I'll call you."

She moved forward and kissed my cheek slowly, the side that hadn't been slapped by Bubbles Dreemer, and then she headed for her car.

I drove back to the DQ parking lot, the smell of Thai food battling with the odor of a decade of indifferent cleaning and those little yellow cardboard things that you hang from your mirror to override whatever has been dropped or invaded the upholstery.

It was definitely a Joan Crawford night. I was always ready for *Mildred Pierce*, but tonight I'd go for *Woman on the Beach*. I knew just where the tape was in the pile next to my television set.

The DQ was still open but I didn't feel like doing any more talking. This had already been the kind of day I had been trying to avoid for the last five years. I told life to leave me alone. It refused to stop knocking at my door, calling me on the phone, and slapping me in the face.

I walked up the concrete steps and moved along the rusting metal railing on one side and the dark offices on the other. When I came to my door, I found an envelope stuck into it with a push pin. The only word on the envelope in penciled block letters was "FONESCA."

I dropped the envelope in my brown bag, opened the door, turned on the lights, and moved to my desk where I put down the bag and opened the envelope.

The single white sheet inside bore a simple, short message in the same block letters as my name on the envelope.

STOP LOOKING FOR HER. ONE INNOCENT PERSON IS DEAD AND GONE. LET IT BE AN END. LET THIS BE A WARNING.

It was unsigned. I put the brown paper bag on the ledge of my office window and went into my small office, which was really what passed for home, a single cot, which I made up every day with an old comforter and two pillows. A chest of drawers. A tiny refrigerator. A closet. A fourteen-inch black-and-white television with a VCR and a stack of tapes and a folding wooden television table. It had taken me minutes to move in three years ago. It would take me ten minutes to move out when the time came.

I found *Woman on the Beach* and did my best not to think, not to think about the murdered man, not to think about Adele, not to think about the pleading face of Marvin Uliaks. I succeeded when the tape came on. The dream world on the tube was mine. Swirling behind it in my mind, deep but hard and always ready to scream, was the image of my wife being hit by that car on Lake Shore Drive. I hadn't been there but I had imagined, dreamed about what it had looked like, about what she might have had time to think, to feel. Each dream was just a bit different. I wanted one solid one to hang on to, but my imagination refused to cooperate, to tell me the truth or a lie I could believe.

Joan Crawford smiled, but there was a troubled look behind that smile. I knew why. I had seen this picture many times. It never changed. Only my dream changed.

I took off my clothes while I watched and hung them in my almost empty closet. I lay in my underwear. Joan was in for pain, lots of pain, lots of anguish. That was her job in film. She bore it well. Better than those of us who have to live it.

I couldn't sleep. I listened to the whishing of cars going down 301. There weren't many of them at this hour and I normally tuned them out, but tonight I listened. I lay there for a while in the dark, then got up and turned on the light.

I reached for one of Lonsberg's books. Maybe a random passage would put me to sleep. When I married, when I had a wife, I always kept books at the bedside, books I could nip at randomly. The Holy Scriptures weren't bad. Poetry, if it wasn't too abstract, was fine. History, popular history, was particularly good. William Manchester was perfect, but I seldom went for fiction. I sat cross-legged in bed in my shorts, scratched my chest, and opened my battered book. I flipped to about the middle of the book and started to read:

Foreceman was angry. Foreceman was mad as hell. Foreceman was ready to tear off arms or heads, to take a bomb to the top of the Barnes Hospital, throw it off, and destroy all of St. Louis except the part and people he cared for. Luckily the Cardinals were out of town. Foreceman knew way down deep where even he couldn't find it that he wasn't going to tear off, blow up, or destroy anything but his own sanity. He had lost everything. Ellen, the factory, the house, the car, two fingers off of his right hand, and three toes, thanks to bad luck, diabetes, and some conspiracy between heaven and hell. He was on his own, a fat little man in a fat world.

He sat in his apartment looking out the window at

the thin layer of snow on the street below and the snow that was still falling from a sky he couldn't tell had a beginning or end.

Okay then. Why was he laughing? What was so damn funny? He didn't own a television set. Not anymore. Not since Ellen and Vickie. He didn't read the papers. He didn't listen to the radio or records. His day was worked out. Get up, shave, eat two fried eggs and white bread. Wonder bread or Silvercup. It had no taste but he wanted no taste except the flabber of egg and the heavy muck of Miracle Whip.

Check the mail. Throw it away unless his check came that day. Walk, walk, walk. He was the fat walking man, hands in his pockets, serious look on his face or sudden unexplained smile. People avoided him. Store clerks didn't meet his eyes. Eggs, hot dogs, cans of sloppy joe, bread, cucumbers, butter pecan ice cream. Walk. They called him the fat walking man. He knew it, heard it. Maybe he didn't hear it. Maybe he imagined it as he made his plans for destroying St. Louis, Nashville, New York, Asheville, places he and Ellen and Vickie and . . . what were the names of the others? What was his father's name? His mother's? Hers was Denise, but his? His father pitched horseshoes in the park with old men who had once been young old men.

At night, just before dark and hot dogs and a half of unpeeled cucumber, Foreceman had his talk with Ellen. She was a kinder Ellen, a more patient Ellen than the one who had lived, but sometimes they argued and she asked him the questions he didn't want to hear. And he answered.

Ellen: What do you want to do?

Foreceman: Erase the past.

Ellen: You can't.

Foreceman: I didn't say I could. I said I wanted to. I want to strap on a gun belt, get a machine gun, fill my pockets with grenades, put on a helmet, and lead a charge.

Ellen: Against who?

Foreceman: The past. I want to destroy the past.

Ellen: Why?

Foreceman: Because it won't come back. If it won't come back, it doesn't deserve to live.

Ellen: You are very crazy.

Foreceman: I know, but that's all I have.

Ellen: The children.

Foreceman: I never had them. Are they alive?

Ellen: Find out.

Foreceman: No. They're part of the past.

Ellen: Or the future.

Foreceman: They hated me. They ran away.

Ellen: They did. And they were right.

Foreceman: They were right. I screamed. I ignored. I think I even beat them. Did I beat them?

Ellen: No.

Foreceman: You're not real so you won't tell me the truth.

Ellen: You beat them.

Foreceman: Did I . . . do things to them? I don't remember.

Ellen: You didn't do things to them. You never did anything to anyone, not to yourself, not to me.

Foreceman: Let's play gin. Let's play Monopoly. Let's play chess. Let's play Yahtzee. Let's play pinner baseball. Let's play pin the tail on the donkey. Let's pretend you like sex with me. Let's take a bath, a hot bath that burns and makes the air cold when we get out.

Ellen: We never did those things.

Foreceman: Then what? Then what the hell what?

Ellen: The children.

And then Foreceman turned her off, had some butter pecan ice cream in one of the two Fiesta ware glasses that were still left, and went to sleep thinking of the destruction of the world, thinking of the destruction of the world of William Clamborne Foreceman.

I put the book down, wondered for a few seconds about the man who could have written this, and fell asleep.

In my dream I did what I had done every weekday morning of my married life. It was part of our marriage agreement. I had been warned by her and her friends. She needed a cup of coffee before she could function even minimally. I wasn't a coffee drinker, but I had always been an early riser.

In my dream as it had been in life, I got up quietly, staggered through the apartment into the kitchen, took a bag of gourmet coffee beans out of the freezer, opened the cabinet next to the refrigerator, and pulled out the small coffee bean grinder. I put a filter in the coffeemaker and filled the plastic tank with tap water.

It was a beautiful dream. The sun was coming through the slightly frosted windows. I could see Lake Michigan between two high-rises as I opened the coffee and began to pour beans into the grinder. Routine. Comfortable. And then it happened as it does in dreams.

The bottom of the bag fell out. Brown beans rained onto the cool tile floor spraying the kitchen, bouncing off cabinets, the refrigerator. The bag should have been empty but the beans kept falling, crashing like a driving rain. The floor was turning pebbly brown and barefooted I danced feeling each small bean under me.

I was panicked. She had heard the thundering beans. She came in. Her hair a morning disarray, her eyes half closed. She saw the mess and tiptoed in slow motion carefully making her way to me, finding clearings in the layers of brown hail.

The phone was ringing.

The smell of coffee rustled through her hair as she touched my cheek.

"I'm so sorry," I said.

The phone was ringing.

She smiled and shook her head as if I had failed to understand some simple truth.

The phone was ringing.

I didn't want the dream to end, but she stepped back and I was awake.

5

THE PHONE WAS ringing in the other room. I rubbed my scratchy face, scratched my itchy stomach, and made it to the phone after five rings. Two more and it would have turned on my answering machine. I decided to start breaking my rule till I found Adele. I picked it up.

"Fonesca," I said.

"Harvey," he said and then gave his Paul Harvey imitation. "Stand by for news."

The phone was cordless. I got the white carton of pad thai and the small carton of white rice, opened them, and fished a white plastic fork from my desk drawer while Harvey talked.

"Vera Lynn Uliaks ceased to exist in 1975," he said. "She worked in a real estate office from 1972 to 1975, filed income tax every year. I've got her social security number, but no trace of her ever having used it or of filing taxes after 1975. No credit cards. No felonies in any state by anyone with that name. The lady vanished. You want to know how much money she made in 1975?"

"No," I said, eating cold tofu.

"That's it," he said.

"Name of the real estate company she worked for?"

"Cornell and Bostik," he said. "They're still there. You want the address and phone number?"

I took them down on the lined pad on the desk.

"Anything else?" he asked.

"Not right now."

"Get me something more to work on. I've got long fingers and the Internet is waiting to invade everyone's privacy."

I hung up, pushed the remainder of my Thai food away, and dialed the number in Arcadia. A very young woman named Faith informed me that the company no longer belonged to Mr. Cornell and Mr. Bostik. Both were dead. A woman named Lorraine Kinch had bought the business at least ten years ago. According to the young woman, there were no records kept from Cornell and Bostik. Since the young woman couldn't have been more than nineteen or twenty, she was not even born when Vera Lynn Uliaks seemed to have disappeared, and according to Faith, Ms. Kinch was busy with a client.

"It's urgent," I lied.

"Well," Faith said after appropriate hesitation. "I'll give you her cell phone number."

She did. I thanked her, hung up, and called the cell phone. Lorraine Kinch picked up on the second ring and said, "Yes."

"Ms. Kinch, my name is Lew Fonesca. I'm searching for a woman named Vera Lynn Uliaks who worked for Cornell and Bostik."

"I don't know any Vera Lynn Uliaks," she said. "There was a young woman who worked in the office when I took it over. She quit. I don't think she wanted to work for a woman."

"And that was it? You never saw her again?"

"No, this is a small town, Mr. . . . ."

"Fonesca," I said.

"I think I heard that she got married and . . . oh, I remember. She . . . I really can't talk now. I'm showing a house to a client."

"Can I call you back?"

"There's nothing to call back about," she said.

"But you remembered . . ."

That was as far as we got. She hung up. I called Arcadia information and got the number for the newspaper.

"Arcadia *News*," a young woman said.

"Who is your oldest reporter?" I asked.

"Our oldest . . ."

"The one who's been there the longest."

"Mr. Thigpen, no, wait, Ethyl's been here longer, I think."

"How long?"

"I don't know," the girl said. "Twenty, thirty years, maybe more. She does social coverage."

"May I talk to her?"

"I'll connect you to her desk. She's there right now."

There was a click, a few seconds of Barry Manilow, and then a no-nonsense older woman's voice.

"Bingham," she said.

"My name's Fonesca. I'm looking for a woman named Vera Lynn Uliaks. She's the sister of a friend and he wants to find her."

"Marvin," she said.

"Yes," I confirmed.

"Slow one."

"Very slow. He lives in Sarasota now. About Vera Lynn . . ."

"She married Charles Dorsey," she said. "I'd say 1975 but I'd have to check."

"I'm impressed."

"Needn't be," said Ethyl. "I'd like to string you along, tell you I have one of those photographic memories like those women on television, but it's not in me. I was Vera Lynn's bridesmaid. Not a big wedding, but I stood up and so did Charlie's brother Clark."

"You know where they went, Charlie and Vera Lynn?"

There was a long pause and then Ethyl Bingham said, "If you're a reporter or something trying to dig up what happened to the Taylor girl, believe me you're wasting your time. It was an accident. I knew Vera Lynn. She had a

temper, yes, but under it . . . It was the rumors, the talk that
drove them off, not some big job Charlie said he had waiting in Ohio. Charlie was doing just fine right here in Arcadia."

"What did he do?"

"He was chief of police."

"And something happened to a girl named Taylor?"

"You didn't know," she said.

"I told you. Marvin wants to find his sister. What was
the Taylor girl's first name?"

"Sarah, Sarah Taylor," she said. "That's all I've got to
tell you."

"What happened to her?"

"She died," said Ethyl Bingham. "She died. I'm sorry. I
don't like ghosts in the morning."

"I know how you feel," I said. "But . . ."

"I'm sorry. That's all I can or wish to say."

She hung up.

I called Harvey and said, "Good Morning, Americans,"
in my best Paul Harvey, which is far worse than Harvey's.
"Vera Lynn Uliaks married a Charles Dorsey in Arcadia in
1975. He was chief of police. A young woman named
Sarah Taylor died in 1975 in Arcadia. There may be a connection."

"If the Arcadia court system and police have a data bank
or the newspaper, I'll get back to you soon. Meanwhile,
I'll work on finding Charles Dorsey and Vera Lynn Dorsey."

"Thanks," I said.

"Just keep mentioning it," he said. "I live on health food,
computers, and sincere compliments."

I shaved with my electric razor and went outside where
the sun was glowing orange and happy. I ignored it and
with my toothbrush and paste moved down to the rest room
shared by the tenants.

An old man, fully clothed, was sitting on the toilet. His
head was back and he was snoring. I moved to the sink
and brushed my teeth. The hot water wasn't working. I
washed cold.

Considering the state of the building, the indifference of

the landlord, and the clients and the homeless, the rest room
was reasonably clean thanks to Marvin Uliaks who swept
and scrubbed once a week and then knocked on every door
in the building holding his hand out and saying, "Bathroom's clean."

Some said "thanks." Some didn't answer. Most gave him
a quarter or even half a dollar. I gave him what I could,
usually a buck. It was worth it.

The homeless guy snoring in the toilet stall had a definite
smell of baked and spoiling human. He woke up with a
snort. There was a partition between us but I could hear
him drop his pants, use the toilet, cough, pull up his pants,
and stagger forward.

He turned to look at me.

"You're the little Italian," he said, pointing at me.

In spite of the heat he wore two sweaters and a three- or
four-day growth of beard.

"I am," I said, washing the remnants of soap from my
face. The bruise on my face provided by Bubbles Dreemer
was almost gone.

"I slept here," the man said, reaching into his pocket for
something he didn't seem to be able to find.

"I guessed."

"Usually sleep in a closet at one of the twenty-four-hour
Walgreens," he said. "Move from one to the other. Used to
be a pharmacist. No, that's not right. I am a pharmacist. I
just don't work as one. It's been more than a while."

"That a fact?" I asked, toweling off my face.

"True as the fact that the sun is out there waiting to bomb
us to early ultraviolet death," he said, searching his other
pocket for whatever was missing. "Not good to spend too
much time in the sun."

"I'll remember," I said.

"You're in the office about five doors down," he said.

"I am."

He failed to find what he was searching for in his second
pocket.

"I'm a bit unsteady today," he said. "Oh, I don't drink.
Never did. No drugs either. It's my mind. Doesn't function
right. I lose days, weeks, get headaches, fall a lot, get to

know the people over there in the emergency rooms at Doctor's Hospital and Sarasota Memorial."

"Sorry," I said.

"It's the way things are," he said with a sigh. "Saw something last night might interest you."

"What was that?" I said, heading for the door.

I had to come within inches of him. Decay.

"The ghost of Martin Luther posted the bans on your door," he said. "I stood in the shadows, and in his robes, a cowl over his head, he posted them on your door."

"A man dressed like a priest?"

"Or a woman," he said. "My eyesight is . . . well, years ago I had glasses but today I'm a living testament to man's ability to endure."

There was a definite note of pride in his voice.

"We endure," I said. "You like Thai food?"

"I consume any food. I'm a human in need of fuel. I have given up the concept of like and dislike of food, lodging, or clothes. It exists and I wander."

"Come on," I said.

He followed me to my office door and pointed to it.

"There is where he posted his conceits," he said.

"You have a name?" I asked, opening the door.

"I had one," he said. "Now I am known as The Digger."

"Why?"

"Who," he said, putting a not clean palm on my shoulder, "the hell knows? But it seems to fit me."

"Wait here," I said, leaving him in the doorway. I retrieved the two cartons of food and my plastic fork and brought it to him.

"Thai, you say?"

"Yes," I said.

"It would probably settle nicely with a root beer," he said, cradling the two cartons.

I fished a dollar out of my pocket and handed it to him.

"I'll accept this food and dollar if you'll accept my thanks," he said.

"I accept, and thanks especially for telling me about Martin Luther's visit."

"Are you a Lutheran?" he asked.

The phone began to ring.

"Lapsed Episcopalian," I said.

"Odd for an Italian," The Digger said.

The phone kept ringing.

"Root beer," I said.

He took the hint and wandered away. I closed the door behind him and went for the phone.

"Fonesca," I said.

"Ed Viviase," the caller said.

Ed Viviase was a detective in the Sarasota Police Department. I liked him. He tolerated me. Considering the fact that I was a depressed process server who basically wanted to be left alone in my room, our paths had crossed more times than chance would account for. Sarasota is not a big city, but I doubted if many other noncriminals who lived and visited here were known by Ed Viviase and the rest of the force.

"We have to talk," he said.

"Let's talk," I said.

"In my office," he said. "Fifteen minutes."

"Fifteen minutes," I agreed.

He hung up. Sarasota Police Headquarters is little more than a block away, north on 301, cross the street to the right, and there it is less than half a block away. Fifteen minutes was plenty of time to walk to his office and wonder why he wanted to see me.

I put on clean slacks and a clean white short-sleeved shirt with a button-down collar. One of the collar buttons was slightly cracked. When it went, I'd probably just throw the shirt in the garbage can and pick up another one at the Women's Resource Center.

The Digger was sitting at one of the canopied metal tables in front of the DQ eating his Thai food and drinking what I assumed was a large root beer. I nodded to him and he nodded back as I stopped at the open window of the DQ. Dave was there. Dave, leather-worn by the sun, the face of an adventurer. He reminded me of Sterling Hayden.

"What do you have ready I can eat while I walk?" I asked.

Dave looked back.

"Double burger with cheese," he said.

"I'll take it."

"You got it."

I paid and said, "How's the sailing?"

"I'm thinking of taking her around the world," he said. "Sell this place and go. A year. Maybe more. You can come. I mean it. You don't talk much. You're a good listener. I could teach you enough so you could help and I'd supply provisions."

"I get seasick," I said, accepting the double burger and handing him two dollar bills.

"You'd get over it," Dave said.

"Can you play tapes on your ship?"

"Songs?"

"Videos," I said. "If I go, Joan Crawford goes."

"Fonesca, you're saying no to a dream here."

"It's your dream, Dave."

"Think about it," he said.

There were customers behind me, a pair of old women.

"I will," I said, knowing I wouldn't as I stepped away and headed for Detective Ed Viviase.

6

THE DOOR TO Viviase's office was open. His name was Etienne. No one called him Etienne, not, according to him, even his wife. He was Ed. That's what it said on the small plaque on his desk: "Detective Ed Viviase."

The last time I had been in the office, there were scaffolds against two walls that were going to be painted the same shade of detective brown as the other two. This time there was no scaffolding, just a large office with very little furniture, three metal desks, a couple of chairs, and a line of file cabinets. Each desk held a computer and stacks of papers and reports threatening to tumble or already tumbled.

Viviase was the only detective in the room. I guess he had seniority. He was closest to the window in the room.

"Lewis," he said, shaking his head as he looked up at me from behind his desk over the glasses perched on the end of his ample nose.

It was getting to be our regular routine.

Viviase was a little under six feet tall, a little over fifty years old, and a little over two hundred twenty pounds. His hair was short, dark, and his face was that of a man filled with sympathy, the smooth pink face of a man whose genes were good and who probably didn't drink. He was wearing a rumpled sports jacket and a red tie. He looked like a policeman, a cup of coffee in front of him, an already tired look on his face though it was a little before ten in the morning.

I knew he had a wife, kids, worries about his older daughter's tuition and bills at the University of Florida, and an inability to resist carbohydrate intake. Ergo, the oversized chocolate-filled croissant on a napkin next to his coffee cup.

"Have a seat," he said. "We'll play a game."

I sat across from him. He held up his cup, wanting to know if I'd like some coffee. I had drunk some of the coffee from the machine down the hall once before. The pain had been bearable.

"Okay," said Viviase, "let's play." He took a long drink of coffee making a face that suggested he was ingesting prison-made whiskey. "I describe two men. You tell me if they resemble anyone you know."

I nodded.

"One man is short, on the thin side, balding, looks like his pet turtle just got mashed on McIntosh Road. With him is a tall old man, denim, flannel, maybe even cowboy boots. Old man stands tall, looks like a cowboy."

I shrugged.

"You want to use a life line? Call a friend who might have an idea?" he asked.

"It sounds like me and Ames," I said.

"That your final answer?"

"Sounds like me and Ames."

"Then," he said, looking at his coffee and donut and settling on a bite of donut, "that would place the two of you at the home of a man who was murdered last night. Man's name was Corsello, Bernard Corsello, sixty-nine, retired shoe salesman from Utica."

"Someone said Ames and I killed this Corsello?"

"No," Viviase said with a shake of his head and a cheek full of croissant. "Three kids driving by Corsello's house said they saw two men go up to Corsello's door. They were on bikes. The kids, not the men. When they drove past the house about five minutes later, they saw two white men fitting yours and Ames McKinney's description getting into a white car, an old white car with a blue top. You renting a car, Lewis?"

"Yes," I said.

"Happen to be white with a blue top?"

"Yes."

He swiveled his chair, took off his glasses, and looked out the window. His back to me now he said, "Corsello was shot, bam, once, right through the stomach, tore a hole in his heart. Bullet dug its way through his back into the hallway wall. Shaeffer hasn't had much time but he thinks it's a nine-millimeter from a Glock. Nice gun, the Glock. Costs a lot but you get your money's worth. Lightweight, easy to shoot, no kickback, almost indestructible. Know anyone with a gun like that?"

"No," I said.

"If your friend Ames were to carry a weapon, what would you guess it would be?" Viviase swiveled back to face me and adjusted his glasses. His right hand reached for the donut and then clasped his left instead. He began tapping his thumbs together.

"Ames isn't allowed to carry a gun," I said.

"I know. I said 'if,'" Viviase reminded me.

"Something old, heavy, noisy, reliable," I said.

Viviase shook his head.

"What did you find in Corsello's house?" he asked.

"I wasn't at Corsello's house," I said. "It was another tall cowboy and short Italian."

He unclenched his hands and downed more coffee.

"Maybe this will help," he said. "We know you didn't kill Corsello, at least not the time the kids saw you. He'd been dead for hours. But you were in there with the body for at least five minutes."

"No," I said.

"Lewie, don't make me bring those kids in here for a lineup," he said. "Waste my time, your time. And I don't like one of the kids. Smart mouth. X-rated mouth. Seen too many movies with that black guy, what's his name, Martin Lawrence."

"We knocked," I said. "The door was open."

"Progress," Viviase said with a very false smile, reaching for his coffee. "Go on."

"We went in, found him dead. Got out and I called nine-one-one."

"Didn't leave your name," Viviase said. "Tape sounds like someone doing a bad imitation of Rex Harrison."

"James Mason," I said.

"You left the scene of a crime, a homicide."

"I panicked. I called the police," I said.

Viviase was shaking his head now. When he stopped, he adjusted his glasses and said, "Why were you there? What were you looking for in his house? What did you find?"

Viviase was well acquainted with Adele, former child prostitute, abused daughter, suspect in a murder. He knew Adele lived with Flo now. He knew a lot but he wasn't going to get anything more from me.

"He called me," I lied. Lying is no problem for me. I have a good memory. It takes a good memory to be a successful liar.

"Why?" Viviase asked, sitting back with his hands behind his head in an I-know-you're-lying pose.

"Don't know, just asked me to come over about six."

"When did he call?"

"Morning," I said to give myself as much room as possible to be sure he hadn't died before my created phone call. "Early morning."

"Why would he ask a depressed process server to come to his house?" Viviase asked.

"I don't know," I said.

"Why did you agree to see him?"

"He said it was important."

"What did you find in those five or ten minutes you and McKinney were alone in the house?"

"We weren't in there four or five or ten minutes," I said. "Maybe two minutes to be sure he was dead and another minute to be sure the killer or someone else wasn't still in the house."

"Michael Merrymen," he said. "Recognize the name?"

"Ames and I went to see him yesterday," I said. "What does he have to do . . ."

"He's the dead man's son-in-law," explained Viviase. "See this file?"

He held up a green folder about two inches thick with papers creeping out. "Michael Merrymen is a lunatic. He has sued and been sued by some of the best and worst people in Sarasota. He has threatened bodily harm, frightened children, and is suspected of destroying the lawns, automobiles, vegetation, and small animals of neighbors. So, question three. Why did you go see Merrymen? He says you did. You and Ames and that Ames almost killed his dog with a baseball bat."

"You said the man's crazy," I said.

"Crazy, not blind. The dog's almost dead."

"Why does Merrymen say we were there?" I asked innocently.

"To spy on him for his neighbors. He claims you represented yourselves as police officers."

It was getting deep now. I almost considered asking for a cup of coffee, but I wasn't that desperate yet.

"We were looking for Merrymen's son," I said.

Viviase slapped the desk with both hands. The coffee cup, croissant remnant, and piles of paper jumped.

"Progress. Fill in."

"Merrymen made no sense. He didn't know where his son was."

"Why were you looking for his son?"

"I think he can help me track down someone I have papers to serve on."

"Who?"

"Can't divulge," I said.

"How does contempt sound to you?"

"Like a word I've heard a lot."

"So, you get a call from the dead guy in the morning . . ."

"He was alive when he called," I corrected.

"I stand corrected. You get a call to come to his house at six. Doesn't say why. Then you go to Michael Merrymen's house to look for his son Mickey. No Mickey. So, in a coincidence that rivals walking into your dear departed wife on a small street corner in Budapest, you go to the house of the grandfather of the very Mickey Merrymen you're looking for."

"A man in Flint, Michigan, got killed by frozen human waste that fell from an airplane last week," I said. "He was a hard hat at a construction site. Took the hat off for an instant to wipe his brow and . . ."

"Very enlightening," Viviase said. "Let's say the kid you're looking for, Mickey Merrymen, lived most of the time in his grandfather's house. Let's say maybe he has inherited some of his father's tendency toward out-of-control lunacy. Let's say he shot his grandfather, took his money, whatever there was of it, and ran. Let's say the kid you're looking for is our prime suspect."

"I'm not after him," I said. "I'm after someone he knows."

"What do we call that? A non sequitur? An abrupt change in subject? Who are you looking for and do you know where Mickey Merrymen is?"

"I don't know where Mickey Merrymen is," I said. "Who I'm looking for has nothing to do with Corsello's murder."

With the palms of his hands, Viviase rubbed his hair and looked down in thought. Then he straightened up and brushed his hair back with his fingers.

"When I find out who you're looking for, who's connected to Mickey Merrymen," he said calmly, "we'll have another talk. One with higher stakes."

"You going to talk to Ames?" I asked.

"What good would it do," he said. "That old man would tell us his name and not say another word. That's what he did the last time. I expect he would do the same again. You can go."

He tossed the end of his croissant into his mouth and washed it down with coffee.

"I hope I've helped," I said.

"Not in the least," he answered pleasantly. "Lewis, you can leave now."

I left.

When I got back to my office, I called Harvey the human computer.

"Got a little something for you, Lewis," he said. I could hear him clacking away at his computer while we spoke. "On April 12, 1975, in the town of Arcadia, Florida, a young woman named Sarah Taylor fell to her death from the window of the city building. Witnesses in the office were Sheriff Charles Dorsey and a Miss Vera Lynn Uliaks. You getting this, Lewis?"

"Yes?"

"The mourning period was all of two weeks before he quit his job and moved away. Vera Lynn packed up and left the same day. Someone found out the ex-sheriff and Vera Lynn were married in Ohio. A small item on the subject appeared in the newspaper."

"Story on Sarah Taylor's fall?"

"Listed as accident. That's all I can get. And I can't track down a Charles or Vera Lynn Dorsey, not in Ohio, not anywhere. I'll keep on it. But I can tell you where to find Clark Dorsey, Charlie's brother."

"Where?"

"Retired," Harvey said. "Former fireman in Arcadia. Lives in Osprey, right off Old Venice Road. Open your white pages. He's listed."

"Thanks, Harve."

"Let me know how it comes out," he said. "Holy piss. I've just broken into the Pentagon files."

"I thought you already did that," I said.

"But they keep changing passwords and access codes. Gets harder all the time."

"Have a good day, Harve," I said.

"It already is," he said.

I pulled out the sheet Lonsberg had given me with the phone numbers and addresses of his son and daughter. Osprey is on the way to Venice, no more than half an hour away, and Venice another ten minutes.

With the neatly folded threat that had been posted on my door tucked into my shirt pocket, I called Ames McKinney and asked him what his day was like.

"Cleaning and contemplation," he said.

I told him the police might be talking to him about our discovery of Corsello's body and told him what I had said. Then I asked him if he wanted to take a ride to Osprey and Venice.

"Armed?"

"Lightly," I said.

"When?"

"Pick you up in ten minutes."

"Can you make it an hour?" he said. "I'm working on the grill."

I agreed and walked over to Gwen's Diner. It was a little early for lunch but I was hungry. Gwen's is a holdover from a few years before the day Elvis supposedly came in in the 1950s. I looked over at Elvis. He was still smiling. There were two booths open. I went to the counter. If you looked out the window from any seat in Gwen's, you could watch the collisions where 301 met the curve at Tamiami Trail.

There was a nonsmoking section in Gwen's, not a real one, just a couple of tables set aside. People in the neighborhood called the place Gwen's II. The original Gwen, if she ever existed, was now long gone. The place was run by a woman named Sheila and her two teenage daughters, one of whom was about to graduate from Sarasota High School a block away, the other was seventeen and working on her second baby. Jesse, the younger one, short, blond, round with child, came up to me when I sat at the counter next to Tim from Steubenville. Tim was a regular, close to ninety. He lived in an assisted living home a short walk away at the end of Brother Geenen Way. He spent as much time as he could at Gwen's reading the newspaper, shaking his head, and trying to get people engaged in conversation over anything from the price of gasoline to the latest school shooting.

There was very little left of Tim from Steubenville. Blue veins undulated over the thin bones in his hands as he turned pages of the *Herald-Tribune* and shook his head.

"Fonesca," he said as Jesse poured me a coffee and waited.

"Fried egg sandwich," I said. "White toast."

"Tomato and onion?" she asked.

"Tomato, I'm working today."

"Fonesca," Tim from Steubenville repeated, tapping my arm.

It was a little after eleven. The place was empty except for me, Tim, and four guys who looked like air-conditioning repairmen in a booth drinking coffee and eating pie.

"Tim," I said.

"You see about this guy in Nebraska," he said, poking a finger at an article in the newspaper awkwardly folded. "Someone stuck a rattler in his mailbox."

"Did it bite him?" I asked.

"No, scared the shit out of him though," Tim said thoughtfully. "How'd you like to get up some morning, walk out to your mailbox expecting your pension check or AAA card, and find a rattlesnake."

"I don't have a mailbox," I said. "Just a slot in the door."

"Not the point, Fonesca."

He shook his head at my density and sipped at his sixth or seventh cup of coffee.

"Point is," he said. "You can be going along, minding your own business, thinking about some old song by Perry Como or Peggy Lee or what you might have for lunch, and bango-bamo, you got a snake hanging on your goddamn nose. Anything can happen. That's the truth of the news, what it really tells you. People don't understand. We don't have to know when there's a train derailed in Pakistan or a drug dealer gets knocked off in Colombia. Who needs to know that?"

I could think of some people but I just nodded at Jesse as she placed a mug of coffee in front of me.

"Point is that the newspapers are telling us that anything can happen, anytime. Careful doesn't take care of half of that. The newspaper is like the goddamn Bible. The Bible says God can do whatever He damn well pleases without giving a reason or making sense. We have to learn to take whatever comes and like it. Arguing with God is like arguing with the news. Same lesson."

"I agree," I said. "Tim, you're a philosopher."

"Used to be a printer," he answered, looking back at the newspaper for more disasters and surprises. "Nothing's changed. Not in thousands of years. Just put in engines, make bigger guns, take the taste out of our food, and why?"

"Why?" I asked as Jesse delivered my egg sandwich cut neatly down the middle with two pickle slices on the side.

Tim reached out and grabbed Jesse's wrist so she would hear the answer. Jesse patiently paused. There were no customers waiting and Tim was the diner's resident character.

"People think they can change things," he said softly. "They can't. They can make bigger, faster, even keep you alive a few years longer, but we all go through the cycle and never know if a rattler's going to come out of the mailbox."

Or what messages will be hung on our doors, I thought. Tim released Jesse's wrist though he couldn't have held it if she hadn't been willing to cooperate in the first place.

"Jesse," I asked, reaching for half a sandwich. "You know a Mickey Merrymen?"

Jesse was a pretty pale girl on the thin side. Her blond hair was short and her look was that of a kid who had a two-year-old at home and another on the way. Jesse's primary claim to respectability was that she was married. Her husband, Paul, also known as The Chink, was a mechanic right across the street in the Ford Agency. The two-year-old, Paulie Jr., was in day care every other day when Jesse wasn't working. Jesse was finishing high school through the mail. Jesse was and looked tired all the time.

"Freak time. Geek time," she said. "Yeah, I know him."

"What do you know about him?" I asked while Tim shook his head and pointed at yet another article to substantiate his world view that, as a matter of fact, was mine too.

"Mickey's a weird bird, an X-man mutant," she said. "Smart, a little nuts, not bad-looking when he cleans up, but a weird bird."

"Get in trouble?" I asked.

She shrugged.

"Look at this. Look at this," Tim said, finding some new truth in the *Herald-Tribune* in front of him. Tim spoke with the quiet resignation of one who knew everything he found would vindicate his philosophy. Tim was a true believer who moved from coffee during the day to the whiskey he must have kept secreted in his room at night and which was still not fully masked by Eckerd mouthwash in the morning.

"Mickey," I reminded Jesse.

"I think he graduated last year, works at the Burger King up the Trail," she said. "Says he's going to college. Or used to say it. Massachusetts Institute of Technicals or something. Father's nuts."

"That's all you know about Mickey Merrymen?" I said, finishing the first half of the sandwich.

"Merrymen?" asked Tim. "Michael Merrymen?"

Jesse and I looked at Tim who smiled and said, "Man's in the paper almost as much as that doctor who's always suing the hospital or someone," said Tim. "Classic paranoid. Sues Albertson's, Barnes & Noble, neighbors, gets himself listed in the crime reports, noise levels, guns. Name it. He's your man. Even tried to run for City Council a few years ago. Couldn't come up with even twenty signatures on his petition. My theory, if you ask me, is he saw the light one morning, maybe turned on his television and saw something or found a rattlesnake in his mailbox and realized the world wasn't a safe place to live in."

"Everyone's out to get him," I said.

"At this point," said Tim, turning a crinkly page of the paper, "he's probably right."

"Adele Hanford," I tried on Jesse who pursed her lips.

"We hung out a little for a while," she said, "before I dropped out. She was wild but straightened out. Won some kind of writing prize even. It was in the paper or somewhere."

"She and Mickey going together?" I asked.

Jesse laughed.

"Anything can happen," she said as a customer came through the door, a nervous-looking woman in a hospital blue uniform, a cigarette in her hand.

"Anything can happen," Tim repeated. "Anytime."

Jesse moved away and I finished my sandwich.

Anything could happen. Anytime. A woman could be

driving home from work one night, her husband at home checking on the pasta, and a car the shape and color of grinning death could cut her in half, crumple her into nothingness.

"Anything," I said, not bothering to finish the last bite of my sandwich. "Anytime."

"Watch out for yourself," Tim said as I dropped three dollars on the counter. "Probably doesn't make any difference but it can't hurt."

"You've brightened my morning," I said, getting off of the red-leatherette stool.

"Glad to help," said Tim.

Ames was waiting for me in front of the Texas Bar and Grille. The temperature had already reached the eighties according to the not-very-bright bantering talk-show abuser out of Tampa who I was listening to on the radio. I can take almost any defect in a car but it has to have a radio. I need voices, sounds. I can deal with thoughts at a second level but I needed noise, voices filling the void of consciousness on the surface. B.J. and M.J. in the morning talking to women who had hit policemen with toilet plungers, Dr. Laura failing to listen to people nearly in tears trying desperately to tell their tales, even the threatening voices of southern-born-again or born-into-it Christian broadcasters telling me what the Scriptures really said. I liked the Sunday morning black Baptist preachers going hoarse with warnings and promises of an afterlife far better than the one Tim from Steubenville read about in the papers.

Ames was wearing a long-sleeved shirt, jeans, and boots. He also wore a thin blue zipper jacket under which, I was sure, rested a weapon of not recent vintage.

He climbed in.

I took Osprey down to Tamiami Trail and turned left when I got the light. Traffic was reasonably heavy for what was now lunch hour for most people.

"We're going to Osprey," I said.

Ames nodded.

I explained about Marvin Uliaks, the note left on my door, Conrad Lonsberg's children in Venice. Ames nodded.

I told him what I knew about Bernard Corsello whose body we had found. Ames nodded.

"Adele," he said.

"Right," I agreed. "We're looking for Adele."

He nodded in agreement. As we passed Sarasota Memorial Hospital, I pushed the AM button on the radio and got WGUL, the oldies station which I knew was Ames's favorite. We listened to Frankie Laine doing "Ghost Riders in the Sky" as we moved slowly past Southgate Plaza and then crossed Bee Ridge.

"Read some of Lonsberg's stuff last night," he said.

"Me too."

"Rereading, I guess," he said.

"And?"

We went over the bridge at Phillipi Creek as Johnny Mercer sang "The Waiter and the Porter and the Upstairs Maid."

"Not my kind of book," he said. "Pushes the knife too deep. Feels sorry for himself. Least he did."

I resisted the urge to turn to Ames in astonishment or to say something about this historic moment when Ames McKinney decided not only to carry on an extended conversation, but to criticize a book. Maybe he was the pod who had replaced Uncle Ira in the old *Invasion of the Body Snatchers*.

I wondered what Ann Horowitz would say about Conrad Lonsberg feeling sorry for himself. I had come to Ann feeling sorry for losing my wife, my life. She had told me that I was feeling sorry for two things, for the loss of the wife who defined who I was and for myself. Ann had said that both feelings were reasonable and that there was no hurry to get rid of either of them. Was Conrad Lonsberg like that? Or had he been when he was a young man and had written those books that met the feelings of a generation of people who felt they had lost something but were never quite sure what it was? Lonsberg gave them something to feel lost about. Were his missing manuscripts all about learning to live with failure?

In Osprey we turned on Bay Street off of Tamiami Trail at the Exxon station and then turned left at the next corner,

Patterson. The house we were looking for was about two blocks down. We couldn't actually see the house. It was deep behind trees and bushes huddled right up to the paved street that had no sidewalk. The mailbox was black, looked almost freshly polished, and had a red metal flag tucked down to show there was no mail to be picked up. The house number was in clear white letters on the box along with the name "Dorsey."

I pulled onto the narrow stone driveway between the trees and drove slowly, leaves and branches slapping against the windshield and top of the car suggesting that visitors weren't frequent.

We came to a clearing after about thirty yards after the assault of the flora. To the left was a blue Ford, vintage 1950 with collector's license tags. I parked next to it and got out.

We turned to face a man at work and a woman reading. They were in front of a building, or rather a collection of small one-story buildings connected to each other. The oldest-looking building on the right was solid white stone. Attached to it was a wooden section that contrasted with the stone section. A third section attached to the wooden one was made of something that resembled aluminum siding. Together they formed a single structure that looked as if it had been built by a blind man, but the man on his knees, with a brick in his hand as he worked on a fourth unmatched section of red bricks, was clearly not blind. He turned his head to look at us, brick in one hand, a bucket of mortar at his side. He wore paint-splattered painter's overalls and a baseball cap that looked like vintage Pittsburgh Pirates. He straightened but didn't get off his knees.

I guessed he was Clark Dorsey. I also guessed that he was around fifty years old. I didn't have to guess that he wasn't happy to see us. His face was a dead giveaway.

The woman was sitting in one of those green and white vinyl beach chairs. There was a round white table next to her and a big umbrella sticking out of a hole in the middle of the table to provide her some shade, but she wasn't taking any chances. She wore a floppy straw hat and sunglasses and I guessed she had a supply of 46 SPF sunscreen nearby.

The woman took off her glasses and examined us as we approached. She was about the same age as the man, lean, hair still dark but showing some gray, few lines, and a wary smile.

"Clark Dorsey?" I asked as we kept moving forward.

The man got up slowly, put the brick on a huge pile of bricks nearby.

"Yes," he said.

"My name is Fonesca, Lew Fonesca. This is my friend Ames McKinney."

The woman I assumed was Mrs. Dorsey didn't move.

"And?"

"I'm looking for your brother," I said.

He turned his head to one side. Something he had wanted to forget had come back to haunt him. I glanced at Mrs. Dorsey. She hadn't responded.

"Why?" he asked, turning his head back to us.

"I've been hired to find his wife. Her brother wants to talk to her," I said.

"That poor son of a bitch," Dorsey said, wiping his hands on his overalls. "I don't know where Charlie and Vera Lynn are and I don't think they'd want to see Marvin even if they knew he wanted to. Marvin's not all there. The whole family . . . Marvin's never really been all there. You talked to him. You can see that."

"Some people spend their money doing strange things like looking for lost sisters," I said. "Others go out on little boards and risk their lives for thrills. And then there are others who build strange houses."

"Your point, Mr. . . ."

"Fonesca," I said. "My point is that people who aren't hurting other people should be able to do what they want to do as long as they don't hurt anybody but themselves."

"I never see Marvin," he said, stepping toward us. "I don't go into town much. Peg has run into him a few times. Even looked him up."

"We had him out here twice since we've been here," the woman under the umbrella said.

"I'm not comfortable with him," Dorsey said.

"Clark's not comfortable with anyone really," Peg Dorsey said with a smile in her voice.

"What can I tell you?" he said with a shrug. "She's right. I used to be a fireman. For twenty years. I've seen enough trouble, enough people. I don't stay in touch with my family. I, Peg and I, we keep to ourselves."

"And you build houses," I said, looking at the oddity behind him.

He turned his head as if he had never before really considered what he had done.

"The white stone one-bedroom came with the land. I added on. I'm not much of a reader. I don't care much for television, movies, or newspapers and we don't have a hell of a lot of friends. So I build. I don't care what it looks like. It's comfortable inside. Each addition is a new challenge. Maybe when I'm done, if I ever get done, I'll cover the whole place with stucco or something."

"No maybe about it," said Peg Dorsey.

"No maybe," Clark Dorsey agreed. "For sure."

"Two feet higher on the metal-sided one, shored with straight I-beams, and the one you're working on at least a foot lower than what you're planning," said Ames.

Dorsey looked at him.

"They'd line up, give you enough headroom," said Ames. "Brick in the whole place. Double your property value."

"Ames used to be in the business," I explained.

"Retired?" asked Peg Dorsey, shading her eyes.

"Business go bad?" asked Clark.

"Business was fine. Partner was as uneven as your roof over there with just as many unmatched parts," said Ames.

The Dorseys waited for me. There was no more coming.

"Marvin just wants to talk to Vera Lynn," I said. "It's all he has."

"You a private detective?" Clark said.

"Just a friend, and I'm not going to charge him more than a few hundred dollars tops, find her or not," I said, "but Marvin's not going to give up."

Dorsey looked at his wife and she looked back at him and nodded.

"Charlie and Vera Lynn don't want to hear from Marvin," Dorsey said.

"Why?"

"Because of what happened," Dorsey explained. "You know what happened in Arcadia?"

"You mean the girl who fell out of the window," I said. "Sarah Taylor."

Dorsey nodded his head and said, "I've got to go inside for a minute. Either of you want water?"

"I'd like that," Ames said.

Dorsey disappeared past his wife and through a door into the white stone section of the puzzle house.

"Clark doesn't like to talk about it," Peg Dorsey said, looking at the door her husband had closed behind him. "He's leaving me to do the talking."

I watched her play with her sunglasses, put them back on, and look in our direction.

"The girl who went out that window, Sarah," she said. "She was a very pretty girl, but a jumpy thing, can't-sit-still type. She got worse, started acting crazy, one day dancing in the street and singing, the next day sitting on the bench near city hall for hours not talking. Sarah was a pretty girl and she was wrong about most things but she was right about one. Charlie had been engaged to Vera Lynn, or as close to engaged as you can be from the time you're both fourteen. They were comfortable together, Charlie and Vera Lynn. Charlie had no trouble with Vera Lynn's brother Marvin who was, let's put this kindly, not fully together from the time he was born."

She paused, bit her lower lip, and went on.

"What made things worse was that Marvin was Sarah Taylor's puppy dog. He has no guile, that Marvin. He adored Sarah, would follow her around, sit with her on that bench, even dance with her in the street. Arcadia wasn't filled with good-looking, smart men with a future. I was lucky. Sarah wasn't. Sarah started to spread the word that she and Charlie had a thing together and that he was dropping Vera Lynn. Some people even believed it. They just saw that pretty girl on the outside and not the one inside. It doesn't matter. If the town is small enough, people want to have a good box of rumors to pass around, especially one involving the young police chief even if the rumor comes from someone like Sarah.

"Well, to make it short, no one really knows what happened in that room that day, the day Sarah went out that window and died. Charlie was there. Vera Lynn was there. They said she fell when it first happened. Then later, next day, Vera Lynn said Sarah jumped. More rumors started. You can't imagine. An old woman named Esther Yoderman who could barely see said she was looking up when Sarah came through the glass. Esther claimed Vera Lynn pushed her. Then she changed her mind the next day and said Charlie threw her out the window. Charlie and Vera Lynn just said it had been an accident."

"But . . . ?" I prompted.

Peg Dorsey shrugged.

"The Dorseys have a temper," she said with a shrug. "They hold it in like my Clark, stay away from people when they can, but everyone knew about Charlie's temper. And since he and Vera Lynn wouldn't say much . . ."

"People drew conclusions," I said.

"Coroner's hearing declared it accidental," she said. "Charlie let his deputy do the investigation since Charlie was a witness for most and a suspect for others. Charlie's deputy was Earl Morgantine, two notches higher on the evolution pool than poor Marvin. Marvin accused Charlie of killing Sarah. Vera Lynn tried to talk to the boy but Marvin ran away, hid in the pastures for days. People could hear him crying and wailing. There was no evidence. It was ruled an accident. Charlie and Vera Lynn packed up. Charlie quit his job. They drove off before Marvin could come out of the woods. That's about it."

"What do you think happened?" I asked.

"Something different each time I think about it," she said, "but getting right down to it, I don't think Charlie or Vera Lynn killed Sarah. And I'll say it right out. I don't care anymore. I just care about what it did to Clark. I'm sorry but that's how I feel."

"Nothing to apologize for," Ames said.

"I suppose," she sighed, shifting in her chair and looking back at the door again. "Clark and I hung on for more than ten years and you would have sworn it had been forgotten, but things like that never are in a small town. So, as soon as he could, Clark retired and here we are."

"Why didn't you move farther away?" I asked.

"Charlie and Clark's mother is still in Arcadia. She wouldn't move, wouldn't come with us. We visit her every two weeks, take her out to dinner or eat at her place. People are polite and don't ask questions."

"You don't have the answers," I said.

"Don't like the questions they don't ask but want to," she said as Clark came out of the door, a tall, clear glass of water with ice in one hand.

He walked over to Ames who took it and shook his head in thanks.

We all watched Ames's Adam's apple bob as he drank the water and the ice tinkled and then he handed the glass back to Dorsey with a thanks.

"There are some questions a man can't live without an answer to," said Ames. "They find the real one or they make one up that works."

Dorsey nodded.

"Marvin just wants to talk to his sister," I said. "Know she's alive. He has something to tell her. I don't know what. It may be that he thinks the Martians are attacking or that he loves her or that . . . I don't know. He wants closure."

I knew what it was like to want closure. I knew what had made me take on the search for Vera Lynn Uliaks Dorsey. If I couldn't have my own closure, I could work at a job that had simple closure. Hand them the papers and walk away. Find the missing person and step back. Let the story play out. In a world of chaos where brilliant, beautiful women said good-bye one morning with a smile and then were mangled by the unknown, there had to be moments of closure or there would be a world of madness. That was why I saw Ann Horowitz. That was why I would find Vera Lynn. Closure for Marvin and maybe for the Dorseys.

"I just want to find her, talk to her," I said.

"My husband and I, we'll talk about it," Peg Dorsey said, looking up at her husband.

Clark Dorsey turned to her and saw a small smile of reassurance. Then he turned to us and said, "We'll talk about it. You have a card?"

I didn't have a business card. I didn't want one. I wasn't searching for more than the business I already had. But I did have a small black notebook in my back pocket with lined pages. I wrote my name and number on a sheet and handed it to Dorsey who pocketed it.

"I'll find her," I said softly. "If you can help me, it'll be faster, easier, cheaper. I'm not out to hurt anyone. And I'm sorry if I've brought some ghosts with us this morning."

Dorsey nodded.

Ames and I got back in the car. Dorsey plunged both hands into his overall pockets. He was a big man, a few years too young for the retirement and isolation he had brought and bought, but who was I to judge. I was trying to do the same thing with my life.

"Well?" I asked as I drove slowly down the stone drive- way of whipping branches.

"They'll call you," said Ames.

"Think so?"

"Could feel it in the glass when he handed it to me," said Ames. "Held it steady, but there was a tightness there. He needs something closed too. House he's working on remind you of somethin'?"

"A kid working with unmatched building sets," I said.

"Three little pigs," said Ames. "Stone, wood. One he's working on is brick. He's getting ready for the wolf to come."

"McKinney instinct?" I asked.

"Book I read once by a man in Chicago named Bettle- heim," said Ames. "Good book. But he had his own wolf at the door blowing hard. Lived a lot of lies. Bettleheim. Couldn't take it anymore. Killed himself."

"You think Clark Dorsey is losing out to a wolf in his dreams?"

"Could be," Ames said.

"People handle their wolves different ways," I said. "You take your gun, hunt them down, and shoot them. Some people can't find their wolves."

"And some people build houses or sit in rooms waiting for the wolf to find them," Ames said.

I had the uneasy feeling Ames was talking about me. I already had a shrink. What I needed was a friend who could ride shotgun.

We didn't say another word till we found Laura Lonsberg Guffey's house in Venice.

Trying to think of nothing is hard to do. Try it for ten seconds. Try to keep memory from coming unbidden. I can distract myself with old movies and work and sometimes with a painful empathy for other people and their problems, but I'm too much a part of the world to find Nirvana. Memory creeps up, as it did now, and leaps at me like a dream wolf.

We drove and the wolf hovered over my shoulder, breathing hot, panting, smelling of both animal and the half-remembered scent of my wife at night.

The wolf was just one shape that haunted me, reminding me that somewhere far behind lived the person who had killed her and driven away. The wolf reminded me.

Today a wolf, later or tomorrow a bear, cat, tiger, dog, something under the bed or in a closet, just outside a door or lurking under the dark surface of a cup of coffee.

She liked her coffee black, her tea unsweetened, herbal, but not mint. Her favorite food was grilled seafood. She wore solids, purples, greens, and grays. Old jewelry. She had a necklace that looked like the one Scarlett O'Hara wore at the ball before the war. But she also liked colorful costume jewelry that contrasted with the solid colors. I always gave her clothes or jewelry for birthdays, anniversaries, and sometimes for no reason but that I saw something that seemed right for her. She always put it on immediately, throwing back her hair, asking me to fasten, hook as I inhaled.

When she was lost in thought, she tapped gently at a

tooth with the thumbnail of her left hand. Her nails were deep red because she knew it was my favorite color.

"We're here," Ames said.

We pulled up in front of a house. The wolf jumped out and disappeared.

7

LAURA LONSBERG LIVED in a condo just off of Venice Beach. She was on the fifth floor of the ten-story building. It was a three-bedroom with a balcony overlooking the Gulf. Her two daughters, she told us when she answered the door, were at school.

We were expected or at least I was. Her father had called from a gas station the day before and said I would be coming.

"You should have called," she said, ushering us in. "I'm usually at work on Fridays."

The living room was moderate in size, big enough for a comfortable bright sofa, some chairs, and a pair of lamps that might have been real Tiffany. The balcony door was open and we could hear the not-too-distant sounds of people on the beach and splashing in the water. A gull landed on the balcony railing, cocked his head to one side, and looked at me. Then he flew away.

Ames and I sat.

"Coffee?" Laura Lonsberg asked. "I've got some hot."

"Fine," I said. "Cream, sugar."

"Black," said Ames.

She left the room and I looked after her. She was in her late thirties, good figure, and the inherited dark blond hair of her father. She also bore a distinct resemblance to him that most people would say made her look plain. I thought she looked strong and determined. I didn't think this was going to take long. She was back almost immediately with steaming blue mugs with the word "Illinois" scripted in orange across them.

She sat across from us, no coffee, legs crossed, hands folded.

"Where do you work?" I asked.

"Hospital, billing department," she said. "I'll save you time so we can get to the real questions. I have two children, daughters. My husband's name is Danny Guffey. I met him in high school, Riverview in Sarasota. His family was poor. Danny's father owned a small dry-cleaning store. My father thought Danny was after my money. He said he would give us nothing till he died. Danny didn't care. My husband is a chiropractor, a good one, a very successful one. He has offices in Venice and in Bradenton, a secretary, a bookkeeper, and two assistants. We have two beautiful girls who along with my nephew will, to anticipate one of your questions, inherit most of whatever my father is worth when he dies."

"You know what happened?" I asked after taking a drink of the coffee. The coffee tasted like raspberries.

"The girl, Adele, took my father's manuscripts," she said. "He wants no publicity so he hired a private detective to find her, one, I understand, who actually knows the girl."

"I'm not a private detective," I said. "I do know Adele. How well did you get to know her?"

Laura Lonsberg Guffey picked up a glass owl from the small table in front of her and looked at it as if it would give her an answer.

"Not well," she said. "I bring the girls over every week or two when the great man feels a need to see them. My husband doesn't go. Sometimes Adele was there. Sometimes we talked. She's bright, has a lot of energy, and has been through a lot."

"She told you about . . . ?"

"Yes," said Laura, rolling the crystal owl from hand to hand. "I read some of the things she was writing. I think my father's right. She's talented."

I said nothing.

"Was I jealous?" she asked. "Not really. I can't write. I'm not interested. My major interest in writing is those manuscripts and the future of my daughters. My father made it clear when I finished college and married Danny that I was on my own. I accepted that. I think he was right."

"And your brother?"

"I'm not sure I know what you're asking, but, yes, he was on his own after he got his B.A. He's a C.P.A. in Sarasota."

"But he lives in Venice?" I asked.

"He prefers it here and doesn't mind the drive," she said, putting down the ball. "You can discuss that with him. As to the rest of your ambiguous question, no, my brother was not happy to be sent into the world with a few dollars and a college degree."

"Your father and brother get along?"

"I'd say so, but I wouldn't call them buddies. Brad has one son, Conrad Junior. Conrad Senior is fond of him. Brad's wife died when Connie was a little boy. Brad's wife and the great man did not get along. She fought the few times they met so they stayed away from each other. Conrad Lonsberg, when his daughter-in-law died, condescended to attend the funeral but drove away when he saw reporters hovering at the funeral home for a glimpse of the famous literary recluse. In any case, the manuscripts, as I said, were they to exist would go to my girls and my nephew."

Silence and then she added, "So, you see there would be no point in Brad or me wanting to take the manuscripts if that's what you're thinking. There's nothing we can do with them. All we can do is sit and wait till he dies. Even Conrad Lonsberg has to die sometime."

"You don't love him?" I asked.

"The great man? He treated my mother reasonably well, but if you're a girl looking for warm, fuzzy, and protection after her mother dies, Conrad is not the one to go to. Now for your next question. Was I worried about Conrad changing his will and putting Adele on it? The answer is 'no.' That's not the way my father thinks. Read his books or his poems. He thinks people have to learn to take care of themselves. His grandchildren seem to be an exception."

"Any idea why Adele might want to take your father's manuscripts?"

"Adele's a sharp kid, more than a kid, but Conrad knows how to hurt," she said, putting the owl gently back on the table. "He wouldn't touch her body, but he could play some painful games with her mind if he wanted to. He knows how to hurt."

"Not one of your favorite people on the planet?"

"No," she said simply. "Anything else?"

"Mickey Merrymen," I said.

"Who?"

It sounded like an honest "who" to me, but I went on.

"Friend of Adele's."

"No. The only other person I ever saw her with was an old woman who drove her to Conrad's a few times. I didn't get her name, but she drove a big car and wore too much makeup. That it?"

"All I can think of," I said. "Ames?"

"Conrad, the great man," Ames said. "You don't call him father or dad."

"I don't think of him that way," she said. "Father is a word you earn by being one."

"You think much of his writing?" Ames asked.

"He is a great man," she answered with a shake of her head. "I really believe that even when I say it with a touch of sarcasm. A great writer."

She gave us the address of her brother's business office in Sarasota and we left. Back in the car, I asked Ames what he thought.

"One good real hug from her father would take away most of the bitterness," he said.

"That simple?"

"In this case, I think maybe so."

The conversation ended and we drove back to Sarasota.

It was late in the afternoon when we got back. We stopped at the Texas Bar and Grille for a quick bowl of chili. I called Brad Lonsberg's office and asked if I could come over for a while.

"Sure," he said. "I'm working on something now. Give me half an hour."

The early-afternoon crowd was straggling into the Texas, some wearily glancing up at the television set where the news was on with no sound, some talking business or baseball. Some not talking.

The phone rang while we were finishing our chili. I noticed but didn't pay any attention until Ed called over, "Lew, it's for you."

I left Ames working on his chili, moved to the bar, and picked up the phone.

"Fonesca," I said.

"Adele," she answered.

"How did you know I was here?" I asked.

"You weren't at your office. I've just been looking."

"Why?"

"Because you've been looking for me," she said. "Don't. By the time you find me they'll all be gone."

"Lonsberg's manuscripts?"

"Every page."

"Why?"

"Because of what he did to me," she said, trying to keep her voice down. "But you tell him. You tell him what I'm doing."

I heard a car horn on the phone. I heard the same horn outside the Texas. I motioned for Ames who wiped his mouth with his napkin and lopped over.

"Mickey's grandfather," I said.

"Mickey's . . . ? What about him?"

"He's dead," I said. "You didn't know?"

"What happened?"

"Someone shot him in his house. The police passed on me but they're probably already looking for Mickey and maybe for you. Let's talk."

"No," she said.

"Ames wants to tell you something," I said, handing him

the phone, covering the receiver, and whispering, "Keep her talking."

Ames nodded and into the phone said, "Got yourself some more trouble, girl?"

I ran for the front door, banged into a table sending a burger flying, and went out into the late afternoon. Flo's white minivan was parked across the street. A young man was behind the steering wheel. Sitting next to him on the cell phone was Adele. As I started across the street Mickey stepped on the gas. He tore rubber and flew down the street. My car was half a block away and who knew which way he would turn.

As I headed back to the Texas, I saw the fire in the trash bin. It wasn't big, but it didn't belong there. I went over to it and looked down. What remained of a manuscript, a short one, was burning. I reached down to save some of it but it was too far along. I did read the title just as the flames hit the top page of the manuscript, *Come Into My Parlor*. The title page was off to the side of the burning bits and pieces. I picked up the title page and blew out the fire in the corner.

I went back into the Texas heading for Ames but was cut off by an angry small bull of a man with hell in his eyes.

"You fuckin' ruined my burger, you little bastard."

"Had to get outside. Emergency. Kid. I'll pay your bill and get you another burger. I'm sorry."

"Maybe sorry don't cut it," he said, stepping in front of me as I tried to walk around him.

"Let him by," came a voice from the bar.

Everyone stopped talking to watch what would happen next. I was only interested in the fact that Ames was still on the phone with Adele.

The little bull didn't move.

Ed Fairing repeated, "Let him by. Your bill's covered. You got an apology."

The bull nodded, stepped aside, and softly said, "I've had a bad day."

I nodded and moved past him to the telephone as the conversation in the room began again. Ames held out the phone to me.

"Adele," I said.

"You found it," she said. "We're going to go around the whole of Sarasota and Manatee destroying the books one at a time, page by page. I'll let you know each time and you can tell him."

"Give Sally a call," I said. "She's worried about you."

"I'll think about it," Adele said.

"She's also responsible for you," I added. "And Flo . . ."

"I called Flo. I'll call you when we burn the next one. That's it."

"Hold it," I said, but it was too late. She had pushed the END button.

"Got an angry child on our hands," Ames said.

"What did she tell you?"

"And each one will go, burning like dying little stillborn suns," Ames said. "She said that's the last line of *Fool's Love*."

We headed for Brad Lonsberg. He had a small office on the second floor over Davidson's Drug Store at the corner of Tamiami and Bahia Vista. Before the Starbucks moved into the middle of the small mall's parking lot, parking had never even been a minor problem. Now, parking spaces were spiked with signs warning that you had to drink your coffee, do your shopping at Kash 'n' Karry, buy your magazines, or get your hair cut in half an hour or find a space at the fringe of the lot. I'm not complaining, just pointing out reality. There was never really a problem finding a parking space in Sarasota. Here people—even if they moved down or are visiting from Toronto, New York, or Atlanta—think parking half a block away from wherever they might be going in Sarasota was a major inconvenience.

Brad Lonsberg's office was down a carpeted corridor on the second floor past the offices of child psychologists, a small gourmet magazine, the business office of a radio station, and the Center for Traditional Chinese Medicine.

His glass door, with his name in gold letters unchipped on it accompanied by "C.P.A." and "Financial Management," was open. Ames and I went in. A harried-looking girl was on the phone trying to be patient. She held up a finger for us to wait a second. We waited while she talked and tried to push back strands of unruly hair. She was dark, pretty, thin, and looked as if she might be seventeen. She was also frowning as she talked.

"I really am sorry, Mrs. Scheinstein," she said with just a touch of authentic Florida in her voice, "but we just got the forms and all, you know . . . if Mr. Lonsberg could get them any faster he'd . . . Yes, soon as they're ready to sign, I'll call you . . . I can't guarantee tomorrow morning . . . It's really up to . . . I'll ask Mr. Lonsberg if he'll . . . Believe me, Mrs. Scheinstein, if . . . I'll see if he's available."

She held the phone away from her and mouthed "just one more minute" to us. Ames and I sat in two of the three waiting-room chairs in front of her desk. She pressed a button and then another one and said, "It's Mrs. Scheinstein. She won't listen. Okay. And there are two men here to see you. Okay."

She pushed another button and said, "Mr. Lonsberg will speak to you now, Mrs. Scheinstein. I'm sure he'll work it out."

She pushed yet another button that obviously disconnected her from Mrs. Scheinstein and said, "Ole bitch," in a whisper. And then realizing what she had done turned to us and said, "Sorry. But some people."

"Some people," I agreed.

"You can go right in," she said. "Mr. Lonsberg's expecting you. At least if you're the men Mr. Lonsberg's expecting."

"We're the men," I said.

As we stepped past her, we could see her reaching with indecision toward the piles of papers and files on her desk and the stack of pink telephone message notes skewered to a pointed post next to the phone. She brushed back her long dark hair, sighed, and reached for a pile of unopened letters.

Ames and I stepped through the door and found ourselves in a small office. The window behind the desk where Lonsberg sat gave a view of the parking lot, Starbucks, Tamiami Trail, and even the white Cutlass we had come in.

The phone was at his ear and he nodded as if the listener could hear him and pointed at the two chairs across from his desk. We sat. Lonsberg looked nothing like his father except for the lanky body. His face was clear, dark, reasonably good-looking in a Peter Fonda kind of way. Laura had inherited her father's looks. I guessed Brad had been blessed by his mother. He had a nice patient smile, a recent haircut, and a shirt and blue tie with white circles on it. His jacket hung on a hanger in the corner.

"Maria," he said calmly, soothingly into the phone, "the government moves in strange ways, its miracles to perform or fail to perform. I have the forms before me. I have your contracts neatly laid out. I'll have this all finished in an hour and I'll bring them by myself for your signature . . . Yes, I'll have an envelope all made out and fully stamped. You sign. I get to Federal Express and you put it from your mind . . . I'll be there between six-thirty and seven . . . No, I'll be happy to do it . . . Give my best to Sam. Tell him not to worry. Yes. Good-bye."

He hung up the phone, looked at us, and said, "I'll bring her a yellow rose from Kash 'n' Karry, hand her the papers to sign, have a glass of very bad Napa Valley wine with her and her husband, and go home a sadder but wiser man. Dealing with the very old isn't particularly easy."

He looked at Ames who looked back.

"Mrs. Scheinstein just had her eighty-sixth birthday," Lonsberg explained. "She still drives. She shouldn't. What she does do is pay her bills on time."

He smiled and with a small sweep of his hand gave us a what-can-you-do look.

"I'm Lewis Fonesca," I said. "This is my colleague Ames McKinney."

He examined us, the smile still on his face, a confident smile.

"I'll try to make this easy for you," he said. "I'll tell you what I know. You ask questions. I get Mrs. Scheinstein's report finished and then if the timing is right I get to see the second half and maybe some of the first half of the Riverview-Booker basketball game. My son Connie's a guard. Great defense. Fair offense. But you want to hear about father, not son."

"Adele," I said.

He kept smiling as he shook his head.

"Met her a few times. She was polite, maybe a little defensive. My father didn't make it any easier on her. I know he liked her. Sorry for the past tense but given the circumstances . . ."

"Given the circumstances," I repeated.

"Conrad Lonsberg knows how to hurt, himself, his children, the feelings of others. A kid like Adele, even a tough kid, could find herself being torn apart by his criticism. It's hard to put your work on the line, your creative work, in front of a legend and listen to him tell you how rotten it is."

"You learn this from experience?" I asked.

"When I was about eight, I tried to read *Fool's Love*. Couldn't understand a word of it. When I was about twelve, I tried some writing. I tried a story, a few poems, got up the nerve to show them to him. He didn't say anything, just read. I can still see his eyes scanning the neatly printed pages. Then he turned up to look at me, handed the pages back, and said, 'You don't have the gift.' That ended my literary career."

"Must have hurt," I said.

"Hurt? I tore up the pages in my room and never thought again about writing. But you know something, he did me a favor. He was right. I didn't have the talent. If he had encouraged me, I might have kept on, even written some stories or a book and got them published because I was Conrad Lonsberg's son. But they wouldn't have been any good and I would have known it. I could have wasted a lot of years. He could have handled that twelve-year-old better. The message was right but the delivery left a lot to be desired."

"So your point is that you've got nothing against your father?"

"I suppose," Brad Lonsberg said. "Either of you like a Coke, coffee, something?"

Ames and I both nodded "no."

"Have you any idea where Adele might have taken your father's manuscripts or why?"

"I've told you. 'Why?' My father is full of 'why's' and

talent. His favorite question to his children. 'Why?' "

"No specific idea of why?" I asked.

"None," he said.

"If she destroys the manuscripts, it could mean you lose millions of dollars, you, your son," I said.

He looked down at the papers on his desk and then over at us.

"Millions of dollars would be very nice," he said. "How's that for understatement. But we can live without it. I wouldn't turn it down but there's something satisfying in not needing it, not having to be tied to a father who's a myth in his own lifetime. I even considered changing my name when I was younger, straight cut. Don't misunderstand, I don't hate my father. In an odd way I love him. We see him fairly often, Connie and I. My wife died when Connie was six, cancer. Connie could use a grandfather. Hell, I could use a father, but I . . . My sister, my father, and I talk about nothing. My father does seem to like his grandchildren but he gives off the sense whenever we're with him that he'd like to look at his watch and get back to his typewriter. As the world knows Conrad Lonsberg still uses the same typewriter his parents gave him when he graduated from high school. I think he would grieve more if his typewriter were stolen than if my sister or I dropped dead."

"So you don't care what Adele does with the manuscripts?"

"Mixed feelings," he said. "But I'd rather see him get them back. He doesn't have much else besides his own lifetime of work."

"And the money?"

"Well, that too," he said, "but I'm doing well, better than the size of this office might show. I've made some good land and stock investments in the county based, I admit in private, on information given by clients. I have plenty of clients, mostly very old, very grateful for attention and often more than willing to set me up as the administrator of their estates, and I do annual audits for major companies all over the country. I specialize in high-tech companies. I've got two lawyers I work with who make it work."

"In short?"

"In short, I'm doing very well financially which results, in part, in my not having to kiss my father's behind when I'm with him. It took me almost forty years but I think I have my father's respect."

"And his love?"

"I'll settle for his respect," said Lonsberg.

"You know a Mickey Merrymen?" I asked.

"That's the kid who picked up Adele once when we were at my father's," he said. "I think that was his name. Tall, young, shy. Stayed outside the gate. My son and I walked Adele out and met him. It wasn't much of a conversation. Seemed like a nice kid, but what can you tell from a few seconds?"

"Sometimes a lot," said Ames.

Lonsberg looked over at Ames as if he hadn't noticed the tall old man in the room before this moment.

"Yes, I guess. I think I've learned to size people up fairly quickly in my business. Being a C.P.A. isn't a glamour job, not like being a writer or a private detective, or a physician, but when people need you, they dump it on you, apologize, and want you to work magic. I've got to get to work. So, I apologize but . . ."

I got up. So did Ames.

"A question," said Ames.

Brad Lonsberg looked up.

"All this big business and you've got a confused kid out there handling things?"

"Daughter of one of my clients, big clients. She just got out of high school," Lonsberg explained. "She looks vulnerable and pretty when people walk in. It balances. Almost. Yes, I'd say she's on the debit side. But it's either pretty, young, and confused or a retiree who wants to go back to work. Tell the truth, I don't think Maria will want to stay much longer. She doesn't like making decisions. Next time I'll try a retiree. Answer your question?"

"It does," said Ames and we went out the door while Lonsberg put on a pair of glasses and looked down at the forms in front of him.

Maria the receptionist-secretary was frantically looking for something among the piles on her desk.

"It was right on top," she said. "Just a second ago."

"Mr. Lonsberg a good man to work for?" I asked.

Still ruffling among the mess, she said, without looking up, "He's the greatest. Patient, calm. Look at me. I'm a boob. I can't find a damn sheet he needs and I had it right . . . here it is."

She held up the yellow sheet in triumph and showed a great set of teeth.

The phone rang. She looked at it with dread.

Ames and I exited.

"What do you think?" I asked as we walked down the corridor.

"He looks like he's letting it all out," Ames said. "I'd say he's holding it all in."

"Think I should check on Brad Lonsberg's tales of the wealth of his kingdom?"

"Might be," he said.

"And if I find he's not the mogul he says he is? What does it mean?"

"Don't know," he said. "Ever think of trying this?"

He nodded at the window of the Center for Traditional Chinese Medicine. The office waiting room was three times the size of Brad Lonsberg's. A lone waiting woman sat reading a copy of *The Economist*.

"They've got herbs, stuff for what ails you," he said.

"What ails me?" I asked as we passed the office heading for the elevator.

"The past," he answered.

"They have pills for that?"

"Pills and they stick needles in you," he said as we reached the elevator and I pushed the button.

"And it works? You've done it?"

"Ed at the Texas comes here. Has his own problems. Liver. Swears on them. Costs some though."

"I haven't got some," I said as the elevator dinged and opened. There were no passengers inside.

"And if you did?" he asked as the doors closed.

I shrugged. I wasn't sure I wanted a quick fix on my

grief. I wasn't sure I wanted a pill or a needle to take away what I was clinging to. Dealing with Ann Horowitz was one thing. She wasn't trying to take away my history, just find a way for me to live with it.

"Cup of coffee?" I asked as the elevator went slowly from the second to the first floor.

"That Starbucks place?" Ames asked.

"Why not?"

"Never been there. Two, three dollars for a cup of coffee with some sweet juice or something."

"It'll be a new experience. On me."

We stepped out of the building and headed across the parking lot toward Starbucks.

"Nice kid," he said.

"Adele?"

"And the girl back there, Maria."

We stepped into Starbucks and both ordered the coffee of the day, Irish something. We sat at a table looking at the other customers reading newspapers, talking business.

"Someone in here named Fonesca?" called a girl with a Hispanic accent behind the desk.

I stood up.

"Phone call," she said.

I crossed the room, inched my way past a big woman in a hat who was filling something that looked like a tall cup of whipped cream with little packets of Equal. The woman handed me the phone.

"Adele," I said before she could speak.

"Finish your coffee, then go back to your car," she said. "I left the title page."

"Adele, did you call Sally?"

"No."

"Will you?"

Long pause.

"I guess."

"Can we talk?"

"We're talking," she said. "But I'm not stopping."

"Mickey's grandfather," I said. "Someone killed Mickey's grandfather."

"It's his fault," she said.

"Lonsberg?"

"It's his fault," she repeated.

"Why?"

She hung up.

"Let's go," I said to Ames, hurrying back to the table.

He took the last of his coffee in one hot gulp and we went out the door past an incoming quartet of Sarasota High School students who had walked or driven over after school, books in hand. The two girls were blond and pretty. The two boys were lean and young-looking. I wondered how Ames and I looked to them.

"There," said Ames, pointing across the parking lot toward Bahia Vista. The white van turned right onto Bahia Vista heading east.

We hurried to the Cutlass. I couldn't smell anything burning, but there was a box on the driver's seat. I hadn't locked the car. We got in and I opened the cardboard box. It was filled with finely shredded paper, shredded so thin that each piece would tear at the slightest touch. One sheet was intact. It read: *Let Me Introduce the Charming Devil.* Conrad Lonsberg's name was neatly typed below the title and he had signed it and written the date, 6/8/88, at the bottom of the page.

I dropped Ames back at the Texas and told him I'd get back to him in the morning. He nodded and leaned onto the open passenger window from where he stood.

"They're all lyin'," he said.

"I know."

"What are you gonna do?"

"Go home, get a banana coconut Blizzard and two DQ burgers, and watch a movie."

At least that's what I planned to do when I left Ames standing on the sidewalk. Oh, I got the banana coconut Blizzard and the burgers but when I got back to my office, I found four messages on my answering machine, a new record.

I pushed the REPLAY button and ate a burger.

Caller one was Marvin Uliaks: "Mr. Fonesca, have you found Vera Lynn yet? I don't want to bother you, you know. I just want to talk to Vera Lynn. So, have you found her yet? Am I calling the right number?" Marvin sounded confused.

Caller two was Conrad Lonsberg: "Progress or setback? I'll be home until ten in the morning." Conrad Lonsberg sounded resigned.

Caller three was Clark Dorsey who had taken time off from constructing his house of irony to say: "Fonesca, my number is 434-5444. Call me." Dorsey sounded troubled.

Caller four was Sally Porovsky: "Lew, Adele called, left a message on my machine. She says she knows who killed Mickey's grandfather, but she's not ready to talk until she's finished destroying the manuscripts." Sally sounded tired.

I was almost finished with my burgers and Blizzard trying to decide who to call first. There was a knock at the door.

"It's open," I called from behind my desk and in came the homeless Digger.

He stood in the doorway, a Neiman Marcus bag bulging in one hand and an envelope in the other. I could smell him, and like a vampire who has to be invited in, he stood waiting, weaving.

"Hypocrisy," he said. "It rules the world."

"I appreciate the information."

"Monks, Luther's ghost itself haunts our rickety abode," he said.

"You saw him again?"

"He just left another message on your door. I watched. There was an aura of the uncanny about him. He floated like a specter."

"A ghost?"

"My imagination is enhanced by a less than vintage wine, I must admit," said Digger, "but while this is not a dagger in my hand, it is certainly palpable to feeling and to sight."

"I thought you didn't drink," I said.

"In great moderation," he said. "And only on special occasions."

He stepped across my threshold, a vampire uninvited, his hand out to place the envelope on my desk.

"Thanks," I said.

I didn't want to say what I said next, but it would have been left hanging and heavy.

"Where are you staying tonight?" I asked.

He pushed out his lower lip and shrugged.

"The lavatory," he said.

I took out my wallet and handed him a five-dollar bill. It was a mistake. It meant he would be back. Maybe not tomorrow. Maybe not the next day or the one beyond, but at some point he would come bearing a note from a ghost, a papal bull, the Sunday *New York Times*, and expect payment.

He took the bill and smiled.

"There's a condition," I said. "You rent a real bed, at least for tonight. Know anyplace?"

"For five dollars?" he asked. "There are crevices of this city of sun and beautiful beaches where hidden people for two dollars a night provide cots and dubious company. I have a friend who lives beneath a stone bench right on Bayfront Park. His head rests on his guitar and the police leave him alone. For fifty cents, he will move over and share his musical pillow."

"A roof, Digger," I said, opening the envelope.

"Then Lilla's it shall be," he said, his head lolling. "A refreshing walk in the evening, a cot, and conversation. Life goes on but the pace is so slow."

"I agree," I said as he staggered out the door and closed it behind him.

The four-folded unlined sheet of paper in front of me was written in the same block letters as the first one left by Digger's monk:

YOU CAN'T BRING BACK THE DEAD. LET THEM REST. YOU CAN ONLY MAKE IT WORSE.

That was it. I have been threatened by pimps, muggers, cops—crooked and otherwise—goons, loons, and the completely mad. This note read less like a threat than a warning, a warning that something bad could come out of the box if I opened it any wider and looked in.

I called Sally. Her son Michael answered.

"It's Lew. Your mom home?"

"Yeah, you ever have zits?"

"Yes," I said. "When I was about your age. Also boils. Two on my neck. Had to be lanced. Hurt like hell."

"I don't have boils," Michael said.

"I know. I was trying to make you feel better," I said. "I understand they have all kinds of things for pimples. Over the counter."

"They don't work," said Michael.

"Soap, water, prayer, and the passage of time," I said.

"Shit," he said. "I thought you might be able to come up with something. You know, like some old Italian remedy. Italian kids don't seem to get it as bad as Jewish kids."

"I always thought it was the other way around."

"Here's my mother."

I heard the clinking of the phone being passed and heard Sally say, "Lew?"

"Yes, Michael and I were just bonding philosophically over adolescent pimples."

"Adele called," she said. "Not long ago. Michael just went back in his room. I think the pimple talk was a result of talking to Adele. He's got a crush on her. God, I'm doing more than showing my age. 'Crush.' They must have a better word for it now, or at least a more graphic one."

"Adele has that affect on men and boys," I said.

"She told me she was all right and that she planned to continue to burn Lonsberg's manuscripts. She asked me to tell her how much trouble she was really in."

"And you told her?" I asked.

"Can't lie to them, Lew. Once they catch me in a lie they never believe me again. I told her Lonsberg wanted the manuscripts back, of course, but I also told her I didn't think he'd be going to the police about them. She had already figured that one out. I told her she had to go back to Flo's or she was subject at worst to criminal charges or to placement in another foster home. She asked me if I'd do that."

"And you said 'no.' "

"I said 'no.' Where could I place a sixteen-year-old former prostitute? The possibilities are few. Flo is perfect for

her. So, I asked her about Mickey Merrymen and his grandfather. She said they had gone to his house, found his body,
grabbed a few things, and left. She wasn't lying, Lew."

"You're sure?"

"You mean would I put my life on the line for it? No,
but I believe her. I told her the police were certainly looking
for Mickey."

"So?"

"She's angry," Sally said. "She's determined. All she
would say is 'He's going to suffer for every page.' Then
she hung up. Hold it." Sally put her hand over the mouth-
piece but I could hear her call out, "Susan, did you shampoo? That was one quick shower . . . No, I'm not calling
you a liar. It's a matter of degree and intensity. I'm sure
your hair is wet and has just had at least a passing acquain-
tance with shampoo. I'll check." Then back on the phone
with me. "Lew, I can cover Adele for a few days, even
that's taking a chance. I'll file a report that she may be
missing. The report will stay buried on my overburdened
desk for a few days, no more. Find her."

"Sunday?" I asked. "Can you get away for a movie?"

"I can get away if I bribe Michael and Susan with a
Scream 3 tape from Blockbuster and a sausage pizza."

"Seven?"

"Check the show times," she said.

We hung up. That left Dorsey to call. I dialed. The voice
came on before the first ring had ended.

"Yes," he said.

"Lew Fonesca," I said.

"My wife is out," he said. "She'll be back soon. So this
has to be fast. I talk to Charlie once or twice a year. He
always calls me, never tells me where he is, but . . ."

"Caller ID," I guessed.

"Yes," Clark Dorsey said as if he had just betrayed his
brother, which was probably just what he was thinking.

"Vera Lynn is alive?" I asked.

"Yes, but I don't know much. He just says, 'Clark, are
you okay?' I say, 'I'm fine.' He says he's fine though he
doesn't sound it. And then he hangs up. That's it. He

sounds worse each time we talk. We're brothers. We were close. Now . . . I think he needs help."

"What number did he call from?" I asked, reaching for an envelope and a blunt pencil.

"I called it back," he said, giving me the number. "It was a phone booth in a rib house someplace not far from Macon, Georgia, called Vanaloosa. A man with a black accent answered, said there were no white people around that neighborhood. Charles must have picked out the phone so I couldn't find him. Maybe you can. He sounded like . . . he sounded like. I can't explain it. Like he was dead and going through the motions. My brother was tough, Fonesca. Big, tough, smart. I don't know if you can resurrect the near dead. My wife thinks what happened to Charles is responsible for our . . . well, responsible for what we are. But he's my brother."

"I'll try to find him. How's the house coming?"

"I bought new lumber like your friend suggested. I'll even out the walls, but the house doesn't seem to care. It just grows, section by section, each room holding less and less."

"Ever think of seeing a shrink?" I asked.

"I don't believe in it," he said.

"I see a shrink," I said. "Good one. I think she'd see you. You might want to give it a try."

"My wife would like it," he said flatly. "But I'm not sure I want to be anything else than I am."

"I know. You get used to it," I said. "Then it's hard to give up the pain."

"Yes, I guess. How do you know?"

"You build more rooms. I crawl back into smaller ones," I said. "I don't like talking about it."

"I know," he said. "Give me your shrink's name. And let me know if you find Charlie and Vera Lynn. I'll pay whatever . . ."

"I've already got a client," I said.

"Marvin," he said.

"What does he want with his sister after all this time?" Dorsey asked.

"Maybe I'll find out," I said.

We hung up. That left Marvin Uliaks and Conrad Lonsberg to see in the morning. I checked my face in the mirror of my small back room. The mark of Bubbles Dreemer seemed to be gone. I shaved with the electric so I could be sure. It was gone.

I went out the door. It was raining. The DQ lights were out. All the lights on the street I could see from the railing were out. Cars swooshed and splashed down 301. No one walked the rainy night, not even a floating monk.

Digger had said he was going to get a cot, but I remembered he had a crevice or a stone bench in Bayfront Park. He might be in the washroom thirty feet away. I couldn't take another conversation with Digger, probably couldn't take one with anyone else.

I held my cup over the railing into the rain, caught enough to brush my teeth and rinse and spit into the night.

I love the rain. I love heavy rain that isolates, keeps people away, sets up a wall if not of silence at least of steadiness. The sound of rain always helps me to sleep. I went back in, locked the door, moved to my room, got undressed, put on fresh underwear, and popped a tape into the VCR cutting off CNN showing people clinging to the tops of trees in a flood somewhere in Africa.

The movie came on. I'd picked it up for three dollars on the third floor of the Main Street Book Store. It was *A Stolen Life* with Bette Davis. Made a good double feature with *Dead Ringer*, both about Davis playing a twin who takes the place of her evil sister. It wasn't Crawford in *Rain* but it would do. The problem was that the film, while in English, had subtitles in Spanish. I ignored the subtitles and watched. Dane Clark was an artist saying something to the good Bette Davis. I dozed to the sound of rain and woke up to see two Bette Davises on a small boat in a storm. The rain continued to tell me to sleep. I did.

8

THE RAIN HAD STOPPED. That I knew before I opened my eyes in the morning. I also knew I hadn't turned off the VCR. The sound of static crackled like burning paper. When I opened my eyes, I found a face looking down into mine. I shot up and cracked foreheads with Marvin Uliaks.

"Oww," he groaned, putting his hand on his forehead and stepping back.

I had a sudden headache from the impact, but no permanent damage.

Was Bubbles Dreemer standing in line in my office to take another crack at me?

"How did you get in?" I asked.

Marvin looked at his hand for signs of blood. There were none.

"Window," he said. "Lock doesn't work."

"How long were you standing there?" I asked, sitting up and holding my head in both hands.

"Awhile," he said. "I didn't want to wake you. You find Vera Lynn yet?"

"I told you I'd let you know, Marvin," I said with irritation.

"I just thought . . ." he started. "You need more money?"

"No," I said. "I do have a lead."

"A lead?"

"Some information on how I might find her, where she might be. Marvin, I don't think she wants to be found."

"I have to talk to her," he said, playing with his hands. It looked as if he were washing them in imaginary water.

"Okay," I said. "But the deal is clear. I find her. Tell her you want to talk to her and she does what she wants to do. If she has a message, I'll bring it."

"I have to talk to Vera Lynn," he said. "Myself. I have to. I have to give her something. Something she needs."

"What?"

He shook his head "no" and reached into his pockets pulling out money.

"Here," he said. "Use it. Find her. Tell her."

He dropped money on the cot. I reached up and stopped him by grabbing his wrists.

"No more, Marvin," I said. "I have enough. I'll use this and that's it."

"That's it," Marvin repeated, stuffing money back into his pockets. "Cross my heart." Which he did. "Hope to die." Which he did not.

"Now if you'd just go to work or wherever you might be going this morning, I'll get up and get to work finding Vera Lynn."

"I'm going. Beauty shop cleanup," he said. "Then . . . I forget. I'll remember. Sometimes I remember five years ago, twenty-five years ago better than yesterday."

"I do the same," I said.

"You do?"

"I thought maybe I was getting a little crazy. I know I'm not smart but I never thought I was crazy."

"You're not. I'll get back to you."

He left. This time through the front door. I gathered the bills he had dumped on my bed. I flattened out the crumpled ones and sorted them. He had dropped almost three hundred dollars. I pocketed them, checked the clock. It was a few minutes after six.

I put on my shorts and a Sarasota French Film Festival T-shirt, grabbed my helmet, and wheeled my bike out the doors and bumped it gently down the stairwell.

I was starting to get on the bike when Dave stepped out of the back door of the DQ, a broom in his hand. He looked more prepared for a day fighting marlins than dishing out shakes and burgers.

"Found something for you on the order counter this morning. Addressed to you," he said.

He leaned the broom against the white wall, went back into the DQ, and emerged with a box. The box was gray and wet. "FONESCA" was printed on the box in all black capital letters.

I opened the soggy package and found a thick manuscript. The top page was clearly typed, *Whispering Love*, a novel by Conrad Lonsberg. There was a clear signature. The date typed at the bottom was May 12, 1990. I lifted the soggy page while Dave stood over my shoulder.

The next pages and all that followed were soaked, the words on them running and undecipherable. The manuscript was ruined.

"She has imagination," I said. "Burning, shredding, soaking."

"The possibilities aren't endless," Dave said.

"But there may be enough."

"What's going on?" he said.

I told him.

"People," he said.

"People," I agreed, tucking the soggy box under my arm.

"I prefer fish and the Gulf waters," he said.

I wasn't much for fish or the Gulf waters, but I knew what he meant.

"You think about that trip," said Dave. "We could probably rig a VCR. When I run out of things to do, I could come down to the cabin and watch you looking the way you look now."

"Haven't had time to think about it more," I said. "I'll get back to you but don't count on me."

"I count only on David," he said.

After I'd brought the useless manuscript to my office and placed it on my desk, I went back to my bike and pedaled the few blocks to the Y.M.C.A., my single extravagance.

I went through the cycle of machines with the others who hurried through so they could shower, put on their suits, and be at their shops or desks or in uniform and possibly even have something to eat before they did what they had to do. It was less crowded today than usual. That's the way it was on Saturdays. That's the way I liked it. I liked swimming alone in the pool, slow, side stroke, on my back, a crawl once in a while, and then a hot shower and bike ride back.

No matter how much I worked out, I didn't seem to look any different, to gain or lose weight. Lew Fonesca's body was intact and healthy. It was his mind that needed a workout. That was the workout I didn't like. Working out was a meditation the way Sunday services used to be for me when I was a kid going to church. No thought. None expected or seen. It was the solitude not the lure of taut muscle or the healthy aerobic heartbeat that drew me.

I got a cheese sandwich with bacon from Dave when I got back to the DQ and then went up with my gym bag and changed into clean clothes. There was no message on the machine. Too early. Fine.

I had Conrad Lonsberg to face. I grabbed the soggy box of manuscript and the bag of shredded story, and the cover pages of the three manuscripts Adele had destroyed, put the cover pages in a brown paper envelope, and drove a few blocks over to the EZ Economy Car Rental Agency. Fred, the older guy, was there alone opening the door.

"Done," he said.

"Trading up," I answered. "I need something that'll get me to Vanaloosa, Georgia, just outside of Macon, and back without a problem."

"Fly," he suggested.

"I don't fly," I said. "I think I told you that."

"Must have been Al you told. Okay," he said. "We'll see what we've got for the trip up south. I understand they have a restaurant in Macon, best fried chicken in the country. Can't remember the name."

"Maybe I'll look for it," I said.

I checked my watch. I was about half an hour from facing Conrad Lonsberg.

The ride to Casey Key in the black '96 Ford Taurus was fast. You would think the tourists would be out on weekends along with the full-time working residents of the Gulf Coast, but they didn't seem to be, not this morning. The sky was slightly overcast but the weatherman on Channel 40 had promised there would be no significant rain. He had the Doppler to prove it, but not the confidence. Doppler and radar had been wrong too often in Florida.

If he were one hundred percent certain it would rain, he would give the rain chance at thirty percent. If he were one hundred percent sure it wouldn't rain, he'd give the rain chance at thirty percent. If you were looking out your window and it was raining, he would say there was a fifty percent chance of rain.

It was cloudy. There was distant rumbling in the sky. No rain. Not yet. Maybe not at all.

I pulled up next to Lonsberg's gate, got out of the car, brown paper envelope under my arm, and pushed the button.

"Who?" came the electric crackling voice of Conrad Lonsberg over the speaker.

"Fonesca," I said, looking up at the camera.

"Wait," he answered.

I waited. The sky was growing darker. I heard his footsteps and the panting of Jefferson on the other side of the gate after about two minutes and then the gate opened. Lonsberg was wearing a pair of taupe chinos today with a short-sleeved gray knit pullover.

Jefferson was wearing a look of eager suspicion.

Lonsberg nodded me in. Jefferson stalked toward me as Lonsberg closed and locked the heavy gate. Jefferson was close, looking up at me and making a sound in his throat I didn't like.

"I think he's considering tearing off my arm," I said, looking down at the dog.

"Jefferson's mostly show," said Lonsberg flatly. "He knows how to bark like fury, growl like a bear, and show his teeth like a cheap textbook drawing of a saber-toothed tiger."

"Admirable."

"It's his job. He won't hurt you."

We stood looking at each other for a few seconds. Then he said, "You have news."

"I have news."

"What kind?"

"Bad," I said.

"Let's walk on the beach."

He turned his back on me and headed toward the water. I caught up with him and Jefferson trotted slightly and uncomfortably behind me.

"Tell it all. Tell it carefully but tell it quickly," Lonsberg said.

"Adele's destroyed three of the manuscripts. Burned one. Shredded one. Soaked the third in water till it can't be read. She made sure to leave the cover pages of each one behind."

I pulled them out. We were standing on the sand now, the Gulf water washing in, waves a few feet high, wind light to moderate as the TV weatherman said. I handed the envelope to Lonsberg, who opened it and pulled out the three single sheets.

"Meet the Charming Devil, Come Into My Parlor, Whispering Love," he read from each sheet. "Not my best work. Not my worst. *Come Into My Parlor* is no loss. *Meet the Charming Devil* . . . I can't even remember it. *Whispering Love*, not a bad novel, not a good one. I was going through . . . through some problems when I wrote it. I wonder if she read them before she destroyed them?"

"I don't know."

"She tell you what she wants?" he asked as he motioned for Jefferson to run down the beach. Jefferson ran north along the beach. He seemed to have something in mind.

"No," I said. "She said something about making you pay page by page. Said she would do it a little at a time and let me know."

He nodded in understanding.

"So what are you doing?" he asked, looking down the beach at Jefferson who seemed to be trying to catch some gulls and having no luck.

"Waiting, trying to talk to her when she calls," I said. "She wants to be caught. She wants to hurt you, taunt you, and be caught."

"If you're lucky, you'll catch her and salvage some of my work before it's all gone," he said without emotion.

Jefferson was loping back toward us down the beach, something flopping in his mouth.

"Luck would be fine," I said, "but I'm not counting on it. I know Adele. She's smart, but she's angry. And she's traveling with a kid named Merrymen. You know him?"

"Merrymen," Lonsberg repeated, leaning down to pick up the dead fish Jefferson had dropped at his feet. The fish had been dead at least two or three days. Crabs had gotten to it and it gave off the distinctive smell of death.

Lonsberg patted Jefferson on the head. The dog's eyes closed in ecstasy. Lonsberg pointed south on the beach and Jefferson took off.

"Merrymen," he repeated. "Young, lanky, decent-looking, quiet, didn't seem bright enough for Adele. Met him twice when he picked her up. The first time he gave me an are-you-a-dirty-old-man look. The second time he just kept his head down, nodded, and got away as quickly as Adele was willing to leave. Jefferson took a definite liking to the kid. Jefferson's not easy to please."

Down the beach the big dog decided to plunge into the water where an incoming wave took him in the face. He weathered it and swam out in search of some treasure for Lonsberg.

"What else?" Lonsberg asked, looking at the dead fish.

"Bernard Corsello," I said. "Mickey Merrymen's grandfather. Someone shot him."

"So, what have I to do with Hecuba or Hecuba to me that I should weep so for her?" he asked.

"Shakespeare," I said. "*Hamlet*, I think."

"I apologize," said Lonsberg. "I was trying to keep you in place. I don't know what place, but . . ."

"I read a lot," I said. "I read and watch old movies. I like the way Shakespeare sounds."

"My favorite is *Titus Andronicus*," said Lonsberg. "Murder, mutilation, racism, hubris, mistakes, lies, rape, cannibalism, madness, and a sense of humor. "None of which are really part of what I write. Which is your favorite?"

"*Macbeth*," I said. "Nice and straightforward. But I'm more a Stephen King man myself."

"Underrated," Lonsberg said. "Overpaid."

"Bernard Corsello," I repeated as Jefferson bounded out of the water with a new treasure in his mouth. "Adele and Mickey Merrymen steal your manuscripts. They go to Mickey's grandfather to hide while Adele destroys your manuscripts. Someone comes looking for them, tracks them to Corsello's, kills the old man, doesn't find Adele, Mickey, or the manuscripts."

"You think I killed this Corsello?" Lonsberg asked with a smile as Jefferson ran up and dropped a large shell at his feet. It was a beautiful turquoise shell without a nick, worn clean and smooth.

Lonsberg picked it up and turned it over. The shell was white inside. He handed it to me.

"A gift from me and Jefferson," he said. "A bonus. I didn't kill any old man. If you talk to Adele, tell her that . . . tell her you told me what she was doing and I said nothing. You can tell her I'm sorry. No, she wouldn't care. Just tell her I said nothing."

"Sorry? About what?" I asked.

"Just tell her I said nothing," he said, looking toward the horizon.

"I'll tell her," I said. It would be the truth.

I put the shell in my pocket. We started away from the beach slowly, Jefferson at Lonsberg's side.

"I met your daughter and son," I said.

"Did you?" he asked but it wasn't really a question. "A lost generation, at least in my family. My grandchildren show some promise even if Laura, my daughter, does teach them to hate me as much as she does."

"I don't think she hates you," I said.

"You don't?" he said, again as if I had made a faulty observation.

"Dislike, maybe. And still . . ." I couldn't bring myself to say it so he did for me.

"Love," he said. "Dislike and love. Almost a good title. Probably also true. And Bradley the C.P.A.?"

"You're not the warmest man in the world," I said.

"Not quite a nonsequitur," he said. "But your point is taken. Bradley wants to be everything I'm not. Warm, out-going, friendly, uncreative, goes fishing with his son, has a good smile. Likable. That the way you found him?"

"Pretty much," I agreed.

"I don't think about my children much or my grandchil-dren as far as that goes," he said as we approached the gate. "I think about my wife. I treated her the way I treated my children. She saw something inside me that kept her com-ing back for more. She gave up trying to make me into something else and accepted what I was. She was a good listener and a more than decent poet. She used a pseudo-nym. Won't tell you what it was. No one's found that out yet. Some avid graduate student will probably make the discovery someday taking weeks or months he could be living to do it. She wanted to make it on her own and she did. *New Yorker, Atlantic*, little magazines."

We were at the gate now.

"I just talked to you more than I have to anyone except Jefferson in the last six or seven years," he said. "You're a good listener, Fonesca. Now, go be a good detective."

He put his hand out and we shook. Strong, firm, but there was a tremble, slight but real, early Parkinson's? I doubted it. Something I had told him? Possibly, but what?

I got in my rented Taurus and pulled out Jefferson and Lonsberg's gift shell. I laid it on the dashboard and looked at it for a few seconds, hoping it held some secret that would come out as if it were a magical gift from the sea. It told me nothing. I wasn't surprised. When my wife was alive I used to watch the skies with a telescope we kept on our small balcony. From time to time I thought I spotted a U.F.O. I was always wrong. She humored me. I wanted to find something out in the skies, something that would alter

the world and open eternity. When she died, I left the telescope behind. Whoever has the apartment now is either
using it, letting it sit in a corner, or has donated it to Good-
will.

On the way back to my office home I stopped at Flo's.
Her car was parked in the driveway. I rang the bell. It
chimed back the music from the ten notes of "If You Loved
Me Half as Much As I Love You." I didn't want to press
the bell again. I didn't have to.

"Who?" Flo called from inside.

"Lew," I said.

"Alone?"

"Alone," I answered.

She opened the door, the barrel of a rifle aimed at my
stomach.

Her hands weren't steady, but steady enough. Her mouth
was slightly open. Tex Ritter sang "High Noon" behind her,
one of Flo's all-time favorites.

"Where've you been?" she asked. "I've been calling you.
Left a message."

"Out looking for Adele," I said.

"Asshole tried to kill me," she said. "I was out driving
in the Ford, pulled into the driveway, and he blasted away
from the bushes."

"Someone tried to kill you?"

"I just said that, Lewis."

"You saw him?"

"No. I heard him. Heard the bullets hit the side of the
car. One went through the window not far from my head.
I ran in, got the gun, and took a few shots in his direction.
Scared him away. While I went for the gun, he had the
balls to open the car trunk. Went back inside and found
whoever it was had gone through the house didn't leave
much mess but the broken window he came through. Just
opened doors, closets, crawl space, didn't find what he was
looking for, and then waited for me to show up."

"He was looking for some manuscripts Adele took," I
said. "He was looking for Adele. He or she. I don't think
whoever it was will come back."

I didn't think this was a good time to tell her that Bernard

Corsello had probably been gunned down for the same reason she had been attacked and that she was lucky to be alive.

"You call the police?" I asked.

"I called you," she said, backing away so I could get inside and she could close and bolt the door. "I don't want cops here asking about Adele and asking why I was out driving when my license is goddamn suspended."

"Whoever broke in took nothing?"

"Not that I can tell, but things were moved, drawers were open in Adele's room, her closet. I've got it all cleaned up now. Guy's coming to fix the window tomorrow."

"He won't come back, Flo," I assured her as Tex sang, "Vowed it would be my life or his'n."

"You got it wrong, Lewis," she said. "I want him back. I'm ready now. I want him back so I can blow his legs off and get him to tell me where Adele is."

"I don't think whoever shot at you knows where Adele is," I said. "They're looking for her."

She leaned the rifle against the wall.

"I can use that thing," she said. "Gus taught me when we were just married. He could shoot a hole through a half dollar thrown into the air. Saw him do it. Did it myself a few times, but I was cold sober then. You want a drink?"

"You made a promise as a bride," Tex sang.

"No, thanks," I said.

She moved across the large living room to the liquor cabinet next to the CD and record player and poured herself a hefty glass of something white.

"You promised to stay sober, Flo," I reminded her.

"That was because I had Adele," she said, taking a drink. "Now I've got nothing again but old songs and lots of bottles and, I almost forgot, someone who's trying to kill me."

"I'll find Adele," I said. "I'll bring her back. Get sober. Make a deal with yourself, a bet. You're a gambler."

She looked old, her sequined green skirt and blowsy white blouse and dark boots belonged on Catherine Zeta-Jones or Charlize Theron or Salma Hayak, but not Flo Zink.

"Okay, I put the bottles away," she said. "Stay sober, wait for that bastard who tried to kill me to show up, and you deliver Adele with no charges against her by Wednesday. Wednesday at high noon," she said as Tex sang, "Do not forsake me, oh, my darling."

"Wednesday, high noon," I said.

Flo looked at her still half-full glass for an answer and said, "Deal."

She dumped the remainder of her gin or vodka into a cactus plant next to the sofa and sat looking up at me.

"Lewis, you brought that girl into my life," she said. "Bring her back. I don't know how much she needs me, but I sure as hell need her."

"I'll find her," I said.

"Then do it," she said, scooting me with one hand.

I went out the front door and moved around Flo's car. There were eight holes in it and the window was broken. I got out my pocket flashlight and dug out a bullet with my pocketknife.

I was on my way home again trying, without much luck, to figure out who had shot at Flo and killed the old man. Lonsberg? I didn't think it was in him, but his life's work had been taken. Did it feel as if a kidnapper had broken in and taken his children? I mean, did it feel like that to him?

And his heirs, Laura, Brad, maybe even Brad's teenage son, afraid Adele would destroy their legacy. Or might it be . . .

The shot hit the front window turning it into an intricate instant insane spiderweb I couldn't see through. The shot had come from a vehicle on my left. That I knew. But I hadn't looked. The vehicle was ahead of me now and I couldn't see through the windshield. I slowed down, opened my window, and guided the car through an empty lane of traffic on Webber Avenue. I sat for a few seconds watching for a car that might have someone in it who wanted another shot at me. I sat for about a minute more before getting out. I opened the clean, empty trunk, found the tire iron, went back inside the car, and smashed the front windshield. It crackled and splashed, shards fell forward though some did fall onto the dashboard. I pushed a few pieces of glass off the shell Jefferson and Lonsberg had given me and then swept the rest of the glass off the hood of the car trying not to leave scratches.

And then I drove back a block to 41 and up to 301 and the DQ with a blast of warm breeze in my face. It was about dinnertime for me but I didn't feel like eating. I knew how Flo felt. I was afraid. I didn't understand my fear. I cared for nothing much besides what was already lost to me. So why should I care about being shot? I didn't know, but I planned to ask Ann Horowitz on Monday.

I drove to EZ Economy Car Rental Agency and went into the small office where the older Fred with the cheerful smile and belly was standing in front of Alan, a big young man in his forties, whose hands were folded in front of him as he listened to his partner. It was Fred who first spotted me.

"Decide against that place near Macon?" he asked.

"No," I said.

"You have the second-best car on our lot," Fred said as Alan turned to me.

"Someone shot a hole through the front window," I said. "It needs a new window."

"Maybe it needs a new driver too," Alan said.

"Window that size will run you over a hundred," Fred said.

"Fine, can you get it done by tomorrow morning?"

"We can get it done," said Alan. "Any bullet holes, other damage to the vehicle?"

"I don't think so," I said.

"Someone tried to kill you in one of our cars," Alan said.

"Looks that way," I said.

"We're going to have to reassess your insurance," said Fred.

"When I turn the car in," I said. "Keys are in the car."

"What happened?" Fred asked. "Mafia catch up with you? That's what I always thought about you, that the Mafia was after you, that you did something to make them mad so you came here to hide."

"I'm from Chicago. I don't know any Mafia. I have enough trouble right here."

"I can dig your plight," said Alan.

"So what are you talking about now, 'Dig your plight,' "

said Fred. "Come down to earth and back from the seventies and help me see if we can find Jerry to fix the window."

Then Fred turned to me and said, "Forgive me, but I'd feel more comfortable with you out of here."

"Like if two guys with Uzi guns run in here and cut us down, especially after I've just had surgery," Alan said.

I nodded in assent and went out on the street. I walked past the bead shop, the Mexican video store, the Tae Kwon Do Academy, and the abandoned gas station. I was walking up my stairs when I noticed that my office lights were on.

I opened my door slowly and found myself looking at a tall young man in the seat across from my desk. He looked up at me as if he had been called into the assistant principal's office for smoking pot in the boys washroom. I played the role and calmly sat behind my desk.

"Mickey Merrymen," I said.

"Yes," he confirmed, his eyes shifting toward the door.

"Adele told me to come to you," he said. "She dropped me off. I taught her to drive."

"That was nice of you," I said, knowing I had no candy or gum to offer him, not even a cup of coffee unless I ran down to Dave's DQ, but Mickey might be gone by the time I got back.

"The police are looking for me," he said nervously. "They think I shot my grandfather."

"Where's Adele?" I asked.

"She'll call soon," he said. "Mr. Fonesca, I wouldn't kill my grandfather. He was good to me."

"How do you know the police are looking for you?" I asked.

"I called my father," the young man said. "He told the cops I was probably the killer. My father and I don't get along. He's a crazy man. Once he had me . . ."

The phone rang and I picked it up quickly.

"Well?" Adele asked.

"Not very," I said.

"Can you help Mickey?" she said. "Taking the manuscripts was my idea. Mickey really didn't know what was going on. He just carried. And he's been good to me. He isn't a genius, but . . ."

"No more destroying manuscripts," I said. "I help Mickey if you promise not to destroy any more of Conrad Lonsberg's work."

"A deal till Mickey's safe," she said. "But if the police get him or you don't get him off, I go back to destroying Lonsberg's work."

"And if I do save him?"

"Lonsberg's not getting his manuscripts back," she said firmly.

"Adele, what's the story here?"

"No story. Not yet. What I'm doing is better punishment."

"For what?" I asked. "For who?"

"Save Mickey," she said and hung up. So did I.

"You know why Adele took the manuscripts?" I asked Mickey who jiggled in the folding chair and held the seat tightly as if he were about to be thrust into outer space.

"No," he said. "She asked me to help her. I did."

"Why?"

"You know Adele?" he asked.

"I know Adele," I said.

"I love her," Mickey said, looking me in the eyes for the first time.

"I can understand that," I said. "Adele's a great, beautiful, and talented girl. But why is she doing this and where is she?"

"I don't know where she is," he said. "Driving around. We hide the van at night and sleep in it. Blankets on top of all those pages. It's kind of creepy, but Adele likes it. She looks through everything and picks out the one she's going to get rid of next. That's all she told me. That's all I know."

"You went with Adele to your grandfather's house and found him dead. You cleared out your things and left him there," I said.

"We had to," Mickey cried. "I didn't want to leave him there like that but Adele said we had to get out of there, that whoever was after her had figured out where we were and had come to get us. I loved my grandfather. I wouldn't hurt him."

"And your father?"

"He's crazy," Mickey said. "Sometimes I think I'm going to be crazy like him."

"Could he have killed your grandfather?"

"Why would he do that? He never even talked to my grandfather. They hated each other."

"That sounds like a motive," I said.

"My father talks like a lunatic. He is a lunatic but he wouldn't kill anyone."

"There's always a first time," I said.

"Am I going to jail?" he asked.

"We're going to talk to a policeman named Viviase. You're going to tell him everything, running away with Adele, finding your dead grandfather, grabbing a few of your things, and running away. You will not mention the manuscripts. You just ran away with Adele. You understand?"

"Then I lie?"

"About Adele, yes."

"Go over it again," he said. "My mind . . . I'm having trouble keeping things straight."

I repeated to Mickey what he should and shouldn't say. He was a slow learner but when he had it right he sounded convincing to me.

"Don't I need a lawyer? On television they always say they·want a lawyer."

"If you get in trouble, just say, 'I don't want to talk anymore without a lawyer.' "

"How will I know if I'm in trouble? I don't even know any lawyers."

"I do. If you get confused, stop talking except to say you want a lawyer. I'll get one for you. You understand?"

"Yes," he said.

"With some luck, I'll be in the room when the police talk to you. If I think it's time for you to ask for a lawyer, I'll just shake my head."

"Which way?"

"Which way what?"

"Which way will you shake your head. Up or down?"

"Like this," I said.

"I'm not usually this dumb," Mickey said, rubbing his hair. "I haven't had much sleep and my grandfather . . ."

I held up a hand to quiet him and picked up the phone. The answering machine was blinking. One call. The call Flo had mentioned. I ignored it, called Viviase, and told him I had someone he was looking for.

"Come with him," Viviase said.

"I was planning to."

Then I told him we'd be right over.

"Be here in ten minutes," he said. "Then we come looking."

"Ten minutes," I agreed.

We hung up. I wondered why he wanted me to come, probably more about finding the body of Mickey's grandfather.

We could get to his office in five minutes if we hurried. I closed the office and led Mickey down the stairs. We stopped at the DQ. I got a double chocolate Blizzard, large. Mickey said he would have the same. We drank as we walked and said nothing.

Mickey might not be the brightest kid with a high school diploma but he was a good witness. He looked and sounded frightened and honest. I was counting on it.

A black car with tinted windows slowed down. I thought of the shot through my window an hour before and stepped back pulling Mickey with me. The car moved on. So did we. I drank the rest of my Blizzard slowly. I wished I were lying in my bed in my underwear watching *Humoresque*.

9

ED VIVIASE'S DOOR was open. He stood in front of his desk, sitting back against it, a coffee cup in his hand. His glasses were off and lying on the desk next to a brown paper bag with grease spots showing through. Next to the bag was a manila folder. I don't like manila folders. They contain too many surprises.

Viviase looked like a tired bulldog.

"This is Mickey Merrymen," I said.

Viviase nodded and drank some coffee. He looked at both of us for a second and then motioned for us to take a seat in front of him. We did. He looked tired. I told him he did.

"Earache," he said.

"Sorry," I answered.

"Not mine, Ernie's. My wife just had some minor surgery, female stuff. I was up with Ernie all night. Medicine, tea, toast, antibiotics. That was after a trip to Emergency. Kid's tough. He insists on going to school tomorrow. I haven't had any sleep. Zero. Zilch. Nothing. So make this easy on me. I am in a very bad mood."

"How old is Ernie?" I asked.

"Sixteen. Goes to Cardinal Mooney. I think he didn't want to miss football practice. What the hell? Donut?"

He picked up the brown paper bag and held it toward us.

Mickey picked out a plain one with chocolate icing. I turned down the offer.

"You sure?" asked Viviase, reaching in for a puffy yellow one with red icing. "If you don't want a donut, I've got a few other things in the bag that might interest you."

"No, thanks," I said, feeling something was coming. He was ignoring Mickey.

He settled the red-icinged donut between his teeth and reached into the bag to pull out the turquoise seashell Jefferson and Conrad Lonsberg had given me the day before. He handed me the shell and then fished a spent bullet out of the bag. He handed me the bullet too.

Viviase took a bite out of his donut as he watched me. I looked at the two objects. Viviase drank. Mickey looked confused.

"Someone took a shot at you," Viviase said. "Bang. End of Taurus window. We fished that," he said, pointing at the bullet, "out of the backseat. Want to guess what ballistics matched it to?"

"The bullet that killed Bernard Corsello," I said.

"Good guess," said Viviase. "Want to make some more?"

"I don't think I'll be so friendly with the EZ Economy Car Rental Agency boys from now on."

"They called in when they saw the bullet hole in the seat," Viviase said. "Good citizens."

"A couple of frightened men with a marginal business," I said.

"All true," said Viviase. "Now, why would the person who killed Corsello want to take a shot at you?"

"I don't know," I said.

"Let's take a guess or two. By the way, that's a nice shell. You don't find many of them that color in that condition. My guess on who took the shot and why? You asked the wrong question to the wrong person, the person who killed Corsello, so he, she, or it decided to take a shot at you."

"Maybe," I said.

"I didn't check this morning, but I don't think you got a private investigator's license in the last day or two or even applied for one."

He finished his donut, slurring his last few words. Mickey was finished too.

"I was just asking questions for a friend," I said.

"No idea who took a shot at you?"

I had a few ideas, but I didn't want to share them with the police, so I said, "No."

"Think they were trying to kill you or scare you?" he asked.

"I think they would have been happy either way."

Viviase suddenly turned to Mickey who had been watching and listening, detached, a little dreamy. Viviase woke him up.

"You have a gun?"

"No," said Mickey, sitting up.

"Your father owns a nine-millimeter," Viviase said. "Hell, he owns four of them. One of them is missing."

"Dad gets a little . . . confused sometimes. You know what I mean. It could be someplace he put it and forgot."

"For the sake of argument," said Viviase, now finishing his coffee, "let's say coincidence suggests that someone took that nine-millimeter, shot your grandfather, and took a shot at Mr. Fonesca here. That make sense to you?"

"I didn't take the gun," Mickey said. "I don't like guns. I don't like dogs. I don't like my father."

"But," Viviase said, "you like girls."

"Yes," said Mickey, looking at me, anticipating.

"Your father, in a moment of coherence, said you've been seeing a girl named Adele Hanford."

I blinked my eyes to let Mickey know it was all right to answer the question. Viviase noted the exchange, folded his arms, and looked back at Mickey.

"I know Adele."

"So do I," said Viviase. "Smart girl."

"Yes," said Mickey.

"She doesn't hate guns," said the policeman, taking in both of us.

"I don't know," said Mickey.

"Who told you your grandfather was dead?"

"I . . ." Mickey looked at me again. It was close to time for a lawyer, but I blinked and he went on. "I don't get along with my father. Nobody gets along with my father. But I'm the one who has to live with him. So I spend lots of time at my grandfather's. I was going to spend the night. My father had his gun out, yelling at the old lady next door, talking to the dog. I don't like the dog. He doesn't like me. So, I went to my grandfather's for the night and found him dead."

"You were alone?" asked Viviase who turned to me and said, "Fonesca, if you blink, nod, even breathe, I book him on suspicion."

Mickey looked confused but said, "I was alone. I found him, got scared, and ran. I knew he was dead. I thought . . . I thought maybe my father had killed him. They didn't like each other. My father didn't like my going to my grandfather's."

"They didn't like each other," Viviase repeated. "Can we escalate that to 'hated each other'?"

"Esca . . . hate, yeah, I guess," Mickey said. "But my father hates almost everybody."

"And he has guns, your father?"

"Yes."

"What would you say if I told you Adele's fingerprints were all over your grandfather's house, door, window, telephone?"

"Lawyer time," I said.

Viviase looked at me and sighed.

"You want a lawyer? Why?"

"I think Mickey wants a lawyer," I said.

"Why? I'm just asking questions. I haven't accused him of a crime."

"You didn't have the time to check out all the fingerprints that must be in Corsello's house. And given the size of your operation, I don't think you checked the whole place."

I knew, for certain, Adele's fingerprints weren't on the phone. I had wiped the phones clean. Viviase was bluffing.

"Adele wasn't with me," Mickey said.

"You want a lawyer?"

"You think I shot my grandfather?"

"No," Viviase said. "But I'm a lousy judge of human character. I even like Fonesca. You'd be surprised at how many people I was sure were innocent turned out to be guilty and how many I was sure were guilty turned out innocent."

"Are we finished?" I asked.

"Nope," Viviase said, picking up his cup, remembering it was empty, and putting it down again. "We have more coincidences to talk about. Early this morning, one of our cars pulled over a car weaving all over Proctor. Driver was definitely DUI. The cop saw holes in the side of the van. He opened the van and found, guess what?"

"More nine-millimeter bullets," I guessed.

"Want to know what they match?"

"The one in my car and the one that killed Corsello?"

"Good guess. Want to guess the DUI?"

"Florence Zink," I said.

"Good. Let's keep it up. You know, connect the dots. Corsello gets shot, someone shoots at you, pops Flo Zink's car full of holes. All the same gun. What's the common denominator here?"

I sat quietly and shrugged. Viviase looked at Mickey who probably didn't know what a common denominator was.

"You miss the thirty-two-thousand-dollar question," said Viviase. "The correct answer is Adele. Mickey's girlfriend, Flo's foster kid, your adopted delinquent. So, I ask you both, where is Adele?"

"I don't know," I said.

"Me either," Mickey said.

"I'd really like to talk to her," said Viviase. "The way it seems, and this is just speculation, a lot of people Adele knows have pissed her off and she's going around shooting them."

"I don't think so," I said.

"She go back on the streets? What?"

I shrugged.

"I do sort of like you, Lewie," he said. "But it wouldn't be hard to make you decide to leave Sarasota, or even leave Florida. I'd classify you as a petty annoyance but this business could move you up to major pain in the ass. You don't want to be a pain in my ass. Not when I'm having a bad day."

"I don't, Etienne," I said in response to his "Lewie." "Can we go or . . ."

"You can go," he said. "Not far. It might be easier, much easier if Adele just drops by to see me."

"Where's Flo?" I asked.

"In the tank," said Viviase. "I talked to her. She asked me to find Adele. She also asked me to find Gus."

"Gus?" asked Mickey.

"Flo's husband," I said. "She can find him in a grave in New Hampshire."

"Want to see her?" asked Viviase.

"Yes," I said.

He finally pushed himself away from the desk, took the bullet back, and let me keep the seashell.

"I'll take care of it," Viviase said. "Fonesca, she's a tough old lady with bad taste in music. This is her second DUI in a week. If she doesn't get sober and stay that way, she's going to lose Adele. It might already be too late."

I motioned for Mickey to rise with me.

"Thanks," I said to Viviase.

"We'll talk again soon," he said, moving behind his desk, sitting down, and picking up the phone.

Mickey and I left the office and went into the hallway.

"What happened?" Mickey asked.

"He's missing a piece and he wants Adele to fill it in," I said.

"The stolen manuscripts?"

"Right. Walk back to my office. Wait for me there."

He nodded as we got in the elevator and headed down. I stopped at the second floor. Mickey went down to ground level. Three minutes later I was signing Flo out of the drunk tank. She recognized me, looked away as I walked her out. She was a mess.

"I have a hangover," she said as we left the lockup.

I held her big canvas bag that passed for a purse. It weighed at least fifteen pounds.

"You're surprised?"

"I don't usually have hangovers," she said. "I just feel queasy, have a beer, and I'm all right."

"A beer won't help you this time," I said.

"No," she agreed as we stepped out into the street.

The sky was still overcast but it wasn't raining.

"They won't let me take my car," she said. "I suppose that means I'll never drive again."

"Not legally," I agreed, starting to walk.

"Where are we going?" she asked as I moved down the sidewalk.

"To get a car and take you home," I said.

"I'll be stranded there," she wailed.

"You have money. There are cabs," I said.

"You're mad at me, Lewis," she said.

"No," I answered. "I've learned not to expect much from people so when they don't deliver I'm not disappointed."

"You're disappointed in me?" she asked.

"Yes," I said. "But I'm not judging you. I'll take you home. You hide, wait till you hear from me, drink yourself to death, and hope I find Adele who'll probably be taken away from you even if I do. If you find the old Flo, have her give me a call."

We walked slowly down to the corner, turned left, and hit the EZ Economy Car Rental Agency in five or six minutes of silence.

"I look like shit," Flo mumbled.

I said nothing as we went through the door. Alan was there handing keys to a customer, a young Hispanic in a trim suit carrying a briefcase.

"Fonesca," Alan said, bright and false. "Your car's ready."

I held my hand out for the keys. Alan looked at Flo.

"The cops told you?" he guessed.

I said nothing.

"We had no choice," Alan said. "You know what kind of profit margin we survive on here? I've got a kid starting college next year. Fred's got a stomach he should donate to Johns Hopkins or the Smithsonian or Barnum and Bailey. We can't afford to fool around with the law."

"You're forgiven," I said. "Keys."

He reached over to the rack of keys, selected the right one, and handed it to me.

"New key chain," he said. "Windshield's new. We patched the bullet hole. Can't even see where it was."

"How close did it come to hitting me?" I asked.

"Not very," Alan said. "Passenger side about chest high."

"Someone tried to kill you?" Flo said, coming a bit out of her fog.

"Someone shot at me," I said.

"Because of Adele?" she asked.

"I don't know," I said. "But that's a good guess. Let's go."

"Ten percent off on the next rental," Alan called as I went out the door with Flo behind me.

Alan followed us out while I helped Flo in and went around to the driver's side. I looked at Alan and said, "You could have called me before you called the police."

Alan nodded.

I got in and drove off heading south. Flo wanted to talk but she didn't have anything to say. I turned on the radio and got two thirty-year-olds talking about the best time of the day to have sex. I changed the station and got a woman psychologist who was setting up brick walls against sex. I wasn't thinking about sex. I pushed another button and got Louis Prima and Keely Smith singing "That Old Black Magic."

"What do I do while I'm waiting if I don't drink?" Flo mumbled.

"Eat, look at the water, watch television, read a book, listen to your records," I suggested.

"Without Adele, something's missing. I fill the something with whiskey sours and gin and fruit."

"Buy a business," I suggested.

"What?"

"You've got money. Buy a business."

"Gus and I had one. I didn't like it. Got on my knees and said thanks to the Lord when he retired."

"Buy one you like," I said, turning west on Oak right near the DQ. We were in Washington Park, clearly marked, a neighborhood of upscale homes, some of the oldest and best maintained in Sarasota. It looks like an MGM 1940s street where Andy Hardy might have a girlfriend. When I wasn't in a hurry I'd bicycle through Washington Park, driving back in time for a few blocks to Osprey, which I did now.

"Like what kind of business?"

"I don't know. Get a small place that specializes in western records or open a little bar where you can get bands in to play country."

"Good advice," she said. "I'll think about it. What about you?"

"Me?"

"Take a big step back to the land of the living," she said. "Hold my hand. I'll teach you to square-dance. You tell me to get a life. I'm telling you right back."

She was right. I had no business telling Flo Zink how to live or die. We were silent the rest of the way to Flo's.

"Think about it," I said, pulling into her driveway. "And let me know if Adele calls."

She opened the door.

"Want to come in for a drink? Beer for you. Sprite for me."

"I don't think . . ."

We could hear the phone inside ringing. Flo left the door of my car open and ran for the house. I got out, leaving my door open too, and followed her as she found her keys, scrambled in, and ran for the phone.

"Hello," she said.

I stood next to her.

"Sorry? You're sorry? You've got a goddamn good reason to be sorry," Flo said, a bit of her old self emerging. "Where the hell are you? What the hell are you doing? . . . I was in jail all night. That's where I was. That's why I didn't answer the fuckin' phone . . . No, I'm all right. I won't be driving for a while, probably never, but I'm all right. Are you coming back? . . . No, I just got some ramrod back and I'm asking you a question? I made it before you and I'll make it again. I've got some plans . . . Yes, I want you back, but this old broad is getting flatter and softer since you started playing games again. I don't much care for the woman you're talking to, but I mean to . . . Fine, here he is. I'm going to take a bath and watch the boats from the deck and think about better times when Gus was alive and kicking ass."

She looked angry now, more than a bit of the old Flo. She handed me the phone.

"Lew?" Adele asked.

"Yeah."

"Is she all right?"

"No," I said.

"Can you help her?"

"Can you?"

"I'm not finished," Adele said. "I've got a lot of work left. You told him what I destroyed?"

"I told Lonsberg what you destroyed," I said.

"How's Mickey?"

"He's confused," I said. "He's in my office waiting for me. Why don't you meet us there?"

"I can't," she said. "I'm not done. There's hurting to be done. Did you read *Plugged Nickels*?" she asked.

"Some of it," I said. "It's not my kind of book."

"Chapter six, first five paragraphs," she said.

"What about them?"

"Read them," she said.

"I'm getting too old for games, Adele," I said.

"I was too old when I was twelve," she said. "My father was screwing me and I was turned over to a pimp when I was thirteen, but you know all that. So a little game playing won't hurt you or me. I missed out on game playing when I was growing up and going down."

"I'll read it," I said. "But I've got a condition."

"No more manuscripts destroyed. Not for a day or two. You bought time by helping Mickey."

"Have you any idea who took a shot at me last night?" I asked.

"Son of a bitch shot at you?" she screamed. "Tell the legend I'm tearing two of his books right now. Tearing them and throwing them into the Gulf. *Rains Rising* and *Childhood on Fire*."

"I thought you weren't going to destroy any more manuscripts. We have a truce."

"Screw the truce," she said. "You want to get killed? Mickey's grandfather was a good man. So are you. Flo's a good woman. Ames is . . ."

"But not you," I said.

"No, not me," she said soberly. "It's in the genes and the jeans. He saw it in me. I thought I could be . . . What's the use. Tell him the titles and take care of yourself and Flo and Mickey."

"I didn't sign on as a baby-sitter," I said. "I signed on to find you. Come to my office. No strings. I won't hold you. Just you, me, and Mickey."

"Battery's low," she said. "Needs recharging. I'll think about it."

She hung up.

"Well?" asked Flo, brushing back her mess of hair.

"I don't know," I said. "She's an angry girl."

"Don't I know it."

I thought but didn't say that Adele was going to get someone very hurt or very dead if she didn't stop this mind game with Lonsberg. What I didn't know was how soon I would find out how right I was.

When I got back to my office and opened the door Mickey Merrymen was against the wall. His father was in front of him, his fist raised ready to strike at an already bloody face.

10

AT THIS POINT I want to make some things clear. First, I am in reasonably good physical shape. I bicycle. I work out four or five times a week. I'm a little on the thin side, a bit taller than short, and I don't have the kind of face that tells people violence lurks behind it ready to explode at some minor infraction of my space or sentiments.
· I could also add at this point that I don't do violence. Most sane and sober human beings could say the same things, but I've seen and imagined too much violence from that very active minority of violent humanity. I couldn't hit anyone. I won't carry a gun.

Ann Horowitz once asked me what I would do if my own life or the life of a loved one were being immediately threatened. I said I would try to save them, but there was no sincerity or passion in my answer. Yes, I would try to save them and I had no intention of letting myself be killed without trying to do something about it. It was the extreme situation Ann had given. Most violent situations did not push me into a corner of the extreme.

And so instead of leaping forward, turning Merrymen

around, and slamming my fist into his nose or throat, I shouted, "No."

Merrymen's fist froze in the air and he turned from his son toward me. Mickey slumped back against the wall.

"They think I killed that old fart," he said, advancing on me. "You and Mickey gave them the idea that I killed Charlie. The cop told me."

Viviase was doing what a good cop should do when he wasn't sure where he was going. He was throwing dust in the air and seeing if it bothered someone enough to lead to answers. In this case, he had turned loose a less than fully sane Michael Merrymen with the idea that his son and I had pointed the finger at him. He wasn't completely wrong.

The fist was up and ready. My plan, to the extent that I had one, was to get through the door and run. There was a flaw in the plan. Either Merrymen would come after me, and I doubted that he could catch me, or he would turn back on Mickey whose teeth were red with blood.

I wasn't sure I liked Mickey, but I was sure I was not going to run out on him. If the Lone Ranger hadn't shown up, I was going to be beaten into something like Tropicana orange pulp, or I'd get in a good or lucky punch and stop Merrymen.

The Lone Ranger arrived. He stepped into the room standing tall, unmasked, years older than I had remembered him from television.

Ames took in the story as he stepped into the room. Just as Merrymen was turning to face him, Ames stepped forward and threw a bony elbow into the younger man's face. Flannel backed by bone hit flesh and Merrymen staggered back.

The phone started to ring. Ames moved to pick it up, which didn't strike me as the thing to do in this situation.

Merrymen, now bloody and broken-nosed, pushed himself away from the wall and headed toward Ames with a gurgling sound that could have been his own animal reaction or the result of blood dripping into his throat.

The phone hit Merrymen in the chin just as Merrymen put his open hand out toward Ames's eyes. This time Merrymen went down. He hit the floor hard and rolled over groaning, his hands covering his face.

"For you," said Ames, handing me the phone.

I took it and Ames moved to help Mickey to his feet.

"Fonesca," I said.

"Horowitz," said Ann. "Are you incapacitated?"

"Huh?"

"If you are going to miss an appointment, you need only dial my number and give me an excuse, preferably the truth."

"Things happened," I explained, looking at the not so very Merrymen.

"That is the nature of life," she said. "You are late. Are you coming?"

"Yes," I said. "Ten minutes."

She was less than five minutes away and I shouldn't have trouble parking at this hour.

"Ten minutes. I'll explain when I get there."

I hung up the phone and used a tissue from the dispenser on my desk to wipe the blood off its corner before putting it down.

"How's Mickey?" I asked.

"He'll be fine," said Ames who had sat the boy on one of my folding chairs.

Michael Merrymen rolled over and looked up at me. He was a mess.

"I'm suing you and that old man," he said, glaring at me.

It was hard to understand what he was saying. His nose was bent to one side and his jaw was swelling rapidly.

"I'm sure you'll win," I said as he sat up still on the floor. "Can you drive yourself to the emergency room?"

He didn't answer, rolled on one side, and managed to get up on wobbly legs. He put his hand on his head and groaned.

"Hit my head," he said.

"I saw," I answered.

"Why are you all after me?" Merrymen suddenly said, his arms outstretched, his eyes moving from me to Ames to his son.

"It's called paranoia," I said.

"Bullshit," Merrymen said, spitting blood on my office floor. I handed him a wad of tissues. He took them and applied them to his face.

"You've got a club in one hand and a target on your back," said Ames, looking into Merrymen's eyes. "Then you scream, 'Here I am.' That's why people are after you."

"You don't understand," Merrymen said.

"All I've got to say," said Ames, turning his back on the ranting bloody man.

"The door's over there," I said.

"You people just don't understand," he shouted. "You don't listen. You don't . . . what's the use. Mickey, if you come home, there's a dog waiting to greet you."

And with that Merrymen staggered out of the door. I looked out of my window and our eyes met. This was not a friendly departure.

"I have an appointment," I said.

"I'll take care of him," said Ames. "You want him here when you get back?"

"Yes," I said.

"I'll get him one of those things you drink from the Dairy Queen and some ice for his face," Ames said.

"I'll be back soon. By the way, what made you arrive just in time for the rescue?"

He reached into his pocket and pulled out the morning's Sarasota *Herald-Tribune*. It was folded so that I could see the small article and the photograph at the bottom. The headline over the photograph read: "Murder Attempt on Motorist." There was a picture of me inset in the small article. The picture was the same one I had taken for my process server's license. I looked like a cockeyed smirking chimp, the very prey any sensible hunter looking for an easy target might take a shot at.

"Thought you might need help," said Ames.

"You were right," I said. "I'll get back as soon as I can."

Ann Horowitz was on the telephone when I arrived. She looked at me over the top of her glasses and motioned for me to close the door and take my usual seat. I did.

"Listen," she told her caller, "my next client just came in. But I'll give you advice. You called to sell me insurance on dying people. It's an interesting idea. I give you money and then wait till my person dies. I check the obituaries or wait for you to call saying, 'Good news, Emily Jacobs just died.' Sensible but an aura of morbidity that I find strange. My question is, 'How do you feel about selling the death?' ... The word 'fine' came too suddenly to your lips as if you wanted to leap over some chasm and come out on the other side with a smile. What if I took my insurance out on your life? Don't answer. You've been doing this how long? Six months. And you are making money as you promise I will. I have a question for you to consider, but I haven't time now to hear your answer. The question is, what do you think is the meaning of your life? Answer it and then call yourself a liar and tell the liar to tell the truth. You have my number. If you want to make an appointment to see me to talk over your answer, call. My charge is one hundred dollars a session. Now, good-bye."

She hung up the phone and settled back.

"No offering?" she asked, looking at my empty hands. "No biscotti, no scone, no rugelach, not even a donut?"

"I didn't have time," I said. "I was dealing with a lunatic in my office who was trying to kill me."

"He didn't succeed," she said calmly. "I've got some raisins in the drawer."

"No thanks."

"We can drink my coffee," she said.

"No thanks," I said.

I had twice tried Ann's coffee. It was thick, bitter, and I never saw her drink it.

"Why did this man want to kill you?" she asked.

"Because he's crazy. He thinks everyone is trying to ... he's paranoid. Nuts. A loony. He beat up his son in my office."

"Your clients sound almost as interesting as mine," she said, opening a nearby drawer and pulling out a clear, small Ziploc bag of raisins that she opened and began to eat.

"We'll compare notes sometime," I said.

"Now is a good time," Ann answered, looking up at her wall clock. "We still have forty-five minutes. So, I'll start with a question. Why does a hermetic, depressed recluse have any clients at all outside of those for whom he serves papers?"

"I don't know," I said.

"Common denominator," she asked.

I'd heard that phrase before today. It had more than a hint of déjà vu.

"People come to me," I said. "I don't ask for them. I don't want them."

"But you don't turn them down," she said, nibbling a raisin. "Why? You've described some of your clients in past sessions. I see a common denominator. I may be wrong but it's a place to start."

"What is it?" I asked.

"They all remind you of the most important person in your life," she said.

"Who?"

"You, Lewis Fonesca. They are all sad cases. People calling out for help with no one to turn to. A runaway wife, a wife whose husband is dying, a runaway girl, an old man who has been robbed by his partner. And you help them as you cannot help yourself."

"Maybe," I said.

"And then what do you do with them?" she asked.

"Do with them?"

"When you solve their problem. What do you do?"

"Nothing," I said.

"You make the survivors part of a family you are rebuilding," she said. "You lost your family and so you are rebuilding one and at the same time you reject it. You are an interesting case, Lewis."

"Thanks," I said.

"I didn't say you were the most interesting case I ever had," she said. "You know Joe Louis the boxer?"

"Of course."

"I treated him once for a while," she said. "Nice man. Paranoid like the man you had in your office. Thought everyone was trying to kill him, particularly the Mafia. He would never give up the idea. He had evidence, proof, a distortion of reality that bordered on the creativity of a Borges. He was more interesting than you are, but you will do. So?"

"So?" I repeated.

"Did anything I just said do anything? How did it make you feel?"

"It made sense, I suppose."

"It made sense," she said in exasperation. "Of course it made sense, but did it feel right to you? Did you have an epiphany? A sudden jolt of understanding?"

"No."

"Sense and feeling are not always in agreement," she said. "You sure you don't want some raisins?"

I accepted some raisins.

"When you feel it, it works. When it just makes sense, it doesn't work. The truth must touch your soul."

"I don't believe in the soul," I said.

"I remember you telling me that many times," she said. "It doesn't matter whether you believe it or you don't. You can deny the sight of a mystic levitating, but he is still levitating. Your denial doesn't change that."

"Levitation is a trick," I said. "Weak analogy."

"Levitation is a trick until you learn to levitate."

"Can you levitate?" I asked.

"No," she said. "But I have touched and had touched the soul. I have an idea. Let's not call it the soul. Let's not call it anything. Your picture was in the newspaper today."

"I know," I said.

"I have an extra copy. Would you like it?"

"No, thanks."

"Someone tried to kill you?"

"I think so."

"Why?"

"Don't you want to know 'who'?"

"No, I'd prefer 'why.' It saves a step."

"Because I'm coming too close."

"To what?"

"Damned if I know," I said.

"Interesting thing to say," Ann said, fishing out the last of the raisins. "Why would this knowledge lead to your damnation?"

"I didn't mean . . ."

"An automatic response from inside, a protective cliché, but one that bears meaning for you. You could have said, 'I don't know,' or 'beats me,' or . . ."

"I'm lost," I said.

"Yes, that is why you came to see me in the first place. Do you know what happened to Henry Hudson?"

"He designed a fat car back in the forties," I said.

"We're close to something," she said with glee, throwing the empty bag in the nearby trash can. "You are dodging. I am throwing. Perhaps you'll stop and I'll hit something."

"Henry Hudson," I said.

"Hudson Bay. Hudson River," she said. "Searched for the Northwest Passage. Got lost, frozen on the massive bay that bears his name. There was a mutiny. The crew was getting sick. The ice was closing in. Hudson was determined to go on. The crew sent Hudson, his son, and others adrift on the icy water and sailed for home. Hudson was never found. No one knows if he made land. There are Indian stories about white men who lived for years on the shore, of Indians they traded with, of remnants of bones or a shack. But never found."

"Interesting. There's a point here?"

"History always has a point," she said. "Historians always make a point. Often they disagree with each other over the point. What is the point of Hudson's story for you?"

"If you keep looking for something that isn't there and you're too stubborn to admit it, you might get yourself killed," I said.

"Or, you might find the Northwest Passage. Samuel Hearne tried and failed."

"Samuel Hearne?"

"Lewis and Clark tried later with more success," she said.

"I'm looking for a truckload of novels and short stories," I said. "Not the Northwest Passage."

"Henry Hudson found the Hudson River and Hudson Bay," she said. "Not unimportant discoveries. Maybe you should . . . what?"

"Look around at what I've found and guard myself from mutineers," I said.

"Close enough," she said. "Session's over."

She rose and so did I. I paid her twenty dollars in cash that I could afford this week.

"One last thing," she said as I went to the door.

I stopped and looked back at her.

"Can you say her name?"

"Catherine," I said immediately.

I stood amazed. I had nurtured, protected my dead wife's name and memory, held it as my own not wanting to let go of my grief, feeling the simple utterance of her name would be a kind of sacrilege to the mourning I did not want to lose. I had spoken her name aloud only to Ann and to Sally.

"You know why you were just able to do that?" Ann asked.

"No."

"Because we talked about life. Because you are slowly rejoining the living, building new friends, a family."

"I'm not sure I want to," I said.

"And that," she said with an air of conclusion, "is what we must work on."

She went back to her chair, picked up the phone, and gave me a small smile of encouragement as I went out the door.

When I got back to my office, Ames was standing against a wall, arms folded. Mickey was sitting in the folding chair holding a see-through bag of ice against his face.

The blood was off the wall and everything was in place. Ames had cleaned up. I would have been surprised if he hadn't. There was no sign of the supposedly adult Merrymen.

"Got some calls," Ames said.

The little red light on my answering machine was blinking and the counter showed three phone calls.

"Any sound important?"

He shook his head "yes." I got my pad and Nation's Bank click pen and pushed the PLAY button.

A man's voice came on, young, serious.

"This is John Rubin at the *Herald-Tribune*. We just got a call from someone who wouldn't leave a name. Caller said that Conrad Lonsberg had all of his manuscripts stolen and I should call you. Please call back."

He left his number, repeating it twice. I wrote it on my pad.

The second voice was Flo's, not quite sober but contrite and possibly coming out of it. In the background I could hear Frankie Laine singing the theme from *Rawhide*. I didn't think it really qualified as country or western, but it wasn't an issue I wanted to take up with Flo who said, "Lewis, Adele called again, said she was all right. Said she was sorry for what she was doing to me but she had to do it if she expected to have any respect for herself. Said she'd come back to me if she lived or didn't get locked up by the cops. I think, overall, that's not a bad sign, is it? I couldn't get her to listen to me. If you want details, give me a call. You know where to find me since my wheels are gone."

The third call was from Brad Lonsberg and he was calm, level-voiced, and mad as hell.

"Fonesca, I just got a call from the *Herald-Tribune*. A man named Rubin asked me if there was any truth to the story that my father's manuscripts have been stolen. I did what I always do when I get calls from people who track me down trying to get to my father. I told him I had nothing to say. He said he was about to get confirmation on the story from you. I don't use foul language. If I did, I'd be using it now. If you're trying to gain fame and a little fortune from my father's relationship to that girl, I'll use whatever power I have in this town to have you . . . Let's just say I would be very displeased if you are talking to the press. I don't like publicity related to my father. It's my rear end I'm trying to protect, not his just so you know this is personal. My guess is if this Rubin has called Laura, he got her number from you. There aren't many people who know who or where she is. So, simply, shut up."

There was a double beep and the tape rewound.

I looked at Mickey whose jaw was swollen and at Ames who stood in the same position he had been in.

"Who do I call first?" I asked Ames.

"Flo," he said. "I'm thinking about paying her a visit. She might be up for a little company."

I nodded and punched in the buttons for Flo's number. She came on after two rings with an anxious "Yes."

"Me, Lew. Ames is going to pay you a visit. You up for it?"

"Ames? Anytime."

I put a thumb up for Ames. The melting ice in Mickey's bag shifted with a tiny clack. Mickey groaned.

"Adele say anything else? I mean besides what you put on the machine?"

"One or two things. Just talk about going back to school if she could. Something about not looking for her. She was in a place no one would look. That's it. What's going on?"

"I'm working on it," I said. "If someone from the *Herald-Tribune* calls you, and I don't think they will, just hang up on them."

"I always do," she said.

"This guy's not selling subscriptions. I'll talk to you later."

I hung up, put a little check mark next to Flo's name on my pad, and hit the buttons for Brad Lonsberg. There were four rings before Lonsberg's voice on the answering machine came on and said, "Lonsberg Enterprises. I'm sorry I'm not available at the moment. Please leave your name and telephone number."

"Lonsberg," I said after the beep. "This is Fonesca. My guess is you're sitting there listening to this message. If you want to pick up, we can talk." He didn't pick up so I went on. "I didn't tell this guy Rubin or anyone else about your father's missing manuscripts. He was playing you. Rubin called and left a message for me while I was out. I'm back now and I'm going to call him and tell him nothing. Just so we're clear, I'm working for your father, but my goal in this is to find Adele and be sure she is all right. If the paper or the police connect Adele with the missing manuscripts, she might be in trouble I couldn't get her out of. If you want to call, you've got my number."

I hung up, checked off Lonsberg's name, and looked up at Mickey.

"I'm not going back to his house," he said painfully. "Never."

"I don't know who your grandfather's house goes to or if it's paid for but it might be you," I said.

"Might," he agreed. "I could live there but . . ."

It struck him.

"The cops might think I killed him to get the house?" he groaned in obvious pain.

"Cops think whatever works for them," I said. "It's possible."

"I'll go to Adele," he mumbled, looking down.

"I thought you didn't know where she was?" I said.

"I don't. I'll . . . I'll just find her and we'll stay in the house for a few days and go to St. Louis. I have an aunt in St. Louis."

"You said 'house,'" I said. "She's not at your grandfather's. It's a marked-off crime scene and she's too smart for . . ."

Then it hit me. I looked at Ames. He had the same thought I had. Adele actually owned a house. When Ames and I had found her father's rotting body there less than a year ago, the little stone house in Palmetto had smelled of filth, rotting corpse, and decaying food. The walls were cracking. I knew a realtor was trying to sell it, but it wasn't much of a prize and the neighbors would be only too happy to tell what had happened there, maybe even show prospective buyers a clipping from the Bradenton *Herald* with the house in uncolorful black and white. My guess, given that it was in a poor neighborhood of the very old and very black and the house was ready to commit suicide and collapse, the asking price was probably around thirty thousand, maybe less. Legally, I guessed, the house belonged to Adele now. I found it hard to imagine her going to it after all that had been done to her by her father in that place, but it made some sense. Or maybe it didn't.

I called the *Herald-Tribune* number Rubin had left and he picked it up after one ring.

"City Desk, Rubin," he said.

"You called."

"What is your connection to the missing Lonsberg manuscripts?" he asked.

Good question. He assumed the manuscripts were missing and I was connected. He wanted an answer, but first he wanted confirmation.

"Conrad Lonsberg, the writer?" I asked.

"Yes."

"What makes you think I have anything to do with Lonsberg?"

"A reliable source," he said.

"Your message says the person who told you about all this didn't leave his name," I said.

It was my turn to be clever. I was looking for gender. Rubin, however, was good.

"The caller left no name. Is it true?"

"I'm a process server. Someone's playing games with you. Why don't you just ask Lonsberg?" I asked, knowing there was no chance of getting Lonsberg to say a word, even a single word if Rubin or some TV crew tracked him down at a hardware store or Publix.

"We're expecting confirmation from Lonsberg's son in a few minutes," said Rubin confidently.

"Fine," I said. "Maybe he knows what you're talking about. You ever read anything by Lonsberg?"

"Me? What has that got to do with this?" asked Rubin.

"It's a trick question," I said. "Think about it. Meanwhile, unless you have some papers you want served or someone hires me to serve papers on you, our friendship is over."

"Maybe not," said Rubin. "I read *Fool's Love* in high school. Required reading."

"And? Did you like it?"

"No."

"Did you tell the teacher you didn't like it?"

"She loved it. I'm not an idiot."

"Neither am I," I said and hung up.

My guess was that he wasn't going to get any confirmation about Lonsberg, Adele, and the missing manuscripts. It was also clear that he made no connection between the dead Bernard Corsello and Adele. If he did, a good reporter would have no trouble tying me to Adele's recent and unpleasantly dark life.

"Let's go," I said, standing.

"Need firepower?" Ames asked.

The last time we had gone to the house in Palmetto Ames had been carrying a very mean shotgun.

"Maybe something small," I said.

"Got to stop at the Texas," he said.

"Right. Let's go, Mickey."

"Where?" Mickey asked.

"To Palmetto," I said. "To Adele's house."

"She's not there," he said emphatically. "She's not there. She'd never go there."

Now that he had confirmed to Ames and me where to find Adele, I grabbed my paperback copy of *Plugged Nickels* and we hurried him out of the office. I closed and locked the door and hustled Mickey to the Taurus. Ames sat with him in the backseat till we got to the Texas Bar and Grille. Mickey, his jaw now swollen to the size of a baseball, suggested the need for the nearest emergency room. He looked at the handle of the back door when Ames got out.

"I can't go," he said.

"Because you promised Adele you wouldn't tell where she was and you're afraid she'll be angry."

"Part of it," he said. "I just want out right now. This is kidnapping."

"You can get out," I said. "Got friends? A place to stay? You need a doctor. We'll take you to one unless you want to walk. You probably have something broken in your face. Hurt?"

"A lot," he said, slumping back.

Ames was back quickly. He climbed in next to Mickey and held up a revolver that could well have been picked up as a souvenir after the gunfight at the O.K. Corral.

I drove straight up Tamiami past the airport and through the carnival of malls and fast-food shops on both sides. When we passed Cortez in Bradenton, we went straight up Ninth while most of the traffic veered to the right to stay on 41.

The malls became small shops and Mexican tamale stands. There were places with rooms for the night, week, or month, cheap. The migrant Hispanic workers who picked tomatoes a few miles away filled the street in picking and packing season. This wasn't the season.

We went past the Planetarium and over the bridge across the Manatee River. On the other side was Palmetto. The last time Ames and I had come here, it had been raining. Today the sky was clear.

I had no trouble finding the street and the house where Dwight Hanford had died. It looked a little different. Someone had cleared the yard of beer cans, decaying boxes, and assorted nausea. Where there had been only crumbled stone and shells, there was now grass trying to stay alive. Grass was in a battle with the shells and rock. It looked like the shells and rock were winning.

There was no vehicle parked on the narrow driveway next to the house. Adele was smart. If she was inside, she had probably parked on some side street within running distance but not within sight.

The three of us went to the door. I nudged Mickey ahead of me.

He knocked and called, "Adele."

No answer.

"Adele, I'm hurt."

Still no answer. I tried the door. It was open. We stepped in, side by side in the dining room that had no furniture. Nothing. A roach scuttled across the room.

In the middle of the floor was a small pile of paper.

I picked it up. It looked like two very short stories by Lonsberg, complete with his signature. The title of one was "Guilty Pleasures" and the other "He Shall Have Nothing."

With the stories in one hand, I followed Ames through the almost empty house to the single bedroom. There was a ruffled mattress on the floor in one corner and a note on the mattress. I picked it up and recognized Adele's writing. It wasn't signed.

"If I got this right, Mr. F.," the note said, "Mickey gave me away. Tell him I expected him to and I'm not angry. I expect disappointments. I expect lies. I expect you have the manuscripts in your hand. They aren't short stories. They are the first twenty pages of two novels. *Guilty Pleasures* was once five hundred ten pages. It's now twenty. *He Shall Have Nothing* was once four hundred thirty-six pages. It's now twenty. Lonsberg can have these forty pages. That leaves him about a thousand pages to reconstruct, the thousand pages that went out with the garbage two days ago."

I showed the note to Ames and Mickey. Ames nodded. Mickey looked as if he were about to cry.

"Let's get Mickey to ER," I said. "And then we better make a delivery to Conrad Lonsberg."

11

THINGS ARE NOT ALWAYS as they seem. Skim milk masquerades as cream.

I don't remember which Gilbert and Sullivan operetta that's from but I remember my wife singing it softly in front of the mirror one morning when she was getting into one of her serious suits for the second or third day of a case she was trying. It was a reminder, a mantra for her. I have tried it on myself many times since. It makes more sense each time.

We took Mickey to the ER at Sarasota Memorial and sat in the waiting room while he was being looked at, treated, and then forgotten for about an hour.

While we sat waiting next to a young black woman with two little girls who kept coughing and jiggling, Ames sat back and closed his eyes. I took the paperback copy of Lonsberg's *Plugged Nickels* from my pocket and found Chapter Five to read the section Adele had told me to read. I was becoming an odd literary expert on bits and pieces of known and unknown works by Conrad Lonsberg. I read:

He knew something was just a bit tilted to one side from the moment Abel Terelli saw his child for the first time. On the outside the baby looked perfectly normal. The first burp even looked like a smile. But there was an imbalance Abel felt in the not ugly infant being held up by the smiling nurse. Did the nurse smile every time she held up a baby? How many times had this middle-aged nurse smiled at babies and fathers? Was it a real smile? Did the nurse feel that slight tilt inside the child that Abel sensed?

Abel looked at the baby again. No, the tilt, the lack of balance, lay behind those dark eyes that looked about trying to find something or someone on which to focus. They finally found the eyes of her father and Abel, whose imagination was admittedly undisciplined, was confirmed in his opinion that the living, pulsing parts of the baby were not normal.

"Is she all right?" he called to the nurse through the glass window.

"Perfect," the nurse answered, looking down at the child.

Did the nurse have a checklist of responses? Was "perfect" the best?

Was "fine" something to worry about? What were the other possible answers? "Imperfect, not well, badly damaged." This was the first day in what Abel Terelli felt, was sure, would be the beginning of that which was worse than a nightmare, the living with a worm of uncertainty that would grow.

Abel was an architect, a creator, a young success, with a beautiful wife, a dark-eyed beautiful child. Then why did the devil, Satan, Lucifer, Beelzebub, Belial, Mastema, the Prince of Darkness, the Lord of Lies, the Accuser, the Evil One, place this child before him? Or was it God testing him? Or was it, as was most likely, the fact that Abel Terelli was slowly, slowly, slowly growing mad?

"He'll be fine," came a voice breaking into my reading. I looked up at a male nurse with thin glasses and a shaved head dressed in hospital blues. Next to him stood Mickey who did not look fine to me. He didn't look tilted like the infant of Abel Terelli, but "fine" was not a word I would have used.

Ames opened his eyes and immediately stood up. It reminded me of that great moment in *The Magnificent Seven* when James Coburn is sitting on the ground with his back to a post, his hat over his eyes, and he suddenly ruefully agrees after being goaded into proving that he is faster with his knife than his challenger with a gun. Quick, name all seven of the actors who played the magnificent seven, I thought as Ames rose. Ask me that one for a million dollars.

"Thanks," I said as Ames put a hand under Mickey's arm to hold him up.

One of the little coughing black girls looked up at me and coughed.

"The desk wants to go over payment again," the nurse said apologetically. There was something about the nurse that made me think he was gay. I didn't care. I didn't want to be here. I didn't want to worry about the hospital bills of this confused and broken kid.

I walked to the woman behind the desk. We had fished Mickey's wallet out when we came in and were asked for insurance. Mickey had a Blue Cross/Blue Shield card in his father's name with Mickey listed as insured.

"Just sign here," the little woman in white behind the desk said.

I pushed the clipboard in front of Mickey and handed him the pen that went with it. He signed. We left.

"Do you have anything at home, your father's place, that you have to pick up?" I asked.

"Yes, no. Some clothes. A little money hidden, you know. Other stuff. Most of my stuff is with Adele."

"Your father home now?" I asked.

"He should be at work," Mickey said.

"You meant it about not going back to live with him?" I asked.

"I meant it," he said.

I looked at Ames who nodded and touched the revolver

in his pocket. We headed down Bahia Vista past Mennonite churches and the huge Der Dutchman restaurant and just past McIntosh turned into Sherwood Forest and headed toward the cul-de-sac where Michael Merrymen lived and did battle against the world.

We didn't make it all the way down the street. There were yellow police barricades up blocking the circle at the end of the cul-de-sac. Two police cars were parked just outside the barricade and one was inside the enclosure.

Outside of the Merrymen house three men were talking. Two of them were uniformed cops. One was Detective Ed Viviase. I considered just backing out, but Viviase's eyes came up and took me in. He recognized the Taurus. He recognized Ames and he may even have seen Mickey in the backseat.

There was no choice. I parked. I suggested that Ames park his Buntline special or whatever it was under the front seat. He did and we got out. The three of us walked slowly between the barricades and headed for the house. Viviase, looking even more solid outdoors than in his office, looked up at the sun and then at us as he came forward to meet us.

"I believe in coincidence," he said in greeting. "I really do. Seen plenty of it. But it's not my first choice when I try to explain things. Fonesca, what are you doing here?"

"This is Mickey Merrymen," I said. "He lives in there with his father."

"Wrong tense," said Viviase, looking at Mickey. "Sorry to tell you this, but your father is dead."

"And the dog?" asked Mickey.

"Dead too. Sorry."

"No," said Mickey. "He won't attack me when I go in and get my things."

"You don't seem surprised your father is dead," Viviase said.

"I don't care," Mickey said. "Yes, I do. I feel . . . I don't know the word?"

"Happy?" Viviase tried.

"Relieved," I helped.

"Relieved," said Mickey. "Yes, relieved. My father was crazy. When my mother died . . ."

"What happened to your face?" asked Viviase.

"His father beat him in my office," I said.

"Curiouser and curiouser," Viviase said, looking at Ames who was blankly looking at the house. "When was this?"

"Three hours ago, something like that. I can pin it down if you need it," I said.

"You with him all the time?" asked Viviase. "I mean since the fight of the century in your office?"

"Ames and I have been with him all the time. Took him to Sarasota Memorial ER," I said.

"So, all three of you can account for each other's time for the last three hours or so."

"Yes," I said.

"Michael Merrymen was shot about an hour ago," said Viviase. "Care to guess about the cause of death?"

"Bullet. Nine-millimeter. Matches the bullet that killed Mickey's grandfather and someone shot at me," I said.

"We'll know in a few hours but that sounds about right to me. Merrymen's nose was smashed and he had a few other signs of getting the shit kicked out of him. That happen in your office?"

"I did it," said Ames. "He was beating the boy. I did what had to be done."

"Okay," said Viviase, rubbing his hands together and looking at the sun again. "Anyone know the UV level today? I forgot my sunscreen."

None of us knew.

"Okay," Viviase repeated. "Let's get back to those co-incidences. If you and I are right about the bullet and the gun and you show up here about an hour after Junior Merrymen's unloved gets shot, I've got to ask once again, 'What is going on here, Fonesca?' "

"I'm not sure," I said.

"But you have some idea."

"Ideas," I created. "I suspect everyone but the four of us and I'm not so sure about you."

"Okay," he said, "we go another way. Someone kills Merrymen, his father-in-law, and takes a shot at you. Merrymen's son turns up in your office and so does his father. Vendetta against the Merrymen?"

"Don't forget the dog," I reminded him.

"Pit bull," said Viviase. "People don't like pit bulls."

"People didn't like Michael Merrymen," I said.

"Everyone hated my father," said Mickey. "Everyone who knew him."

"I've looked at his record," said Viviase. "We're talking to the neighbors. I have a feeling we'll wind up talking to half of Sarasota County before we're finished unless . . ."

"Unless . . ." I repeated, knowing what was coming next.

"Unless you tell me what this killer is looking for?" he said. "Someone went through this house. Someone went through Bernard Corsello's house. I've got a feeling whoever it is, is still out there looking. I have a feeling that you know what they are looking for. I have more than a feeling that I'm going to wind up arresting you for obstruction of justice and withholding evidence. It could be worse, your friend with the nine-millimeter might kill someone else and you'll need a very good lawyer."

"I've got one," I said.

"Werring," said Viviase with distaste. "You know how many times his firm has been investigated by the Bar Association for violations of everything from fixing juries to lying about jet lag?"

"I guess a lot," I said. "But he's a good lawyer."

"I need my things," Mickey said.

"Not for a few days," said Viviase. "It just struck me. You've suddenly inherited both your grandfather's and your father's houses and who knows what else?"

"He was with us," I repeated.

"Plenty of money to go around," said Viviase, becoming irritated.

"Did either of them have money or own the houses?" I asked.

"Don't know," said Viviase. "Fonesca, I'm taking Merrymen Junior here. You and Wyatt Earp go away. One more person gets shot or shot at by whoever we're looking for and you will not be a happy man."

"Death doesn't make me happy," I said.

"I'm glad he's dead," said Mickey.

"Son, we have a lot of talking to do and I want to get out of the sun. Let's go in the house and see if maybe you can tell us if something is missing?"

Then Viviase said, "I'll let him call you when and if you can pick him up."

Viviase turned his back on us and walked with Mickey at his side. Ames and I headed back for the Taurus. I stopped at the phone at the gas station at Beneva and Bee Ridge and called Lawrence Werring's office and got his secretary. I told her I wanted to speak to Harvey. She told me I wanted to speak to Mr. Werring.

Werring came on almost immediately.

"Gone out of business, Fonesca?" he asked calmly.

"No," I said.

"Good, then I have papers for you to serve on three people, today."

I couldn't afford to lose Werring's business or Harvey so I said, "I'll be right there."

A hundred fifty dollars wouldn't be bad either. Before I could ask Werring if he could transfer me to Harvey, he hung up. I called back. This time I was allowed to get through to Harvey.

"Lewis," he said. "Challenge me."

I told him what I wanted.

"Make it harder."

"How about having it done in an hour?" I said.

"I accept the challenge," he said.

We went back to my office, stopping at the DQ for burgers and fries. Dave asked if I wanted to finally try sailing next Saturday. Just a test to see if I might like it. Ames was also invited. We both turned him down politely and went up to my office.

Two messages on the machine.

The first was from Rubin, the *Herald-Tribune* reporter.

"Man named Merrymen was just found murdered," he said. "His father-in-law was murdered, too. Merrymen's son knows a girl named Adele Hanford. You had something to do with a case involving the death of a couple of people last year including Adele's father. The same source who told me about the missing Lonsberg manuscripts called ten minutes ago. We'll have a story tomorrow morning. You want to give me a call so we get it right? I'm planning to squeeze your name somewhere into it."

Young man's smart, I thought, and leaned back wanting to tell Ames to walk back to the Texas, wanting to unplug the phone, wanting to watch a western, an old one with John Wayne, Randolph Scott, Tim Holt, or "Wild" Bill Elliott, wanting to sleep without dreaming.

I pushed the button and got the second message. It was from Conrad Lonsberg. He didn't give his name.

"Four o'clock, my house."

Ames had finished his burger and was emptying a container of root beer.

"Feel like going for a ride?" I asked.

He nodded.

We went off to serve the papers. All were for the same case, a civil action about some property in Towles Park. Towles Park, not three blocks from where I lived, had been trying to make a comeback after years of being a small collection of ramshackle old houses. It was now an artist's colony of sorts. The houses repaired and painted bright colors. Shingles over the doors with cute names, even a small restaurant I'd never been to. One of the houses that hadn't made a comeback was the issue. I didn't care.

The first two papers were delivered into the hands of the witnesses or litigants, I didn't know which, within fifteen minutes. Number one was a waitress at the Sunrise Deli on Webber and Beneva. Number two was a Japanese cardiologist on Arlington. Number three had no address, wasn't in the telephone book. Just the name, James Nuttley.

"Know him," Ames said.

"Who is he?"

"Homeless, sometimes. Tried working at McDonald's, Kentucky Fried, Burger King. All dumped him. Ed Fairing tried him as a bartender for a few days. You read Omar Khayyám?"

"Not recently," I said as we drove east on Main Street.

"What does the vintner buy half so precious as that he sells," Ames said.

"Nuttley drank more than he sold," I said.

"Lasted two or three days. Ed gave him a few dollars and walked him out the door. Sun's up, weather's warm. Got a few places to try. Five Points first."

I turned the car around and headed back to Five Points Park. A group of the homeless, a small group, heads down, were sitting on the grass across the street from the Golden Apple Dinner Theater. I slowed down.

"The one with his hands in his pockets," said Ames.

I parked illegally, leaving Ames in the Taurus, and ran over to the small group. Nuttley looked up at me with clear eyes silently saying, "What's the world going to do to me now?"

I handed the folded paper to the bewildered man and hurried back to the car where I filled in the form stating I had delivered all three of the papers.

We brought the form back to Werring's office where his secretary prepared a check and took it in for the boss's signature. She was back in less than a minute.

"New record," she said.

"I got places to go and people to see," I explained. "Starting with Harvey."

Ames and I went down the corridor and into Harvey's computer room. The counter next to him was lined with cans of Sprite.

"I did it in forty minutes," he said, proudly handing me a brown clasped envelope. It felt as if it contained a magazine. "I can probably get more but I don't know what it would be worth."

"We'll see after I read this," I said.

"You just serve some papers?" he asked.

"Yes," I said.

"Dinner at Michael's at the Quay, Friday," he said. "You pay. We can go early and catch the early bird specials."

"If I'm in town," I said.

"I'm bringing a date," he said.

Harvey was a good-looking man and now a sober man. He had told me that he was staying away from women until he felt alcohol-safe. So either he did feel safe or he was taking a chance. Either way, I owed him. I would see if Sally was available.

"Use your phone?" I asked.

Harvey nodded and went back to his computer screen.

I got Sally at her desk after the fifth ring.

"Lew," I said.

"She didn't call," she said. "I'm going to have to turn her in."

"One more day," I said. "I want to go over some things with you first. I've got an idea or something that resembles one. This evening?"

"I'll probably be out on cases or in my office late tonight," she said. "I've got a client and her kids with me right now."

"It's important," I said.

"My office, seven o'clock," she said and hung up.

I checked my watch. Just enough time to drop Ames back at the Texas, read what Harvey had dug up, and get to Lonsberg's.

"Been a busy day," I said to Ames when he stepped out of the car.

"You know where to find me," he said.

I nodded and watched him go into the Texas. Then I opened the envelope Harvey had given to me and began to read. It didn't take long. With the remains of Conrad Lonsberg's two manuscripts and the envelope with the material from Harvey, I got some gas and headed toward Casey Key fairly sure of what was going on now, but needing Sally to fit one more piece together if she could. I needed the world's foremost expert on Adele. Sally was it.

I got to Lonsberg's five minutes late. There was a car parked near the gate, a blue Toyota a few years old. When I parked, a kid in jeans, a white shirt, and a blue blazer jumped out of the Toyota. A camera dangled around his neck. He ran like an athlete and looked like one, a young Paul Newman, but this guy had the nose of my uncle Guiliarmo, big, arched. It gave him the look of a preening bird.

"Fonesca?" he said when he approached, no sign of being out of breath.

"Rubin?" I guessed.

He nodded and took my picture before I could protest.

"Lewis Fonesca in front of Conrad Lonsberg's house," he said. "I've got enough. You want to give me a little more? Your explanation?"

"I'm a process server," I said.

"And you're serving all those papers under your arm to Conrad Lonsberg?"

"No comment," I said, heading for the door.

"You get my message on your machine?" he asked, taking another picture.

"I got it," I said. "No comment."

He took another picture.

"We can deal here," the kid said. "I give you this roll of film if (a) you get Lonsberg to talk to me, (b) you talk to me, or (c) you give me something, documents, something I can go on."

"I like your tenacity," I said, pushing Lonsberg's bell.

"Then?"

"Publish and be damned," I said.

Rubin smiled and readied his camera. I heard the crackling over the speaker that let me know someone was on the other side.

"Fonesca," I said. "A reporter is camped out here. If you don't want your picture taken, don't show yourself when you open the door."

I turned to Rubin who shrugged.

"Tenacity," he said. "Eventually I'll get it."

"You're wasting your time sitting here," I said.

"My day off," he answered. "We're a *New York Times* paper. I can get a story like this on the wire, in the *Times*, byline. Get invited back to my Journalism Department at the University of Missouri to tell how it's done. I like my work, Mr. Fonesca. I'm staying with it."

The door opened a crack and I jumped in knowing Rubin was taking my picture as I did so.

"You're late," said Lonsberg. Jefferson was at his side looking up at me and panting. I thought of the dead pit bull at Merrymen's. I thought of the dead Merrymen. I thought of the shell Jefferson and Lonsberg had given me and I thought of the brown packet and fragments of manuscript I handed him.

We walked back to the house saying nothing. Lonsberg looked at the manuscripts but didn't read them. He took the pages out of the brown envelope Harvey had given me. He scanned a few pages before we reached the house.

Lonsberg's pickup was parked in front of the house. Two little girls were jumping in the back of the pickup enough to make it rock. Jefferson looked at them for an instant and then accompanied us into the house where his daughter Laura sat in an uncomfortable-looking wooden chair with a drink in her hand.

"Mr. Fonesca," she said. "Would you like some iced tea?"

I said I would and she went to get it as Lonsberg took the same chair she had left though there were more comfortable-looking ones in the room. He slowly went through Harvey's report. Laura returned with the tea and handed it to me. I said thanks and we sat watching Lonsberg read as we listened to Lonsberg's granddaughters screaming in the truck outside.

When he was finished, he laid the report on top of the manuscript fragments on a nearby table and looked up at me.

"It's over," he said.

"Over?" I asked.

"Forget about the manuscripts. Forget about finding Adele. I'll give you cash, right now, five thousand, and you walk away."

I looked at his daughter. She looked a bit green.

"It's gone too far," I said. "Two men are dead. Someone took a shot at me and a friend of mine. I think it's someone looking for those manuscripts. But for a man who writes like you do, you keep overlooking the fact that it's Adele I'm after. Mr. Lonsberg, if I don't find her or the police don't find her, Adele could be killed. You could be killed. Your daughter could be killed."

Laura stopped drinking.

"Brad and my grandson are coming for dinner tonight," he said. "We'll all talk about it and get back to you."

"Your son is all right?"

"He's hiding from the press," he said. "In addition, he's got the flu or something, but he's all right."

"Tell him to be careful," I suggested.

"I'll tell him what I think needs telling," Lonsberg said. "You won't stop looking?"

"For your manuscripts? I just stopped looking. For Adele, I've just started looking."

"If you find anything, call Laura," he said. "I'll be in touch with her."

"Okay," I said.

"Okay," he repeated, rising. "I'm in reasonably good health. I've got a book or two and who knows how many stories left before I die. I've got a legacy to work on."

"Then I'd better leave you to it," I said.

"I'll walk Mr. Fonesca to the gate," Laura said.

Lonsberg didn't object. He looked down at the manuscript fragments and brown envelope as we went through the door.

"Nice kids," I said, looking at the two girls who seemed to have lost none of their energy.

"They are," she said as we walked. "I don't think my father has any more books in him. Not now."

"How about an autobiography?" I suggested.

"My father?" She laughed and shook her head. "He'd rather die."

"It would be worth a lot of money," I said.

"Millions probably," she said as we neared the gate. "But you don't know my father."

"I'm beginning to," I said.

"Brad and I will get along without the money," she said. "But my father has this idea of a legacy. I think he feels guilty about not publishing and giving us a life of luxury while we grew up. He'll try to work. Brad and I won't try to talk him out of it. There is no Conrad Lonsberg without his writing. If he couldn't write, he'd look in the mirror and ask himself who he was. I have a feeling he wouldn't have an answer. Or worse, the wrong answers. Were you serious about someone killing people, that we might be . . . ?"

"I was serious," I said.

"Mr. Fonesca," she said.

"Lew," I responded.

"Lew, my real fear is that my father has taken on the same look you wear, depression, despair, weariness."

"We both earned the right to wear it," I said.

"Maybe someday you'll tell me your story," she said.

"Maybe . . . someday. Take care of your father and watch out for yourself and your brother."

I went out the door and she closed it behind me immediately.

Rubin was standing there. The afternoon heat had forced him to remove his jacket and his white shirt was stained with sweat. He took my picture and I moved toward the Taurus.

"I see you don't have those papers with you," he said.

"If you plan to camp out here," I said, "you're in for a long wait. It's my understanding that Mr. Lonsberg isn't going out anymore today or tonight. And if you plan to follow me, I'll make a call to whoever is the editor-in-chief at your paper and tell them you're stalking me. And if that doesn't work, I call the police. Not good publicity for an ambitious young reporter. Besides, I'm going home."

He shrugged. It was a you-win shrug, but one I knew wouldn't stop him from digging. In an odd way I didn't want him to stop. He was working hard. He was working with enthusiasm. He was looking for something like the truth and he wanted to get somewhere in life.

We were direct opposites. I wondered if I had ever been like Rubin. I think I was close once, but that was long ago and far away.

12

JOHN GUTCHEON SAT at the reception desk on the first floor of the three-story Building C in the complex of identical buildings marked A, B, C, and D. The complex was just off of Fruitville and Tuttle. Gutcheon sneezed and wiped his nose with a fresh tissue from the box on the corner of his desk.

Building C housed some of the offices of Children's Services of Sarasota. Buildings A, B, and D had a few empty offices but most were filled by dentists, urologists, a cardiology practice, investment advisers, jewelry and estate appraisers, young lawyers, a dealer in antique toys, and at least three allergists. There are a lot of allergists on the Gulf Coast. John Gutcheon was in need of one or more of them. His eyes were watering and he looked ready to reach for the tissues again.

John was busy on the phone guiding people, giving advice he wasn't supposed to give, directing calls, taking messages, or transferring them to voice mail. A computer sat on a small, precarious wooden platform that slid out of his gunmetal desk and when he wasn't on the phone John

Gutcheon folded mailings and put them into envelopes, copied handwritten reports onto the computer and printed them, or warded off people who had come to the wrong place for help.

"Do you know who that was?" he asked, hanging up the phone and looking up at me as he folded his hands on his desk like a third grader.

"Pete Ward," I guessed.

"Pete . . . ?" Gutcheon said, looking at me with pursed lips in the expectation of a pale punch line.

John Gutcheon was thin, blond of hair, about thirty, and openly gay. He had a sharp tongue to ward off the potential invaders of his life choice and sexual preference and a wary air of conspiracy for those he accepted and who accepted him. I had made the second list but it was difficult for John to keep the pointed words from shooting out like little darts.

"That was Thomas Wardell's assistant," he said, proudly tilting his head down and looking up at me expecting me to recognize the name. "And who is Pete Ward?"

"Was a third baseman for the Chicago White Sox when I was a little kid," I said. "Solid player, go for any ball hit his direction. That was in the days before AstroTurf," I said. "AstroTurf ruined the game, football too. Hitting AstroTurf is like landing on a concrete sidewalk."

"I'm fascinated," Gutcheon said, sniffing back.

"Thought you would be," I said. "Who's Wardell?"

"Wardell Galleries on Palm Avenue," he said as if I should now know from at least the context.

I did.

"Should I be impressed?" I asked.

"They are going to show two of my paintings during the next art walk," he said. "You are the second person to know. Actually, you're the fourth including Alex Wardell, his secretary, and me."

"Congratulations," I said. "I didn't know you painted."

"Sanity behooves me to paint," he said. "They're painting the building. I can't breathe but I'm happy."

"What kind of paint?" I asked.

He looked up at me and sighed.

"Sherwin-Williams or something like that," he said.

"Something cheap. Children's Services is putting up that eight-million-dollar building downtown for offices and meeting rooms for those who lead us in our mission to save the children of this county. The turnover rate of social workers and therapists is a mind-boggle."

He pointed to his computer screen and blew his nose.

"None but those most in need of work or dedicated to the point of insanity stay more than a year. Their caseloads are enormous. Their salaries low. The paperwork is staggering and the work is heartbreaking. So, I take it back. They're not using Sherwin-Williams. They're using something mixed by ex-convicts in a basement somewhere in a vacant office of Building B. God, I sound bitter. It's become a lifestyle even when I've had good news."

"I meant what kind of paint do you use," I said. "On your paintings."

"Watercolors," he said, blowing his nose and wiping his eyes with the back of his hand. "I specialize. Dark, gothic backgrounds, decaying buildings, castles, full moons, dark clouds, dense woods, and always a single bright beautiful flower, usually an orchid so bright in hue that it doesn't need the sun or moon."

"Hope," I said.

"In the flower, yes," he said. "Hope, a little beauty, but even the darkness and decay have a fascinating beauty, at least to me and apparently to some degree to Mr. Wardell."

"Good luck," I said.

"You and Sally are invited to attend, not expected to buy," he said. "My only hope is that they don't have that huge bowl of Hershey's candy kisses for browsers."

"Let's hope. Is . . . ?"

"You're in luck," he said before I could finish my sentence. "She got in about five minutes ago. I think she has a client call in, let's see, about an hour. I'll tell her you're on the way up."

He sneezed.

"Bless you."

"That would be nice," he said, picking up the phone as I headed for the elevator. It was open. I stepped in and pushed the button for the third floor.

Sally was at her desk. She was brushing back her hair with one hand and thumbing through a file thick with papers and reports on her desk. She and the other workers, some of whom were out, a few of whom, male and female, were huddled with clients and their parents or foster parents.

"I'm so busy, Lew," she said. "Court in the morning and I can't find the case study report. Gone, missing. I was sure it was here. Gone. Or maybe I've flipped past it ten times but my mind is among the missing."

"Normal day," I said, sitting next to her.

"Perfectly normal," she said. "Adele?"

"Nothing," I said. "You?"

"Haven't heard from her again."

She stopped going through the papers, put both hands to her hair to try to get it to cooperate, and sat back looking at me.

"Five minutes, Lew. I'm sorry. That's all I've got."

"Michael Merrymen is dead, Mickey's father. Mickey's grandfather too."

"And?"

"I think I know who killed Merrymen and Corsello and took a shot at me and Flo," I said.

"Who?"

I told her.

"Why?"

I told her.

"Now," I said. "If I'm right, how do we get to Adele? How do we stop her? Ames and I can try to protect her but you'll have to put her together when we find her."

"Not 'if' you find her?"

"I'll find her. Maybe you can help with that part, but I'll find her," I said.

Sally nodded. She wore little makeup, still carried a few more pounds than she would like, and had on a serious blue court suit that needed ironing or pressing. She looked serious. She looked dark and pretty, her mouth and eyes large, her cheeks and forehead unlined. Adversity, the loss of a husband, two kids to raise, and a job that could break a hangman's heart didn't destroy her looks or determination.

"Assuming you're right," she said.

"Assuming," I agreed, leaning forward.

I listened to her talk. She let her eyes wander toward the photograph of her children on her desk as she talked, making sense, suggestions, pointing out possibilities, ways I could handle the situation with the least harm to the fewest people. She made sense. It was her job. She did it well. Then she looked at her watch.

"Got to find that case study," she said with regret, touching my hand.

"Friday night I owe Harvey a dinner at Michael's at the Quay," I said. "Can you?"

"No kids?"

"If possible," I said.

"Possible," she said. "I need it."

She got up and glanced around and so did I. She stepped close to me and gave me a kiss. It wasn't long and it wasn't deep, but it was full. There was promise.

"Soon," she said softly.

I knew what she meant. We had been seeing each other for almost half a year. We had never gone beyond some very close fully clothed kisses. The memory of my wife wouldn't go away. Ann was working with me but I couldn't and wouldn't lose those memories, the good ones and the ones of her death. Before I came into her overly busy life, Sally had decided that she couldn't add a close relationship to a man to her existence. Celibacy might not be perfect, was her belief, but it beat the entanglements of a relationship. In some ways, I was about all she could handle or want from a man for now. We were a perfect match. A good-looking widow with two kids, and a short depressed Italian process server losing his hair. God had brought us together.

"Don't take a chance you don't have to," she said.

"I'm not suicidal," I said.

"There are suicides and suicides," she said.

"I've gone a long way with Ann Horowitz," I said. "I don't want to die. I just want to stay depressed and hide."

"Progress," she said. "I've got to get back to the file. Call me."

I said I would as she went back to work. I took the elevator down, waved at John, who was on the phone, and went back to my office.

Marvin Uliaks was waiting at my door. When I got out of the car after parking at the DQ I looked up and there he was waving down at me.

I hurried up the steps and was twenty feet from him when he called, "Find her yet?"

I hadn't found anyone yet, not Adele, not his sister, but I had high hopes.

"I have a good lead on where she is, Marvin," I said, opening my office door.

Marvin followed me in. I didn't turn on the lights, just pulled up the cord on the blinds Ames had installed the last time my window had been broken. There was plenty of sun. This was Florida. Heat. Sun. Rain. Five months of spring. Seven months of summer. Nothing in between.

Marvin wore dark baggy pants and an oversized white T-shirt that had "TITUS" printed in silver, with a picture of Anthony Hopkins in a helmet staring at me when I turned.

"You need more money?" Marvin said as I sat behind my desk and looked at my answering machine. Two messages.

"No," I said as Marvin reached into both baggy pockets. My "no" was emphatic. It stopped him.

"Where is she? I gotta talk to her. I gotta find her. You unerstan'?"

"A few days, maybe a week," I said, thinking that I would have to go to Vanaloosa, Georgia, to find the long missing Vera Lynn to deliver her brother's urgent message.

"A few days. Maybe a week," he repeated softly to himself as if he were trying to commit it to memory. "A few days. Maybe a week. Okay. You sure you don't need money?"

"A few days," I said.

He moved to the door, turned, and stood looking at me.

"A week at most," I said.

"A week at most," he repeated. He kept repeating it as

he went through the door. I remembered the newspaper photographs of Marvin as a baby. I didn't feel like answering my machine, but I pushed the button and heard the voice of Adele.

"Five more, short stories, have been sent to sea on a plastic raft. Tell him. No titles this time. Let him guess."

Then there was a pause. I expected her to hang up but she came on with a different, less confident voice.

"Lew, I don't want to hurt Flo or Mickey. The wrong people are getting hurt. I'll call you back."

I was pretty sure I could hear her start to cry when she was hanging up. That was a good sign. I needed good signs.

The second call was from Richard Tycinker's secretary. Very businesslike she said, "Mr. Tycinker has some papers for you to serve. To be precise, an additional summons for Roberta Dreemer. Come by as soon as you can."

I hung up. All this and Bubbles too. I could turn down the job or call back and say I would need more money to take it on, but I didn't need more money. I needed to never see Bubbles Dreemer again. But I knew what I was going to do. I would have to face Bubbles. My hand went up to my cheek. The only impression I still had of the enormous Bubbles was not the physical one she had given me but a fuzzy, dreamlike, and definitely unpleasant memory of a confrontation I would like to avoid. Why was it that I kept having to face people I wanted to avoid? Question for Ann. I wasn't suicidal but I had to admit to myself that what I was planning to do in a few hours was distinctly a confrontation I would prefer to avoid even more than taking on Bubbles Dreemer.

I checked my watch. Nearly five. Time had grown restless. Maybe I had time to simply grab a burger from the DQ and watch a few chapters of *The Shadow*. It was too early for Joan Crawford or Bette Davis. They were for the nights to hold off the dreams. I needed a jolt of Victor Jory's Lamont Cranston taking on simple evil and hiding his identity.

I called Ames, told him what I planned, and asked him if he wanted to join me. He immediately asked if he should drive over or I should pick him up. I told him I would pick him up. End of conversation.

I went out, locked the door, walked past the DQ parking lot, and crossed 301. I went into the Crisp Dollar Bill. There were a few people at the bar I didn't recognize, both men, one in a suit looking at the drink in his hand, hoping it had answers, the other hunched over, thick, tanned arms flat on the bar. He wore a solid black short-sleeved shirt and a look that definitely said, "Leave me alone."

My booth was empty. I sat deep in the corner listening to Country Joe and the Fish sing about Vietnam. Billy looked over at me from behind the bar where he was busy leaving the muscular guy in the black T-shirt alone.

"What have you got healthy?" I asked.

"Is a steak healthy?" he asked.

"Why not?"

"Onions?"

"Grilled?"

"You got it," said Billy. "Beer?"

"Beck's," I said.

Billy nodded, happy to be doing something instead of pretending to do something. The evening group, never a crowd, was hours away. Billy brought my beer. Country Joe finished singing. The guy in the suit stopped looking at his glass, took its contents in with a single long gulp, dropped some bills on the bar, got off the stool, looked at the door, shook his head, and left.

I was alone with Billy, the bad news black shirt, my thoughts, and now a Mozart string quartet. I glanced at the black shirt whose hands and arms were still on the bar to see if he was a Mozart man. He didn't move. I could see his face dimly in the window behind the bar.

The steak Billy finally brought was thick, rare, and covered with grilled onions. There were fries on the side. I reached for the ketchup and Billy plunked down a second Beck's I hadn't ordered.

"Drinks are on him," Billy said, nodding toward black shirt. "He says he's celebrating."

"He looks it," I said. "Tell him thanks for me."

"My pleasure," Billy said with a perfect touch of small irony.

The steak was good. I ate half the fries, drank the second Beck's, and checked my watch.

Billy was going classical. It seemed to calm black shirt. Three more customers came in. I recognized one, the clerk at the Mexican food market across the street and four or five doors down. His name was Justo. Justo nodded at me and headed for the pinball machine. Justo was about fifty, a purist. No video games for Justo, just pinball. He stacked up his quarters and Billy kept him supplied with whiskey on the rocks.

The pinball game wasn't loud, but it was a pinball game and it didn't go with Mozart. Billy switched to a John Philip Sousa march by the Boston Pops after he had taken all the drink orders.

Black shirt ordered drinks around for everyone again. I didn't want a third beer. I had a killer to deal with and a body built for no more than two beers even with a full stomach.

Everyone lifted their glasses to black shirt who turned his head toward me and said, "I'm getting married."

I nodded.

"I'm celebrating," he said in a surprisingly high voice.

"Congratulations," I said, paying Billy at the bar.

"Yeah," he said with little enthusiasm.

I left, spirits not in the least uplifted.

I had time for one episode of *The Shadow*. Victor Jory disguised himself as a sinister Chinese merchant. The bad guys kidnapped the lovely Margo Lane who screamed at least once a chapter and three times in this one, and a bomb was about to blow up a building where the city moguls were meeting.

The phone rang. I got to it before the answering machine kicked in and picked up. It was Adele, reasonably calm and definitely sure of what she wanted and what she had decided to tell me.

"Did you read the section in *Plugged Nickels*?" she asked.

"Yes."

"Good," she said and then asked me not to interrupt till she had finished what she had to say. I told her I would be quiet. And I was. I knew or had guessed much of what she told me, but there were a few things I hadn't been close to.

"That's it," she said when she was finished.

"Ames and I are on the way to Conrad Lonsberg's now," I said. "They'll all be there. I'll take care of it. Don't destroy any more manuscripts till . . ."

"You trying to make a deal?" she asked.

"No, a request. Hold off. Are you someplace safe?"

"Yes," she said.

"Call me back at eleven tonight," I said. "Thanks for telling me. I know it was hard."

"It was more than hard," she said.

At ten minutes to seven I got up, zipped on my blue jacket, and went to pick up Ames.

He was standing in front of the Texas in his slicker, hatless, ramrod straight. I didn't know what weapon was under his coat but I was sure it was large and formidable. He climbed in.

"Peacefully, if possible," I said.

"If possible," he agreed.

We started driving. I had explained why we were doing it this way instead of going to the police. I definitely didn't have enough evidence for an arrest. I might be able to convince Ed Viviase that there was a reasonably good chance I was right, but the police, the lawyers, wanted evidence or something they could label evidence. And so we drove.

We drove straight south on 41 missing all the lights. Traffic wasn't heavy but there was some. A little red sports car cut us off as we neared Stickney Point Road and then zipped past a big light blue Lincoln and cut it off. The sports car was in a hurry. I wasn't.

We pulled up in front of Conrad Lonsberg's gate at fifteen minutes to eight. I guessed dinner would be over. Both Brad's and Laura's kids were certainly there, but it was a school night. They would be heading home soon. There might be a better way of doing this but this was the most direct. I pushed the button with Ames at my side and waited.

A voice crackled on, "What?"

"Fonesca," I said. "Important."

The speaker went off and we waited. We could see the sun starting to set from where we stood. I tried not to dream about what could have been and to concentrate on what was.

Laura opened the door, one of her little girls at her side.

"Hi," the girl said.

"Hi," I answered.

Ames bowed his head and held up his right hand. The girl giggled.

"Did you find them?" Laura asked.

"No," I said.

"We just finished dinner," she said. "My father's not in . . . well, let's say Brad and I are seeing his dark side when the kids aren't in the room. I've got to get the girls home and in bed and Brad twisted his ankle and doesn't want to be here at all. You sure you want to walk in on this?"

"I'm sure," I said.

Laura looked up at Ames.

"My friend Ames McKinney," I said. "He's keeping me company."

"Come on in," she said, opening the door. "But I don't think the great man's going to welcome this visit. He had me call the editor of the *Herald-Tribune* today to warn them to keep a reporter away who follows my father whenever he leaves the house."

"Rubin," I said, "the reporter's name is John Rubin. He's doing his job."

We followed Laura. Ames chatted with the little girl who switched from a hop to a skip.

"You look like a cowboy," the girl said.

"Never was," said Ames. "But I take that as a compliment."

"You talk like one too," she said.

"Thank you."

We were at the house. There were three vehicles at different angles in front of the house. The second of Laura's daughters, slightly older than the one at Ames's side, was down at the shore with a tall boy, who I assumed was Brad Lonsberg's son Conrad Jr.

"Nice sunset," I said.

Laura looked toward it as if she hadn't considered this possibility before.

"Yes," she said.

"Maybe your little girl would like to join her sister and cousin on the beach and watch it go down," I suggested.

Laura looked at me. There was no doubting now that what I had to say was serious. I wanted the children out of the way. She paused and turned to the little girl.

"Go down with Jenny and Connie," she said. "Contest. Whoever finds the biggest shell wins. You can search till the sun goes down."

"What's the prize?" she asked.

"Five dollars," said Laura.

"Five dollars?" the girl said in openmouthed disbelief.

"Five," Laura repeated. "Bring your biggest when there's no more sun."

The girl went running and Laura opened the door. We walked in. Lonsberg and his son were in the living room. So was Jefferson, who lay on the floor, looked up at us, and then put his head back down to return to his dozing. Brad Lonsberg sat in a chair to the right. Conrad stood, hands in pockets.

"Does it have to be now?" Lonsberg said, looking at Ames.

"If not now, when?" I said.

"Now then," he said, looking at Ames.

"My friend Ames McKinney," I said.

"Good to meet you," said Ames, holding out his hand. "Read everything you've written."

"You mean everything I've had published," Lonsberg said. "Which I hope is not the extent of your reading or the extent of what will be published."

Lonsberg and Ames shook hands.

"This is my son Brad," Lonsberg said.

"Hello," said the younger Lonsberg, still seated.

"Brad twisted his ankle," Laura explained.

"I don't think so," I said.

Everyone looked at me. Two beers and a big steak with

grilled onions were not enough for this moment and I wanted to get it over with quickly.

"You don't think so? About what?" asked Laura.

"About your brother's twisted ankle," I said.

"What the hell are you talking about?" Brad Lonsberg asked, sitting up.

"I think there's a good chance you were bitten by a dog," I said.

"Jefferson didn't . . ." he began.

"Michael Merrymen's dog just before or just after you shot him and Merrymen," I said.

Far away, through the open window of the living room, we heard a girl shriek with delight at the discovery of a large shell.

Brad Lonsberg glared at me, almost motionless.

"I think you should leave, Mr. Fonesca," Laura said firmly.

"I think he should stay," Conrad Lonsberg said softly.

Taking this as an invitation either to coffee and biscotti or to continue, I continued.

"Both murders were committed by someone who apparently and desperately wanted to get your father's manuscripts back before Adele destroyed them," I said. "Whoever killed Merrymen and Corsello."

"And don't forget his dog," Brad Lonsberg said, shaking his head.

"I'm trying to," I answered. "So, who would benefit most by their being found? You and your sister and your children."

"And me," Conrad Lonsberg said.

"And you," I agreed. "No one else could sell them or publish them. They are all copyrighted. Adele might also find a fanatic collector, which I understand exist, but that's not what she's after."

I felt a little like Charlie Chan with a room full of suspects—only it wasn't who had done it that was the mystery but why.

Ames stepped back, probably getting ready for the suspect to pull a gun. Ames was my number two son or one of Nick Charles's alerted cops. Only I already knew who did it.

"Why would Brad kill people to get our father's manuscripts?" asked Laura.

It was the wrong question, but she didn't know that.

"I had a friend check both of your financial records," I said. "Right into your bank accounts. What he found surprised me. I gave the information to your father."

Laura and Brad Lonsberg looked at their famous father who now looked old compared to Ames who stood almost at his side. Conrad Lonsberg looked away.

"Neither of you is wealthy but neither of you is exactly facing poverty or gambling debts or a failing business. In other words, no matter how mercenary you might be, you can afford to wait for your father to die. Sorry," I said, turning to Lonsberg.

"You don't have to be sorry for telling the truth. You might feel sorry for its existence in certain cases."

"What's your point here?" Laura said. "If the manuscripts were gone, Brad and I would have no inheritance."

"Yes," I agreed, "but would you commit murder to save what Adele had stolen?"

"Why not?" asked Laura. "My father's work is very valuable. What if one of us simply wanted to preserve what he has written and damn what they are worth in dollars?"

Through the window again the voice of a child, this time a boy whose voice had already changed, saying, "This is twice as big, midget."

"Could be," I said. "But neither of you has said anything that would support that. You still want the truth?" I asked Lonsberg.

He shook his head "yes."

"What kind of man are you? What kind of father? What kind of grandfather?"

"A little distant," he said. "Eccentric maybe."

"What do you think about your children?" I pressed on, suddenly thinking about my wife, about the children she and I would never have.

"They're very important to me." he said.

"More important than your writing? If someone had said

thirty, twenty, ten years ago. Or today. If you had to stop writing or stop seeing your children and grandchildren, what would your answer be?"

Lonsberg lilted his head just a little to the left and said, "Irrelevant question."

"No," I said. "I think it's part of the reason your son wanted to kill Adele. Want to tell the truth?"

"I'd die without my work," he said, suddenly standing straight.

Brad Lonsberg laughed and shook his head.

"There's your answer, Fonesca. His work over his children."

"It's a decision I don't have to make," said Lonsberg.

"I could have given you the answer," Brad said. "He writes about love, gets into the minds and even the goddamn souls of children. He respects them, almost bleeds for them. Compassion and understanding for the children he created like Zeus from his head. More than for the ones he created with the juice of his body."

It was Conrad Lonsberg's turn to laugh. It wasn't much of a laugh.

"That was a damn good comparison," he said. "You should try writing."

"I did," Brad said with venom. "When I was a kid. I showed you a short story. You looked as if you didn't want to read it. When you did, you gave it back and said, 'Your characters don't come alive.' That was it. 'Your characters don't come alive.' "

"You don't care if Adele destroys the manuscripts," I said.

"I don't give a shit," Brad said. "I'd help her if I could. So, why would I go looking for them and kill people?"

Laura looked at me curiously. Conrad Lonsberg looked at Jefferson who was sound asleep.

"You weren't after the manuscripts," I said. "You were after Adele. You wanted to kill Adele."

"Why the hell would I want to kill Adele? Dad, will you get this lunatic out of here?"

"No," said Conrad Lonsberg.

"Then I will," said Brad, starting to get out of the chair.

He was a big man, in good condition. He would be slowed down by his leg, but I was still no match for him.

"Best sit down again," Ames advised.

"Get the fuck out of here. Both of you," Brad said, starting to sound more than a little frantic.

Ames stepped forward and opened his slicker just like a cowboy in an Italian western. There was a very large gun in his belt.

"You're going to shoot me?" Brad said with a laugh.

"He's done it before," I said.

"He'd kill me because you think I want to kill Adele?"

"Before you got a step away from that chair," said Ames evenly.

"I think all of you know why Brad wants Adele dead," I said. "Why he was looking for her. Why he wanted to find her before I did. He took a shot at me. I'll give you the benefit of the doubt. You were trying to scare me off. Maybe you were just trying to frighten Flo Zink away so you could check her trunk. Did you think she was in there? Maybe at that point you were just looking for manuscripts."

"Say it," said Conrad Lonsberg.

"Adele is pregnant," I said. "The baby is Brad's."

"You're crazy," Brad said, squirming.

"Adele told me about an hour ago."

"If she's pregnant, I didn't do it," Brad said, pointing at himself.

"DNA," said Conrad Lonsberg.

"DNA," gasped Brad, "DNA? How different is yours than mine? If she's pregnant, you're more likely than . . ."

"I used to do research for the Prosecuting Attorney's Office in Cook County," I said. "Your father and you don't have exactly the same DNA. And I think you know it. You wanted Adele dead and hidden before anyone found out she was going to have a baby or could prove it was yours."

"DNA," Lonsberg said. "I'm leaving. I'm taking Connie and leaving. Don't bother me again and, Dad, don't bother calling me again."

This time he did stand up, a little wobbly, and faced Ames.

"You going to shoot me for trying to leave?"

Ames looked at me. He would have had I given him a nod.

"If the dog did bite you," I said, "he has your blood on his teeth. More DNA evidence. And I have the two notes you pinned on my door. The police should be able to match your handwriting."

"Notes?" Brad Lonsberg said, looking genuinely puzzled. "I didn't leave any notes on your door."

I looked at him. His indignation seemed real on this one. He hadn't left the notes on my door.

"Do either of you believe any of this?" Brad went on, looking at his father and sister.

"Before your wife died she left you when she found you having an affair with a fourteen-year-old girl four years ago. My friend with the computer found out," I said. "She filed for divorce. Civil case. Could have been statutory rape but the police never found out or didn't care. No evidence. Your wife died. Divorce proceedings ended. You said she died of cancer. The records show . . ."

"Hit-and-run," said Laura. "Never found who did it."

"We have an idea now," I said. "Don't we? This time we have a damn good idea."

"This time?" asked Lonsberg.

"My wife died in a hit-and-run accident. I didn't want her to. I wasn't having an affair."

"So this is some kind of vendetta," said Lonsberg. "Your wife gets killed in a hit-and-run and so does mine. You blame me and you want me to pay."

"Not for my wife's death. Maybe a little of that too," I said. "I have some sick ideas. I see a shrink. Do you?"

"So Brad wanted to kill Adele to keep from being charged with statutory rape?" Laura said.

"I think your brother loves his son," I said. "Just a guess. The way he feels your father doesn't and never has loved either one of you. You told Adele that," I said, looking at Laura. "Whatever your father has to leave, Brad wants to go to his Connie and your girls. He doesn't want any of it to go to Adele's child and his. That part I figured out, but so did Adele."

"You are out of your mind," Brad said.

The voices of the children told us they were heading back to the house. Brad looked toward the window. Jefferson woke up and looked toward the window.

"I know that," I said. "I told you. I see a therapist twice a week."

"You need one," said Lonsberg.

"That's why I go," I said. "But that doesn't make me wrong. The police might find that nine-millimeter you used in your house. Simple ballistics. You didn't throw it away after killing Corsello and shooting at me. You still need it for Adele."

"They can look," he said and headed for the door.

His father stepped in front of him.

"He's right," Conrad Lonsberg said. "I believe him. I knew she was pregnant. She told me. I told her to work it out with you. I didn't think you'd kill people. I . . ."

"You're an amazing man," Laura said to her father, holding back tears and flashing anger. "You know so much about people who don't exist and nothing about those closest to you who do."

"Genetics or environment," Lonsberg said. "Possibly a combination. Like most talent. I don't know where it came from, haven't spent much time trying to figure it out. So, what do we do now?"

Conrad Lonsberg was looking at me.

"You agree not to disown your grandchild and Brad goes to the police and confesses," I said. "He says he did it to get back the manuscripts. He thought Merrymen had taken them, that Merrymen had a grudge against him. He protects Adele and your grandchild."

"And the world finds out my manuscripts have been stolen," said Lonsberg. "I'll be a prisoner in my house. Or I'll have to move again. B. Traven."

No one asked him who B. Traven was.

"I agree," he said. "She's destroying my family and the manuscripts not only to get back at my son, but to get to me for not protecting her, not standing by her."

"That's something else she told me," I said.

"Then maybe she's right," Conrad Lonsberg said.

The voices of the children were right outside the door now.

"Brad?" asked Laura.

Brad Lonsberg shook his head in agreement. He had only one thing going for him, his love of his son.

"Your grandson is sixteen," I said to Lonsberg. "What month was he born?"

Lonsberg knew where I was going but he answered.

"June," he said.

"Adele is four months younger than Brad's son," I said.

"Let's just go," Brad said. "Now."

"Who tells Connie?" asked Laura.

"Dad," said Brad with some satisfaction. "He explains it all to him. I'll talk to him later. Tell him the truth about Conrad Lonsberg. Tell him the whole truth including what you know and didn't do."

Brad Lonsberg brushed past his father. I nodded to Ames as the children came through the door each holding a big shell, but none was better than the one Jefferson had given me.

"Where you goin'?" asked the lanky boy who looked strikingly like his grandfather.

"Your grandfather will explain," Brad said. "I'll talk to you later. You can go home with Aunt Laura tonight."

"You won't be home?" asked the boy.

"Ask your grandfather."

"I've got the biggest shell," the boy said, holding it out to his father.

Brad Lonsberg took it and said, "This is the most beautiful shell I've ever seen."

Then he looked at his father and went out the door. I followed, barely looking at the two little girls. I would have liked two little girls, a son, a life. I didn't look back at Laura or Conrad Lonsberg.

13

AMES AND I ACCOMPANIED Brad Lonsberg to the police station where he told the woman at the desk that he wanted to see Detective Viviase and that he wanted a lawyer. The young woman, short-haired, serious, in full uniform, told Brad Lonsberg that Viviase was off and wouldn't be back till morning.

I suggested that she call him and tell him that the murderer of Bernard Corsello and Michael Merrymen was there to give a statement.

"The dog," Ames reminded me.

"He killed a dog too," I said.

"Dog?" she asked, looking at the odd trio in front of the desk.

"Merrymen's dog," I said. "Just tell Viviase."

"And who are you?" she asked.

"Just describe me," I said. "He'll know."

"I'm making a flat statement," Brad Lonsberg said. "Just that I killed them. No why. Nothing more. Then I call a lawyer."

"Suit yourself," I said.

"If you get free," Ames said, "I'll shoot you dead on the street."

"He's fond of Adele," I said.

Lonsberg sat quietly, his leg in obvious pain, while the young woman called Viviase. Ames and I walked out. I drove Ames back to the Texas. The late crowd was there and the voices inside were soft.

"Want to take a trip with me?" I asked.

"You need me?"

"Maybe," I said. "Probably not."

"When?"

"Probably tomorrow and the next day," I said.

"What time you want me ready?" he asked.

"Early, around seven."

"That's not early," he said.

"It is for me. Do you want to know where we're going?"

"Makes no matter," he said.

He walked into the Texas and I pulled away.

The phone was ringing when I entered my office. It was eleven on the dot.

I told Adele what had happened and asked, "What now?"

"I don't know," she said. "I don't want his money. I don't want my baby to have any of his money."

"Then you're going to destroy the rest of the manuscripts even though we made a deal?"

"Deals are made to break," she said. "My father taught me that among other things."

"If your father taught it," I said, "it must be wrong."

"I'll think about it," she said. "I'm not sure I believe you."

"Read tomorrow's *Herald-Tribune*," I said. "And meet me somewhere with the manuscripts in two days."

"Why not tomorrow?" she asked.

"I have to go to a town near Macon," I said.

"I'll call you on Monday," she said. "Tell you where to meet me. Can I ask you a favor?"

"Ask."

"Will you call Flo and Sally before they read it in the paper?"

"I'll call them," I said.

"Thanks," Adele said and hung up the phone.

Before I called Flo and Sally I tracked down Rubin at the *Herald-Tribune*. He was there finishing a story for the next day.

"Rubin," I said. "Recognize my voice?"

"Sure," he said.

"I'm not giving you permission to tape," I said, hearing an odd click on the line.

"Okay."

"Go over to the police station right now," I said. "Drop what you're doing. I have a feeling the murderer of a man named Corsello and another named Merrymen just turned himself in."

"That's not my story," he said.

"Find out the name of the killer," I said. "It's your story."

I hung up, called Flo, told her Adele was fine, and then decided it was too late to call Sally. I'd call her early in the morning before she picked up the newspaper.

I opened my desk drawer and pulled out the two notes Digger had seen the monk pin to my door. I read the top one:

STOP LOOKING FOR HER. ONE INNOCENT PER-
SON IS DEAD AND GONE. LET IT BE AN END.
LET THIS BE A WARNING.

It didn't sound like Brad Lonsberg, and Digger, even given his relative lack of connection to the real world, had said the person who had left the note was small. The person had probably been wearing a raincoat and hood, enough to make Digger see a monk.

Some words in the message jumped out at me. "Innocent, gone, her."

It wasn't a warning to stop looking for Adele. It was a warning to stop looking for some other woman. There was only one other woman I was looking for, Marvin Uliaks's sister Vera Lynn Dorsey.

I went to bed. No Joan. No Bette. I had lived and seen enough melodrama for one night. I slept without dreaming and woke early. Digger was back in the bathroom wearing

relatively clean pants and a gray sweatshirt that had "Rat-
tlers" written on the front with a picture of a coiled rattlesnake under it. Digger was shaved and looked sober.

"Rained last night," he explained. "Ran out of the money
you gave me so I had to come here."

I started to reach into my pocket.

"No," he said, trying to stand tall with some dignity
while I stood shirtless washing myself.

"Five dollars for more information on that monk who
left the note on my door," I said, soaping my face and neck.
"Payment for services."

"That's different," said Digger. "What can I tell you?"

"You said the person was short."

"Very short."

"Shorter than me?"

He nodded his head. "Shorter than you."

"Could the person have been a woman?"

"Women ain't monks," said Digger.

"Maybe it was a woman in a raincoat," I said as I finished washing.

Digger looked up and then over at me. "Could'a been.
Sometimes I've got a little imagination."

I rinsed, dried myself with the towel I had brought from
my room, and handed Digger a five-dollar bill. He pocketed
it quickly and deep.

"Thanks," he said.

"You earned it," I said and went back to my office where
I dressed, threw some clean underwear, socks, a clean shirt,
and my razor in the Burdine's cloth bag I had in the closet
and went back out into another sunny day.

I picked up Ames who had a small duffel bag in his hand.
He was wearing dark pants and a long-sleeved blue shirt.
No slicker. No jacket. No visible weapon. He climbed in
next to me and reached back to place the duffel bag on the
floor of the backseat. It dropped a few inches with a metallic clank. I knew where Ames had stored his artillery.

We paused at a 7-Eleven for donuts and coffee and then
headed straight up I75 North. There were a few slowdowns,
once along the Bradenton exits for road construction, and
then near the Ocala exit.

We stopped at a Shoney's for lunch. There wasn't much to say or see on the drive. Trees, a few rivers, exit signs that promised Indian Reservation gambling, clubs that promised nude women twenty-four hours a day, flea markets.

At lunch, Ames finally spoke.

"Adele," he said. He didn't make it a question.

"I talked to her last night," I said. "I'll see her when we get back."

"Is she keeping the baby?"

"I don't know," I said, working on a burger. "She sounded like she was planning to."

Ames shook his head and pushed away the empty plate that had recently held a chicken fried steak and a lot of green beans.

"You think she should abort?" I asked.

"I don't like Conrad Lonsberg's son," Ames said. "Child will be half his. Carry his blood. The girl's barely just sixteen."

It wasn't the position I expected from Ames.

"So, you think she should abort?" I asked.

"Nope," he said, getting up. "I don't believe in killing babies. Maybe she can give it up. Maybe she and Flo can raise it. Maybe it's none of our business."

I nodded. That was pretty much the way I felt.

I turned on the radio to listen to talk shows, voices as we passed the turnoff for Gainesville and later crossed I10. Left for a long time on I10 took you to Tallahassee. Right for a long time took you to Jacksonville. I hadn't been to either one. I had seen almost none of Florida outside of the Sarasota area. This was by far the longest trip I had taken since I had come down from Chicago and parked forever in the DQ parking lot.

Vanaloosa was a little hard to find. It was on the map, not far from Macon, which was a large circle. Vanaloosa, about ten miles outside of town, was a dark dot. We got off of I75 and headed for Vanaloosa.

When we got there it was dark. After asking a few questions at a Hess station just inside the town, we made our way to Raymond's Ribs. The night was dark and the neighborhood filled with run-down homes. The faces we saw in cars and in front of the houses were black.

Raymond's was small, little more than a shack. Four cars were parked in front of it. As we got out of the Taurus, we could smell the rib sauce. It hit me with memories. My wife and I loved ribs. There were lots of rib places in Chicago and we . . . No, not now. A fat black man with a big white paper bag came out the door of Raymond's Ribs as we walked in.

There wasn't much there: a wooden counter, a small area for customers to stand and order, no tables or chairs, and an open grill behind the counter sizzling with ribs being tended to seriously by a small black woman. Serving the customers was an old black man who took orders. There was a phone on the counter.

A young couple and a slight man with a small beard who kept looking at his watch were ahead of us. When it came to our turn, there was no one behind us.

"Can I get you?" the old man said.

"Ribs and slaw for me."

"Same," said Ames.

"Full ribs, half ribs?"

"Full," I said.

Ames nodded. The old man turned to the woman at the grill and gave her our order. She wiped her hands on her work dress and started the order while I started talking.

"You Raymond?"

"That's right," he said.

"Get many white customers?"

"Fair number," he said with clear pride. "We got the best ribs in the county."

"In the state," the woman at the grill said. "Best outside of New Orleans."

"Best outside of New Orleans," Raymond agreed with a smile.

"Last week a white man made a long distance call from your phone," I said.

Raymond stopped smiling.

"I don't remember that," he said.

"The white man who made that call must have paid for it," I said.

Raymond shrugged and looked back at the woman at the grill. She had her head down.

I took the folded Arcadia newspaper clipping from my pocket, unfolded it, and laid it on the counter.

"He's about twenty years older now," I said. "Recognize him?"

Raymond glanced at the clipping and shook his head "no."

"You police?" he asked.

"No," I said. "We're trying to find him and his wife. His wife's brother wants to get in touch with her. Family reunion."

Raymond looked down at the clipping again and thought.

"That's Mr. Cleveland," he said. "Regular customer. Doesn't talk much. Regular customer. Never knew till now he had a wife."

"What's his first name?"

"Don't know," said Raymond. "Comes in once, sometimes twice a week, orders enough for four people, says hi and good-bye, and that's what I know. Here's your order."

The woman placed a white bag on the counter and went back to her work.

"Knives, forks, napkins are in the sack," Raymond said. "Fourteen dollars even."

I paid the bill while Ames picked up the bag.

"We're not here to hurt Mr. Cleveland or his wife," I said. "Her brother just lost contact with her."

Two teenage boys and a girl came in. One of the boys was saying, "Singin'? You call that shit singin'? I call that shit 'shit.' "

"You might try Collier Street," Raymond said softly. "You might ask around. I wouldn't do it at night though. Wait till morning."

"Thanks," I said.

Ames and I left. The teenagers didn't look at us. We went back to a Motel 8 we had passed coming into Vanaloosa. The room had two beds, a television, and a small table.

We watched the tail end of a Will Rogers film on AMC while we ate.

"Good ribs," Ames said.

"Very good," I agreed.

Besides "good night," that was all of the conversation we had before we turned off the lights a little before midnight.

When I woke up in the morning, Ames was sitting in a chair reading.

"I need a shave and shower," I said.

Ames nodded. I looked at the cover of the book he was reading.

It was Conrad Lonsberg's *Fool's Love*.

When I came out of the bathroom clean, shaven, and dressed, Ames, now wearing a loose-fitting gray jacket, stood up, handed me the book, and pointed to a paragraph on page 148.

"Went back to it," Ames said.

I sat on the bed and read the paragraph.

There was no Amy now. There was no Sherry. She sat in the diner with an enormous double order of corn flakes topped with strawberries, drowning in half and half. She thought about who she should be now. She thought about the baby inside her who was just beginning to kick. She needed a name for him or her. She needed a name for herself. Not something exotic. She knew now that exotic just wasn't in her and stylish wasn't in her and New York wasn't in her. And going back to her mother was defeat. She wasn't a quitter. She would never quit. She had six hundred dollars in her purse and two lives inside her. She paused with a big spoonful of corn flakes in her hand and decided. Her name was from that moment Diane Lowell. If the child was a girl, her name would be Laura. If it was a boy, his name would be Bradley.

I handed the book back to Ames who picked up his duffel bag and followed me out the door. It was just after eight in the morning. We had toast, coffee, and fruit at the motel's morning continental breakfast that was served in the lobby. And then we were on our way.

Collier Street wasn't hard to find. It was one of those run-down side streets on which some developer had thrown up one-story white-frame houses back in the mid-1940s for the wave of servicemen coming back from the war and getting married and raising families in whatever jobs were available in Vanaloosa or for commuting to Macon.

Fifty years later, the houses were long past the wrecker. They were occupied by black families where the breadwinners were women who cleaned house for the Macon middle class and businesses. How did I know? Because it looked exactly like neighborhoods I had seen from California to Florida.

The houses were sagging and dead or dying. A few of them had been shorn up and coaxed like punch-drunk boxers into standing up for one more round.

Three little girls were jumping rope when we parked. They were the only people in sight. We could hear them chanting something to the beat of the rope against the cracked sidewalk. The girl doing the jumping was about eleven. She jumped tirelessly and smiled at us as we watched and waited and the girls kept chanting something about babies.

Finally the girl jumped out of the twirling rope and looked at us.

"We're looking for this man," I said, showing the girl Dorsey's photograph. "Know him?"

The other two girls moved in to take a look. None of them recognized him.

"He lives on this street," I said.

"Only white people on this street live over there," the jumping girl said, pointing to a house across the street. "Old white people."

"You know their name?" I asked.

"Them's the Clevelands," answered another girl. "They never go out. But them's the Clevelands."

"He goes out sometimes," one of the other girls said.

"Sometimes at night," the jumping girl agreed. "Not much."

I thanked them and Ames nodded.

Behind us, one of the little girls whispered, "They gonna see the witch."

We crossed the street. The girls went back to their chanting and jumping.

The morning already promised a hot day.

The Cleveland house looked as if it couldn't take another punch. The porch sagged and the paint flecked. The screen door had been patched so many times that it looked like modern art, and the dirt lawn, with only a barren little tree, had long given up.

I knocked at the peeling frame of the screen door. Nothing. I knocked again and heard a shuffle inside. It stopped. I knocked again and the shuffle moved toward the door and then the door opened, but just a crack.

"What?" came a man's voice.

"Mr. Cleveland?" I asked.

"So?" he asked in return.

"My name is Fonesca. This is my partner Mr. McKinney. We'd like to talk to you for a minute or two."

He hesitated and started to close the door.

"It's about your wife," I said.

The door stopped closing.

"My wife isn't well," he said.

"I've got a message for her," I said.

"No," the man said, closing the door.

"Mr. Dorsey," I said, hoping to penetrate with the bullet of his real name, "I think you're going to have to deal with us, either now or tomorrow or the next day. We can keep coming back and draw attention to you or you can let us in and get it over with."

If he hadn't opened the door, we would have left and I would have gone back to Sarasota and told Marvin where she was. But Dorsey didn't call my bluff. The door opened and we went through the screen door into a darkened hall. I could see the thin outline of a man in front of me. He backed away and we followed. When we stepped into a small living room, there was enough light coming through the drawn shades to see that the man was dressed in a badly faded blue shirt and equally faded blue pants. His mouth was partly open and his teeth were bad but they were all there. In his right hand he held a Smith & Wesson .38 with a six-inch barrel, a favorite with cops. Charles Dorsey used to be a cop.

The most striking thing about Charles Dorsey was that I knew he couldn't be more than fifty, but he looked at least twenty years older, older than Ames. His hair was white, his shoulders bent, and his eyes a vacant, faded blue.

"Who are you?"

"My name is Fonesca, just the way I told you."

There were chairs to sit in, even a sofa, but they were old with a washed-out, ghostly pattern and I was sure that dust would rise from them if we sat. Dorsey didn't ask us to sit.

"He sent you, didn't he?" Dorsey said, pistol moving between me and Ames.

"He?"

"Her brother," he said.

"I just want to talk to your wife for a minute," I said.

"No," he said.

Something stirred in the doorway and I turned to the sound of sagging wooden floors. My eyes met the deepest, darkest, and most melancholy eyes I had ever seen. The eyes were set in a soft balloon of a face resting on a huge, neckless, round body. Vera Lynn Uliaks Dorsey walked with a cane to support her mass. Her breathing was pained and labored.

"They're from Marvin," Dorsey said.

Her eyes opened wide in fear.

"He wants to talk to you," I explained.

"Charlie," Vera Lynn croaked.

"We've spent our lives hiding from him, Vera," Dorsey said with almost a sob in his voice. "I'm beginning to think our lives aren't worth that damned much anymore."

With that he gave me his full attention.

"How much is he paying you to kill us?" he asked.

"Kill you? He doesn't want to kill you. He wants to see his sister."

"His sister is dead," Vera Lynn said, sagging into a nearby chair that groaned under her weight.

"Dead?"

"Her name was Sarah. Sarah Taylor," Vera Lynn said. "My parents adopted Marvin. The Taylors adopted Sarah when their mother went mad and killed herself. Arcadia's not that big. We all knew each other."

"Whole family, Marvin and Sarah's mother and father, way back, were a little mad," said Dorsey. "Sarah thought I was in love with her. She said I promised to marry her. She came to my office. Vera Lynn was there with me. We told Sarah that Vera Lynn and I were getting married, that she had to stop bothering me. And then . . ."

"She acted crazy, threatened," said Vera Lynn, her eyes looking beyond me into the past. "I lost my temper . . . I said things . . . and she . . ."

". . . jumped out the window?" I finished. "That's . . ."

"Crazy," Dorsey said. "Sarah had talked to Marvin, told him lies about me, and when Sarah died he blamed us for it."

"And he was right," Vera Lynn said.

"He wasn't," wailed Dorsey. "We didn't know she was that crazy."

"We should have been more gentle with her," said Vera Lynn to no one.

"We've been over it and over it," cried Dorsey. "You want to die now? You want these men to shoot you?"

"I'm past caring," she said. "We ran from him when he came for us in Arcadia, and we ran from every other man he sent for us every place we moved. He found us."

"We're not here to kill anybody," I said, but the Dorseys weren't listening to me. They were off in a conversation they must have had a thousand times on a thousand mornings, afternoons, and nights.

"No more," Vera Lynn said. "No more."

Dorsey's hand dropped slowly as he spoke and the gun pointed toward the floor. I wanted to tell them to forget the whole thing, that I would just go back to Sarasota and tell Marvin it was over. And that's what I would have done if Dorsey had given me the chance to explain. What he did instead was lift his .38 and take aim at me. I read the look in his eyes. It said something like: "Charles Dorsey is no longer in command of this vessel. Charles Dorsey has nothing to do with what's going to happen next. He's somewhere else. When it's over, he'll come back and won't even know what he had done."

"Best put that down," Ames said, showing a gun about twice the size of Dorsey's.

Dorsey looked at the gun in Ames's hand and started to lower his weapon. It fired. Intentionally, unintentionally. I don't know. And then the gun clattered to the floor. Then he started shuffling over to Vera Lynn, who was slumped forward, a rivulet of blood snaking down her once-white dress. Dorsey tried to stop the massive body of his wife from sliding onto the floor. He didn't have a chance.

"She's dying," he wailed. "I shot her."

"She's dead, Mr. Dorsey," I corrected, walking over to him as the body of Vera Lynn Uliaks Dorsey rolled onto the floor.

"I killed her?" Dorsey asked, looking at Ames.

"You did," Ames said, putting his weapon back under his jacket.

"She'd be alive if you hadn't come."

"That's one way of looking at it," Ames said, picking up the .38 Dorsey had dropped by the barrel.

"The phone," I said.

"We have no phone."

Dorsey sat cross-legged on the floor cradling his dead wife's head in his lap. The dust in the house and the taste of death got to me. I went for the door and into the sun. The bright day had gotten brighter. The warm sun had grown hot and the children across the street had stopped jumping rope and were looking at me, probably wondering about the gunshot but maybe not too surprised to hear it in this neighborhood.

Ames came out behind me holding Dorsey's weapon by the barrel.

"You got a phone?" I asked.

"Sure, yes," said the girls.

"Go call the police. Nine-one-one. Tell them there's been a shooting at . . ." I turned my head to look at the number on the house. "Three six two Collier. Can you do that?"

"Sure," said the tallest girl.

She turned and ran into the nearest house. One of the remaining girls called, "Anybody dead?"

"Most of the people who ever lived," I said.

Before the Vanaloosa police arrived, Ames hid his gun in some bushes behind the Dorsey house. Then we came back and we waited. The police were in no hurry to get to this neighborhood. When two policemen in their thirties, one black, one white, trying to show that cop look that said, "I've seen it all," arrived, Ames turned Dorsey's gun over to them and they were careful not to touch the grip.

"Didn't want to leave it where he could get at it," I explained.

He nodded, looking down at the dead woman and the pleading face of the old man on the floor.

"She's a big one," the cop whispered, turning back to us. "What happened?"

"Don't know," I said. "Mr. Cleveland was a friend of my father back in . . ."

"This your father?" he asked, looking at Ames and noting the clear differences between us.

"No, Mr. Minor is just a friend. My father asked me to stop in and say hello. We're headed up to Chicago. We could hear noises when we got to the porch and then a shot. We went in and found them like that."

I nodded at the tableau on the floor.

Dorsey was too far out of it to contradict me or pay any attention. He had been waiting and planning to go mad for almost half his lifetime. His moment had come.

"That the way it was, Mr. Cleveland?" the policeman asked.

Dorsey shook his head "yes," tears in his eyes.

"You shoot her, sir?" he asked.

"I shot her," Dorsey agreed.

The young policeman closed his notebook.

"We'll leave the rest for a detective," he said.

"We can stay around town for a day or so if you need us," I lied. If we didn't have to give up our names or anything that might lead them to us, I had no intention of being anywhere but Sarasota by that night.

"Wouldn't think so," the young cop said. "You didn't actually see him shoot?"

"No," I lied.

"Then . . ." the cop said with a shrug. "This kind of thing happens around here, only they're not usually white and sometimes it's the husband who gets it and most times it's not as clean as this."

I said nothing. Both cops talked for a while.

"All right if we leave?" I asked.

"You know next of kin, any family?" he asked.

" 'Fraid not," I said with regret. "Just a name and an address where I was supposed to stop and say hi."

The cop turned his back on us and looked down at the weeping Dorsey. Ames and I walked to the door at a normal pace and tried to keep from running when we got outside.

One of the little girls, the one who had telephoned, asked, "She dead?"

"She's dead," I said, getting in.

"Ding dong, the witch is dead," one of the girls behind her said. It gave them all an idea. They picked up their rope. This time one of the smaller girls jumped while all three chanted the song from *The Wizard of Oz* turning it almost into rap.

We were back in Sarasota by nightfall. We stopped twice. Once to get gas, another time to pick up a sack of tacos and drinks from a Taco Bell. We didn't say a word on the way back. I dropped Ames at the Texas with his duffel lighter by one gun.

"Sorry about the gun," I said.

"I'll go back for it maybe someday," he said. "Maybe not. I guess maybe not."

I parked in the DQ lot and crossed the street to the Crisp Dollar Bill. The place was fairly crowded, at least for the Crisp Dollar Bill. About a dozen people, drinking, talking, laughing, looking up every once in a while at a tennis match. B. B. King was singing "Ain't That Just like a Woman" above the soundless television as I sat in a booth, not my usual one. That was taken. I was in the one in front of it.

Billy gave me a questioning look and I returned an answering one. He brought me a Beck's.

"Crazy Marvin's been looking for you," he said.

I nodded "yes" and drank some beer. When I looked up a few minutes later, Marvin Uliaks entered, spotted me, and moved forward eagerly to sit across from me.

"Figured I'd find you here when you weren't in your office. Saw that black car you been riding parked at the Dairy Queen."

"You figured right," I said.

"Any luck, Mr. Fonesca?" he asked, squirming.

"Not for Vera Lynn," I said. "She's dead."

"What?"

"You're too late, Marvin," I said. "You can't kill her. She's dead."

"Kill her?" he asked, those eyes wide with confusion. "I didn't want to kill her, Mr. Fonesca. I wanted to tell her I forgave her, about Sarah. I was bad to Vera Lynn a long time ago. I was dumb. I said some bad things to her and Charlie Dorsey. I just wanted to find her and tell her I was sorry. All these years. I didn't know how to find her. I just wanted to forgive her."

"For what she did to Sarah?" I asked over a burst of laughter at the bar and B. B. King now doing "Early in the Morning."

"Yeah," he said. "Now I lost two sisters, Mr. Fonesca. Sarah and Vera Lynn. I lost 'em."

I looked at Marvin and I could see from his battered face that he was telling the truth. Charles and Vera Lynn Dorsey had spent two decades running away from nothing but their own guilt.

"I guess I got no sisters now," Marvin said.

"You've got change coming, Marvin," I said, pulling out my wallet.

He put his hand on top of mine to stop me.

"No favoring," he reminded me.

I put my wallet back in my pocket.

"Let me buy you a drink," I said.

"Just a Pepsi will do," said Marvin, sitting up with dignity. "You got any sisters, Mr. Fonesca?"

"No," I said, trying to get Billy's attention behind the bar.

"Too bad," said Marvin softly. "Too bad."

I hardly heard him. The air was full of music.

14

WHEN I GOT BACK to my place, the answering machine
told me I had three messages. I couldn't listen to
them. I went into my room, took off my clothes, put on
clean underwear, and went to bed. I fell asleep, waking in
the morning from a nightmare I couldn't fully remember
though I knew it had something to do with a huge inflated
white balloon chasing me on a beach. The ringing of my
phone woke me from the dream as something punctured
the balloon. The balloon was still screaming as the phone
rang.

The answering machine kicked in and I could hear
Adele's voice. I got up quickly but was too late. She had
hung up after a very short message.

I fast-forwarded past the three messages before it and
heard Adele's voice say, "Lew, I read the paper yesterday
morning. Meet me at Spanish Point at noon."

My watch said it was a little after eight and the sun
coming through the window confirmed the fact. I turned to
the window and saw Digger's face pressed against it. Being
pressed against the glass actually improved his battered fea-

tures. He was squinting in, looking toward me, leaving fingerprints on the window. I scratched my head and still in my underwear opened the door.

"Is this a bad time?" he said.

"It's a bad day," I said, heading back to my answering machine.

"I brought you somethin'," he said, reaching into his pocket.

It was a white plastic cup.

"Waitress at Gwen's said you take your coffee with cream and sugar," Digger said, holding out his offering.

"Thanks," I said.

"I'm working now," Digger said.

He was, in fact, slightly better dressed than usual. His pants were ancient jeans showing a lot of white and his solid blue short-sleeved shirt was wrinkled. Over the pocket of the shirt stitched in white was "Bobby Jones Golf."

"You're a caddy?" I asked, taking the lid off the coffee.

"No, no," he said, stepping in and closing the door. "Manpower. I signed up. I go to this place over on Fruitville and they send you out on day jobs, loading trucks, packing stuff up in boxes, digging holes. Six bucks an hour. Worked yesterday. They pay right when you come back from a job. Minimum wage, which is all I need."

"Congratulations and welcome to paradise," I said, toasting him with my warm coffee.

"Yeah," he said, what looked like a thoughtful smile on his face.

"You should share the news with your friends."

"I have," said Digger. "My friend who sleeps under the bench in Bayfront Park and you. You're my only friends. I ain't crabbing about that. It's all I can handle. Had too many friends before I hit the skids, the bottle, and the bottom."

"I've got to get to work, Digger," I said.

"Had to give them my name at Manpower," he said pensively. "For a second there I couldn't remember. Been Digger so long. But you should know in case I forget. Name's Ben, Benjamin Kanujian, but don't call me that. Call me Digger. I'm goin' to Manpower now."

"Thanks for the coffee," I said.

"What're friends for?" he said as he closed the door behind him.

I thought it was a good question. I thought about my balloon dream as I listened to my answering machine. There had been that television series, *The Prisoner*, where a big white balloon rolled around keeping people from escaping from an island. That show had given me nightmares when I was a kid. And there was Vera Lynn in her white dress punctured by a bullet from her husband's gun. Maybe I was missing something. I'd check it out with Ann Horowitz if I remembered.

Two of the messages were from Adele, one saying that she had read the article, the other saying that she'd call, which she had this morning. The final message informed me that if I didn't pick up and serve the papers on Bubbles Dreemer this morning, someone else would be found to do it.

I shaved, washed and dressed, and made a phone call.

I was lucky, Clark Dorsey didn't answer the phone, but maybe it wasn't luck, maybe his wife always answered.

"Mrs. Dorsey, this is Lew Fonesca," I said.

"You found them, Charles and Vera Lynn?" she asked almost in a whisper.

"I found them," I said.

"Clark is working on the new room," she said. "I can get him."

"No," I said. "You can tell him or not tell him. It's up to you. Vera Lynn is dead and Charles doesn't want to be found."

"Vera Lynn is dead," she repeated flatly. "How?"

"An accident," I said. "But you were right."

"I was right? About what?"

"You put those notes on my door telling me to stop looking for Vera Lynn, didn't you?"

There was silence.

"I'll tear them up," I said.

"I put them on your door," she said, her voice so low that I could barely hear her. "After Sarah's death and . . . I just didn't want anyone else hurt. I didn't want my husband to go through any more."

"You don't have to tell him," I said.

"I probably won't," she said. "Thank you."

She hung up. She had been right. If Ames and I hadn't gone to Vanaloosa, Vera Lynn would be alive. She wouldn't be in my dreams. She and Charles Dorsey would probably have lived on entombed in that house torturing and supporting each other till she died of obesity or he went crazy.

I picked up a copy of yesterday's *Herald-Tribune* at Gwen's and read Rubin's front-page bylined story as I ate the breakfast special, two eggs, two slices of bacon, grits, and coffee for two dollars. Brad Lonsberg had, according to the story that included separate photographs of Brad and Conrad Lonsberg, turned himself in to the police and confessed to two murders. Brad had given no reason for his actions. I doubted he ever would. The photograph of Conrad Lonsberg was recent. The writer had been snapped as he loaded a bag of groceries into his pickup truck. Conrad Lonsberg was looking directly at the camera with clear exasperation.

There would be many more pictures of Conrad Lonsberg now. He could run or hide but he was surely a hot news item again. *People, US, Time, Newsweek*, the wire services, and the television networks probably had a twenty-four-hour vigil outside his gate.

I finished my breakfast and headed for the trailer park. What I had for Bubbles was a summons for a court appearance. I needed her signature. I did not need a knee in the groin or a fist in my face.

Maybe Bubbles had been part of my dream. Chased by a giant white bubble. I drove into the trailer park across from the Pines Nursing Home, parked in front of Bubbles's trailer, and procrastinated by taking out my notebook and writing what I could remember of my dream and what connections I had made. It didn't take long. I took the court appearance order and my clipboard with the statement requiring her signature clipped to it. I had two black ballpoint pens in my shirt pocket. I approached the trailer looking at the small dingy windows. There was no sign of life.

I knocked and stepped back hoping I could outrun her to my car. I had left the engine running and the door open.

I was about to knock again when she opened the door wide.

"Roberta Dreemer, I've been instructed to give you this summons and to ask for your signature to confirm that you've received it."

She was wearing a faded red T-shirt and a green skirt that didn't match. I readied myself for an attack. I got tears.

"Give it to me," she said, snatching the summons and the board.

I handed her the pen. She cried. She signed and returned the pen and clipboard to me. Then she looked at the paper in her hand.

"I don't deserve this," she said, still crying. "Believe me, I don't deserve this."

"I believe you," I said, stepping back.

"You know a good lawyer?" she asked.

"Depends on what you can afford to pay?"

"I can pay with shit," she said. "Look at this place. You think I've got any money."

"If you want me to, I'll ask around," I said.

"I'd appreciate that," she said sincerely, trying to hold back her tears now.

"That's okay," I said.

I left her standing in the doorway looking at the papers I had given her. I drove away slowly reminding myself of what I often forgot. You never really know what to expect from people.

I drove down Tamiami Trail to Osprey passing Sarasota Square on the way and arrived at Spanish Point at noon on the dot.

I had never been to this particularly historic site before but I knew a little about it from Dave at the DQ who took his boat down here frequently and liked to know about what he was seeing and where he was stopping. He was a walking encyclopedia of Florida coastal history.

More than four thousand years ago, people lived on Spanish Point. There is a burial mound and two middens or shell mounds that contain evidence of the lives of these people. These ancient Floridians fished, hunted, made shell, bone, and wooden tools, fished with nets, cooked their food, and buried their dead. The place was named Spanish Point just after the Civil War by its first white settlers, the Webb family, thousands of years after its original inhabitants were long gone. The Webbs heard about the supposedly beautiful spot from a Spanish trader they met in Key West. The family farmed at Spanish Point for forty years and are buried there.

I parked looking for the white minivan. There was none. I paid my seven-dollar entry fee.

The Point was eventually purchased by the widow of Potter Palmer. In fact, I knew that she and the Palmers had purchased much of the Sarasota area in the early part of the twentieth century. Berthe Matilde Honore Palmer—I got most of this part from the flyer a young woman handed me when I paid the entry fee—built an estate on the Point. In 1980 the Potter family turned the Point over to the Gulf Coast Heritage Association, Inc. That too was in the flyer.

There are more than thirty acres at Spanish Point with jungle walks, a sunken garden, and lots of other things. I skipped the jungle walk and headed for the water in search of Adele. Adele loved the beach. She could lose herself in daydreams when she looked out at the Gulf waters.

It was a hot day. Few tourists. The beach was empty except for me and two women. Waves from Little Sarasota Bay were coming in gently.

Adele was seated cross-legged in the sand near the water's edge throwing small shells into the water. Flo sat next to her wearing a big, broad-brimmed hat, sunglasses, and a blue dress with the image of a dolphin leaping between her breasts. Adele wore jeans, sandals, and a multicolored man's shirt with the sleeves rolled up.

Flo had watched my approach. Adele didn't look up till I was next to them. She was a beautiful girl and while she was gaining weight from the pregnancy, she had lost the last of her baby fat. Her face was unblemished. Her blond hair brushed back, cut short. She was smiling.

"Hi," I said.

"Hi," Adele answered.

"How are you doing, Flo?"

"Clean and sober and, goddammit, signed up for AA." She definitely sounded sober.

Flo was smiling too. They both looked as if they were having a good time. That made two out of three.

"The bastard's manuscripts are in the minivan, what's left of them," Adele said, still cross-legged and looking back into the bay. "I parked the van in the lot at Pine View School."

Pine View was the public school for the gifted in Sarasota County. It was no more than five minutes from where we sat.

"Here," Adele said, reaching into her pocket, fishing out the keys to the van, and flipping them to me. I caught them.

"Good catch," she said.

"I used to play Little League," I said. "Good field. Couldn't hit. I was small so I got walked a lot."

"I'm keeping the baby," Adele said, turning her head back to the water and folding her arms on her knees.

"That's fine, but . . ." I began as Flo jumped in.

"Sally's going to help me legally adopt Adele. She'll become Adele Zink. When the baby's born, Adele's going back to school. I'll hire someone to help and I'll take care of the baby."

"I want to just get rid of the past," Adele said. "Throw it in the ocean, starting with my father's name. I could have gone back to my mother's last name, Tree, but I want to be a different person. I don't want Lonsberg, Hanford, or Tree tying me and my baby to the past."

"Like the girl in *Fool's Love*," I said.

"I suppose," she agreed. "How can someone who can get inside a person's head so perfectly be such an asshole?"

"Conrad Lonsberg?"

"Who else?" Adele said.

"How did you get here?" I said. "To the Point?"

"I drove," Flo said, still smiling.

Flo's license was suspended and Adele had none. I hoped they would make it back to Flo's carefully and wondered who was going to drive.

"Be careful going back home," I said.

"I've got a daughter and grandchild to protect," said Flo. "Can you beat that, Lew? I'm gonna be a goddamn mother and grandmother just like that. I wish Gus had lived to see it."

I knew what I was going to do: drive to Pine View, leave the Taurus, and drive the minivan to Lonsberg's. I'd get past whatever reporters and cameras happened to be there, say nothing, and hope I could get Lonsberg to open his gate so I could drive in. I didn't want to talk to Lonsberg though I wouldn't have minded seeing Jefferson. Maybe he would have another shell for me.

After a day or two I would call Laura. I didn't want to. I didn't want to talk to a Lonsberg again in my life, but she deserved something from me. I wasn't sure what it was. Maybe a chance to thank me. Maybe a chance to say I had ruined her life.

"We've picked out a name for the baby," said Flo. "Adele suggested Gus if it's a boy but I don't think that's a good name."

"No offense," said Adele, "but I'm not too taken with the name Lewis."

"I've gone through phases about it myself," I said.

"So we came up with Ames," said Flo.

"I want to be there when you tell Ames you're naming a baby after him," I said.

"You'll be there, but we're going to wait and see if it is a boy," said Flo.

"We asked Sally if she had any ideas for girls' names," said Adele. She turned and looked up at me. "She came up with a good one, thought you'd like it."

"And?" I asked.

"Catherine," Adele said.

I sat next to Adele. I couldn't stand. Catherine was my wife's name. Sally and Ann Horowitz were the only ones I had mentioned it to.

"You all right?" Adele asked, putting her hand on my shoulder.

I turned my face to the water so she couldn't see it.

"If you don't like the name Catherine . . ." Adele began.

"No," I said, holding back a threatened rush of confusion, gratitude, and tears. "It's perfect."

Turn the page for a preview of
Stuart Kaminsky's latest . .

Not Quite
Kosher

Coming soon from Forge Books

1

YOU SURE?"

Wychovski looked at Pryor, and said, "I'm sure. One year ago. This day. That jewelry store. It's in my book."

Pryor was short, thin, nervous. Dustin Hoffman on some kind of speed produced by his own body. His face was flat, scarred from too many losses in the ring for too many years. He was stupid. Born that way. Punches to the head hadn't made his IQ rise. But Pryor did what he was told, and Wychovski liked telling Pryor what to do. Talking to Pryor was like thinking out loud.

"One year ago. In your book," Pryor said, looking at the jewelry store through the car window.

"In my book," Wychovski said, patting the right pocket of his black zipper jacket.

"And this is . . . ? I mean, where we are?"

"Northbrook. It's a suburb of Chicago," said Wychovski patiently. "North of Chicago."

Pryor nodded as if he understood. He didn't really, but if Wychovski said so, it must be so. He looked at Wychovski, who sat behind the wheel, his eyes fixed on the door of the jewelry store. Wychovski was broad-shouldered, well built from three years with the weights in Stateville and keeping it up when he was outside. He was nearing fifty, blue eyes, short, short haircut, gray-black hair. He looked like a linebacker, a short linebacker. Wychovski had never played football. He had robbed two Cincinnati Bengals once outside a bar, but that was the closest he got to the real thing. Didn't watch sports on the tube. In prison he had read, wore glasses. Classics. For over a year. Dickens, Poe, Hemingway. Steinbeck. Shakespeare. Freud. Shaw, Irwin and George Bernard. Ibsen, Remarque. Memorized passages. Fell asleep remembering them when the lights went out. Then two years to the day he started, Wychovski stopped reading. Wychovski kept track of time.

Now, Wychovski liked to keep moving. Buy clothes, eat well, stay in classy hotels when he could. Wychovski was putting the cash away for the day he'd feel like retiring. He couldn't imagine that day.

"Tell me again why we're hitting it exactly a year after we hit it before," Pryor said.

Wychovski checked his watch. Dusk. Almost closing time. The couple who owned and ran the place were always the last ones in the mall besides the Chinese restaurant to close. On one side of the jewelry story, Gortman's Jewelry and Fine Watches, was a storefront insurance office. State Farm. Frederick White the agent. He had locked up and gone home. On the other side, Himmell's Gifts. Stuff that looked like it would break if you touched it in the window. Glassy-looking birds and horses. Glassy not classy. Wychovski liked touching real class, like really thin glass wineglasses. If he settled down, he'd buy a few, have a drink every night, run his finger around the rim and make that ringing sound. He didn't know how to do that. He'd learn.

"What?"

"Why are we here again?" Pryor asked.

"Anniversary. Our first big score. Good luck. Maybe. It just feels right."

"What did we get last time?"

The small strip mall was almost empty now. Maybe four

cars if you didn't count the eight parked all the way down at the end by the Chinese restaurant. Wychovski could take or leave Chinese food, but he liked the buffet idea. Thai food. That was his choice. Tonight they'd have Thai. Tomorrow they'd take the watches, bracelets, rings to Walter on Polk Street. Walter would look everything over, make an offer. Wychovski would take it. Thai food. That was the ticket.

"We got six thousand last time," Wychovski said. "Five minutes' work. Six thousand dollars. More than a thousand a minute."

"More than a thousand a minute," Pryor echoed.

"Celebration," said Wychovski. "This is a celebration. Back where our good luck started."

"Back light went out," Pryor said, looking at the jewelry store.

"We're moving," Wychovski answered, getting quickly out of the car.

They moved right toward the door. Wychovski had a Glock. His treasure. Read about it in a spy story in a magazine. Had to have it. Pryor had a piece of crap street gun with tape on the handle. Revolver. Six or eight shots. Piece of crap, but a bullet from it would hurt going in and might never come out. People didn't care. You put a gun in their face, they didn't care if it was precision or zip. They knew it could blow out their lights.

Wychovski glanced at Pryor keeping pace at his side. Pryor had dressed up for the job. He had gone through his bag at the motel, asked Wychovski what he should wear. Always asked Wychovski. Asked him if he should brush his teeth. Well, maybe not quite, but asked him almost everything. The distance to the moon. Could eating Equal really give you cancer. Wychovski always had an answer. Quick, ready. Right or wrong. He had an answer.

Pryor was wearing blue slacks and a Tommy Hilfiger blue pullover short-sleeved shirt. He had brushed his hair, polished his shoes. He was ready. Ugly and ready.

Just as the couple inside turned off their light, Wychovski opened the door and pulled out his gun. Pryor did the same. They didn't wear masks, only hit smaller marks that lacked surveillance cameras, like this Dick and Jane little jewelry store. Artists' sketches were for shit. Ski masks itched. Sometimes Wychovski wore dark glasses. That's if they were working the day. Sometimes he had a Band-Aid on his cheek. Let them remember that or the fake mole he got from Gibson's Magic Shop in Paris, Texas. That was a bad hit. No more magic shops. He had scooped up a shopping bag of tricks and practical jokes. Fake dog shit. Fake snot you could hang from your nose. Threw it all away. Kept the mole. Didn't have it on now.

"Don't move," he said.

The couple didn't move. The man was younger than Wychovski by a decade. Average height. He had grown a beard in the last year. Looked older. Wearing a zipper jacket. Blue. Wychovski's was black. Wychovski's favorite colors were black and white.

The woman was blonde, somewhere in her thirties, sort of pretty, too thin for Wychovski's tastes. Pryor remembered the women. He never touched them, but he remembered and talked about them at night in the hotels or motels. Stealing from good-looking women was a high for Pryor. That and good kosher hot dogs. Chicago was always good for hot dogs if you knew where to go. Wychovski knew. On the way back, they'd stop at a place he knew on Dempster in Chicago. Make Pryor happy. Sit and eat a big kosher or two, lots of fries, ketchup, onions, hot peppers. Let Pryor talk about the woman.

She looked different. She was wearing a green dress. She was pregnant. That was it.

"No," she said.

"Yes," said Wychovski. "You know what to do. Stand quiet. No alarms. No crying. Nothing stupid. Boy or a girl?"

Pryor was behind the glass counters, opening them quickly, shoveling, clinking, into the Barnes & Noble bag he had taken from his back pocket. There was a picture of Sigmund Freud on the bag. Sigmund Freud was watching Wychovski. Wychovski wondered what Freud was thinking.

"Boy or girl?" Wychovski repeated. "You know if it's going to be a boy or a girl?"

"Girl," said the man.

"You got a name picked out?"

"Jessica," said the woman.

Wychovski shook his head no and said, "Too; . . . I don't know; . . . too what everybody else is doing. Something simple. Joan. Molly. Agnes. The simple is different. Hurry it up," he called to Pryor.

"Hurry it up, right," Pryor answered moving faster, the B&N bag bulging. Freud looking a little plump and not so serious now.

"We'll think about it," the man said.

Wychovski didn't think so.

"Why us?" the woman said. Anger. Tears were coming. "Why do you keep coming back to us?"

"Only the second time," said Wychovski. "Anniversary. One year ago today. Did you forget?"

"I remembered," said the man, moving to his wife and putting his arm around her.

"We won't be back," Wychovski said, as Pryor moved across the carpeting to the second showcase.

"It doesn't matter," said the man. "After this we won't be able to get insurance."

"Sorry," said Wychovski. "How's business been?"

"Slow," said the man, with a shrug. The pregnant woman's eyes were closed.

Pryor scooped.

"You make any of this stuff?" Wychovski asked, looking around. "Last time there were some gold things, little animals, shapes, birds, fish, bears. Little."

"I made those," the man said.

"See any little animals, gold," Wychovski called to Pryor.

"Don't know," said Pryor. "Just scooping. Wait. Yeah, I see some. A whole bunch."

Wychovski looked at his watch. He remembered where he got it. Right here. One year ago. He held up the watch to show the man and woman.

"Recognize it," he said.

The man nodded.

"Keeps great time," said Wychovski. "Class."

"You have good taste," the man said sarcastically.

"Thanks," said Wychovski ignoring the sarcasm. The man had a right. He was being robbed. He was going out of business. This was a going out of business nonsale. The man wasn't old. He could start again, work for someone else. He made nice little gold animals. He was going to be a father. The watch told Wychovski that they had been here four minutes.

"Let's go," he called to Pryor.

"One more minute. Two more. Should I look in the back?"

Wychovski hesitated.

"Anything back there?" Wychovski asked the man.

The man didn't answer.

"Forget it," he called to Pryor. "We've got enough."

Pryor came out from behind the case. B&N bag bulging. More than they got the last time. Then Pryor tripped. It happens. Pryor tripped. The bag fell on the floor. Gold and time went flying, a snow or rain of gold and silver, platinum and rings. Glittering, gleaming little animals, a Noah's ark of perfect beasts. And Pryor's gun went off as he fell.

The bullet hit the man in the back. The woman screamed. The man went to his knees. His teeth were clenched. Nice white teeth. Wychovski wondered if such nice white teeth could be real. The woman went down with the man, trying to hold him up.

Pryor looked at them, looked at Wychovski, and started to throw things back in the bag. Wait. That wasn't Freud. Wychovski tried to remember who it was. Not Freud. George Bernard Shaw. It was George Bernard Shaw with wrinkled brow looking at Wychovski, displeased.

"An accident," Wychovski told the woman, who was holding her husband, who now bit his lower lip hard. Blood from the bite. Wychovski didn't want to know what the man's back looked like or where the bullet had traveled inside his body. "Call an ambulance. Nine-one-one. We never shot anybody before. An accident."

Wychovski knelt and began to scoop up watches and the

little gold animals from the floor. He stuffed them in his right pocket. He stuffed them in his left and in his right. A few in the pocket of his shirt.

It was more than five minutes now. Pryor was breathing hard trying to get everything. On his knees, scampering like a crazy dog.

"Put the gun away," Wychovski said. "Use both hands. Hurry up. These people need a doctor."

Pryor nodded, put the gun in his pocket and gathered glittering crops. The man had fallen, collapsed on his back. The woman looked at Wychovski crying. Wychovski didn't want her to lose her baby.

"He have insurance?" he asked.

She looked at him bewildered.

"Life insurance?" Wychovski explained.

"Done," said Pryor with a smile. His teeth were small, yellow.

The woman didn't answer the question. Pryor ran to the door. He didn't look back at what he had done.

"Nine-one-one," Wychovski said, backing out of the store.

Pryor looked both ways and headed for the car. Wychovski was a foot out the door. He turned and went back in.

"Sorry," he said. "It was an accident."

"Get out," the woman screamed. "Go away. Go away. Go away."

She started to get up. Maybe she was crazy enough to attack him. Maybe Wychovski would have to shoot her. He didn't think he could shoot a pregnant woman.

"Joan," he said stepping outside again. "Joan's a good name. Think about it. Consider it."

"Get out," the woman screamed.

Wychovski got out. Pryor was already in the car. Wychovski ran. Some people were coming out of the Chinese restaurant. Two guys in baseball hats. From this distance, about forty yards, they looked like truckers. There weren't any trucks in the lot. They were looking right at Wychovski. Wychovski realized he was holding his gun. Wychovski could hear the woman screaming. The truckers could

probably hear her, too. He ran to the car, got behind the
wheel. Pryor couldn't drive, never learned, never tried.

Wychovski shot out of the parking lot. They'd need another car. Not a problem. Night. Good neighborhood. In
and gone in something not too new. Dump it. No prints.
Later buy a five-year-old GEO, Honda, something like that.
Legal. In Wychovski's name.

"We got a lot," Pryor said happily.

"You shot that guy," Wychovski said, staying inside the
speed limit, heading for the expressway. "He might die."

"What?" asked Pryor.

"You shot that man," Wychovski repeated, passing a guy
in a blue BMW. The guy was smoking a cigarette. Wychovski didn't smoke. He made Pryor stop when they'd
gotten together. Inside. In Stateville, he was in a cell with
two guys who smoked. Smell had been everywhere. On
Wychovski's clothes. On the pages of his books.

People killed themselves. Alcohol, drugs, smoking, eating crap that told the blood going to their heart that this
was their territory now and there was no way they were
getting by without surgery.

"People stink," said Wychovski.

Pryor was poking through the bag. He nodded in agreement. He was smiling.

"What if he dies?" Wychovski said.

"Who?"

"The guy you shot," said Wychovski. "Shot full of holes
by someone she knows."

The expressway was straight ahead. Wychovski could
see the stoplight, the big green sign.

"I don't know her," Pryor said. "Never saw her before."

"One year ago," Wychovski said.

"So? We don't go back. The guy dies. Everybody dies.
You said so," Pryor said, feeling proud of himself, holding
G.B. Shaw to his bosom. "We stopping for hot dogs? That
place you said? Kosher. Juicy."

"I don't feel like hot dogs," said Wychovski.

He turned onto the expressway, headed south toward
Chicago. Jammed. Rush hour. Line from here to forever.
Moving maybe five, ten miles an hour. Wychovski turned

on the radio and looked in the rearview mirror. Cars were lined up behind him. A long showroom of whatever you might want. Lights on, creeping, crawling. Should have stayed off the expressway. Too late now. Listen to the news, music, voices that made sense besides his own. An insulting talk show host would be fine.

"More than we got last time," Pryor said happily.

"Yeah," said Wychovski.

"A couple of hot dogs would be good," said Pryor. "Celebrate."

"Celebrate what?"

"Anniversary. We've got a present."

Pryor held up the bag. It looked heavy. Wychovski grunted. What the hell. They had to eat.

"Hot dogs," Wychovski said.

"Yup," said Pryor.

Traffic crawled. The car in front of Wychovski had a bumper sticker:

DON'T BLAME ME. I VOTED LIBERTARIAN.

What the hell was that? Libertarian. Wychovski willed the cars to move. He couldn't do magic. A voice on the radio said something about Syria. Syria didn't exist for Wychovski. Syria, Lebanon, Israel, Bosnia. You name it. It didn't really exist. Nothing existed. No place existed until it was right there to be touched, looked at, held up with a Glock in your hand.

GLUCK, GLUCK, GLUCK, GLUCK, GLUCK.

Wychovski heard it over the sound of running engines and a horn here and there from someone in a hurry to get somewhere in a hurry. He looked up. Helicopter. Traffic watch from a radio or television station? No. It was low. Cops. The truckers from the Chinese restaurant? Still digesting their fried won ton when they went to their radios or a pay phone or a cell phone or pulled out a rocket.

Cops were looking for a certain car. Must be hundreds, thousands out here. Find Waldo only harder. Wychovski looked in his rearview mirror. No flashing lights. He looked up the embankment to his right. Access drive. The tops of cars. No lights flashing. No uniforms dashing. No dogs barking. Just GLUCK, GLUCK, GLUCK. Then a light.

Pure white circle down on the cars in front. Sweeping right to left, left to right. Pryor had no clue. He was lost in Rolexes and dreams of French fries.

Did the light linger on them? Imagination? Maybe. Description from the hot-and-sour soup-belching truckers? Description from the lady with the baby she was going to name Jessica when Joan would have been better. Joan was Wychovski's mother's name. He hadn't suggested it lightly.

So they had his description. Stocky guy with short gray hair, about fifty wearing a black zipper jacket. Skinny guy carrying a canvas bag filled with goodies. A jackpot pinata, a heist from St. Nick.

Traffic moved, not wisely or well, but it moved, inched. Music of another time. Tony Bennett? No, hell no. Johnny Mathis singing "Chances Are." Should have been Tommy Edwards.

"Let's go. Let's go," Wychovski whispered to the car ahead.

"Huh?" asked Pryor.

"There's a cop in a helicopter up there," Wychovski said, looking up, moving forward as if he were on the roller-coaster ride creeping toward the top where they would plunge straight down into despair and black air. "I think he's looking for us."

Pryor looked at him, then rolled down his window to stick his head out before Wychovski could stop him.

"Stop that shit," Wychovski shouted, pulling the skinny Pryor inside.

"I saw it," said Pryor.

"Did he see you?"

"No one waved or nothing," said Pryor. "There he goes."

The helicopter roared forward low, ahead of them. Should he take the next exit? Stay in the crowd? And then the traffic started to move a little faster. Not fast, mind you, but it was moving now. Maybe twenty miles an hour. Actually, nineteen, but close enough. Wychovski decided to grit it out. He turned off the radio.

They made it to Dempster in thirty-five minutes and headed east, toward Lake Michigan. No helicopter. It was still early. Too early for an easy car swap, but it couldn't be helped. Helicopters. He searched this way and that, let his instincts take over at a street across from a park. Three-story apartment buildings. Lots of traffic. He drove in a block. Cars on both sides, some facing the wrong way.

"What are we doing?" asked Pryor.

"*We* are doing nothing," Wychovski said. "*I* am looking for a car. I steal cars. I rob stores. I don't shoot people. I show my gun. They show respect. You show that piece of shit in your pocket, trip over thin air, and shoot a guy in the back."

"Accident," said Pryor.

"My ass," said Wychovski. And then, "That one."

He was looking at a gray Nissan a couple of years old parked under a big tree with branches sticking out over the street. No traffic. Dead-end street.

"Wipe it down," Wychovski ordered, parking the car and getting out.

Pryor started wiping the car for prints. First inside. Then outside. By the time he was done, Wychovski had the Nissan humming. Pryor got in the passenger seat, his bag on his lap, going on a vacation. All he needed was a beach and a towel.

They hit the hot dog place fifteen minutes later. They followed the smell and went in. There was a line. Soft, poppy seed buns. Kosher dogs. Big slices of new pickle. Salty brown fries. They were in line. Two women in front of them were talking. A mother and daughter. Both wearing shorts and showing stomach. Pryor looked back at the door. He could see the Nissan. The bag was in the trunk, with George Bernard Shaw standing guard.

The woman and the girl were talking about Paris. Plaster of? Texas? Europe? Somebody they knew? Nice voices. Wychovski tried to remember when he had last been with a woman. Not that long ago. Two months? Amarillo? Las Vegas? Moline, Illinois?

It was their turn. The kid in the white apron behind the counter wiped his hands, and said, "What can I do for you?"

You can bring back the dead, thought Wychovski. You

can make us invisible. You can teleport us to my Aunt Elaine's in Corpus Christi.

"You can give us each a hot dog with the works," Wychovski said.

"Two for me," said Pryor. "And fries."

"Two for both of us. Lots of mustard. Grilled onions. Tomatoes. Cokes. Diet for me. Regular for him."

The mother and daughter were sitting on stools, still talking about Paris and eating.

"You got a phone?" Wychovski asked, paying for their order.

"Back there," said the kid taking the money.

"I'm going back there to call Walter. Find us a seat where we can watch the car."

Pryor nodded and moved to the pickup order line. Wychovski went back there to make the call. The phone was next to the toilet. He used the toilet first and looked at himself in the mirror. He didn't look good. Decidedly.

He filled the sink with water, cold water, and plunged his face in. Maybe the sink was dirty? Least of his worries. He pulled his head out and looked at himself. Dripping wet reflection. The world hadn't changed. He dried his face and hands and went to the phone. He had a calling card, AT&T. He called Walter. The conversation went like this.

"Walter? I've good goods."

"Jewelry store?"

"It matters?"

"Matters. Cops moved fast. Man's in the hospital maybe dying. Church deacon or something. A saint. All over television, with descriptions of two dummies I thought I might recognize."

"Goods are goods," said Wychovski.

"These goods could make a man an accessory maybe to murder. Keep your goods. Take them who knows where. Get out of town before it's too late, my dear. You know what I'm saying?"

"Walter, be reasonable."

"My middle name is reasonable. It should be 'careful' but it's 'reasonable.' I'm hanging up. I don't know who you are. I think you got the wrong number."

He hung up. Wychovski looked at the phone and thought. St. Louis. There was a guy, Tanner, in St. Louis. No, East St. Louis. A black guy who'd treat them fair for their goods. And Wychovski had a safe deposit box in St. Louis with a little over sixty thousand in it. They'd check out of the motel and head for St. Louis. Not enough cash with them without selling the goods or going to the bank to get a new car. They'd have to drive the Nissan, slow and easy. All night. Get to Tanner first thing in the morning when the sun was coming up through the Arch.

Wychovski went down the narrow corridor. Cardboard boxes made it narrower. When he got to the counter, the mother and daughter were still eating and talking and drinking. Lots of people were. Standing at the counters or sitting on high stools with red seats that swirled. Smelled fantastic. Things would be alright. Pryor had a place by the window, where he could watch the car. He had finished one hot dog and was working on another. Wychovski inched in next to him.

"We're going to St. Louis," he said behind a wall of other conversations.

"Okay," said Pryor, mustard on his nose. No questions. Just "okay."

Then it happened. It always happens. Shit always happens. A cop car, black-and-white, pulled into the lot outside the hot dog place. It was a narrow lot. The cops were moving slowly. Were they looking for a space and a quick burger or hot dog? Were they looking for a stolen Nissan?

The cops stopped next to the Nissan.

"No," moaned Pryor.

Wychovski grabbed the little guy's arm. The cops turned toward the hot dog shop window. Wychovski looked at the wall, ate his dog, and ate slowly, his heart going mad. Maybe he'd die now of a heart attack. Why not? His father had died on a Washington, D.C., subway just like that.

Pryor was openly watching the cops move toward them.

"Don't look at them," Wychovski whispered. "Look at me. Talk. Say something. Smile. I'll nod. Say anything."

"Are they coming for us?" asked Pryor, working on his second dog.

"You've got mustard on your nose. You want to go down with mustard on your nose? You want to be a joke on the ten o'clock news."

Wychovski took a napkin and wiped Pryor's nose as the cops came in the door and looked around.

"Reach in your pocket," said Wychovski. "Take out your gun. I'm going to do the same. Aim it at the cops. Don't shoot. Don't speak. If they pull out their guns, just drop yours. It'll be over, and we can go pray that the guy you shot doesn't die."

"I don't pray," said Pryor, as the cops, both young and in uniform, moved through the line of customers down the middle of the shop, hands on holstered guns.

Wychovski turned, and so did Pryor. Guns out, aimed. Butch and Sundance. A John Woo movie.

"Hold it," shouted Wychovski.

Oh God, I pissed in my pants. Half an hour to the motel. Maybe twenty years to life to the motel.

The cops stopped, hands still on their holsters. The place went dead. Someone screamed. The mother or the daughter who had stopped talking about Paris.

"Let's go," said Wychovski.

Pryor reached back for the last half of his hot dog and his little greasy bag of fries.

"Is that a Glock?" asked the kid behind the counter.

"It's a Glock," said Wychovski.

"Cool gun," said the kid.

The cops didn't speak. Wychovski didn't say anything more. He and Pryor made it to the door, backed away across the parking lot, watching the cops watching them. The cops wouldn't shoot. Too many people.

"Get in," Wychovski said.

Pryor got in the car. Wychovski reached back to open the driver-side door. Hard to keep his gun level at the kid cops and open the door. He did it, got in, started the car, and looked in the rearview. The cops were coming out, guns drawn. There was a barrier in front of him, low, a couple of inches, painted red. Wychovski gunned forward over the barrier. Hell, it wasn't his car, but it was his life. He thought there was just enough room to get between a white minivan and an old convertible who-knows-what.

The cops were saying something. Wychovski wasn't listening. He had pissed in his pants, and he expected to die of a heart attack. He listened for some telltale sign. The underbody of the Nissan caught the red barrier, scraped, and roared over. Wychovski glanced toward Pryor, who had the window open and was leaning out, his piece of crap gun in his hand. Pryor fired as Wychovski made it between minivan and convertible, taking some paint off both sides of the Nissan in the process.

Pryor fired again as Wychovski hit the street. Wychovski heard the hot dog shop's window splatter. He saw one of the young cops convulsing, flapping his arms. Blood. Wychovski and Pryor wouldn't be welcome here in the near future. Then came another shot as Wychovski turned right. This one went through Pryor's face. Through his cheek and back out. He was hanging out the window making sounds like a gutted dog. Wychovski floored the Nissan. He could hear Pryor's head bouncing on the door.

The cops were going for their car, making calls, and Pryor's head was bouncing something out of the jungle on the door. Wychovski made a hard right down a semidark street. He pulled over to the curb. Wychovski grabbed Pryor's shirt, pulled him back through the window, and reached past him to close the door. Pryor was looking up at him with wide surprise.

Wychovski drove. There were lights behind him now, a block back. Sirens. The golden animals lay heavy in his pockets and over his heart. He turned left, wove around. No idea where he was. No one to talk to. Just me and my radio.

Who knows how many minutes later he came to a street called Oakton and headed east, for Sheridan Road, Lake Shore Drive, Lake Michigan. People passed in cars. He passed people walking. People looked at him. The bloody door. That was it. Pryor had marked him. No time to stop and clean it up. Not on the street. He hit Sheridan Road and looked for a place to turn, found it. Little dead end. Black-on-white sign: NO SWIMMING. A park.

He pulled in between a couple of cars he didn't look at,

popped the trunk lock, and got out. There was nothing in the trunk but the bag of jewelry. He dumped it all into the trunk, shoved some watches in his pocket, picked up the empty canvas bag, closed the trunk, went around the side to look at Pryor, who was trying to say something but had nothing left to say it with. Wychovski pulled him from the car and went looking for water.

Families were having late picnics. Couples were walking. Wychovski looked for water, dragging, carrying Pryor, ignoring the looks of the night people. He sat Pryor on an empty bench next to a fountain. Pryor sagged and groaned. He soaked George Bernard Shaw and worked on Pryor's face with the pages. It made things worse. He worked, turned the canvas bag. Scrubbed. He went back for more water, wrung the bloody water from the bag. Worked again. Gunga Din. Fetch water. Clean up. Three trips, and it was done. George Bernard Shaw was angry. His face was red under the dim park lamp.

"Stay here," he told Pryor. "I'll be right back."

Wychovski ran to the parking lot, not caring anymore who might be watching, noticing. He opened the trunk and threw the bag in. When he turned, he saw the cop car coming down the street. Only one way in the lot. Only one way out. The same way. He grabbed six or seven more watches and another handful of little golden animals and quickly shoved them in his bulging pockets. Then he moved into the park, off the path, toward the rocks. Last stand? Glock on the rocks? Couldn't be. It couldn't end like this. He was caught between a cop and a hard place. Funny. Couldn't laugh though. He hurried on, looking back to see the cop car enter the little lot.

Wouldn't do to leave Pryor behind unless he was dead. But Pryor wasn't dead.

Wychovski helped him up with one arm and urged him toward the little slice of moon. He found the rocks. Kids were crawling over them. Big rocks. Beyond them the night and the lake like an ocean of darkness, end of the world. Nothingness. He climbed out and down.

Three teenagers or college kids, male, watched him make his way down toward the water with Pryor. Stop looking at us, he willed. Go back to playing with yourselves, telling lies, and being stupid. Just don't look at me. Wychovski crouched behind a rock, pulling the zombie Pryor with him, the water touching his shoes.

He had no plan. Water and rocks. Pockets full of not much. Crawl along the rocks. Get out. Find a car. Drive to the motel. Get to St. Louis. Tanner might give him a few hundred, maybe more for what he had. Start again. No more Pryor. He would find a new Pryor to replace the prior Pryor, a Pryor without a gun.

Wychovski knew he couldn't be alone.

"You see two men out here?" He heard a voice through the sound of the waves.

"Down there," came a slightly younger voice.

Wychovski couldn't swim. Give up or keep going. He pushed Pryor into the water and kept going. A flashlight beam from above now. Another from the direction he had come.

"Stop right there. Turn around and come back the way you came," said a voice.

"He's armed," said another voice.

"Take out your gun and hold it by the barrel. Now."

Wychovski considered. He took out the Glock. Great gun. Took it out slowly, looked up, and decided it was all a what-the-hell life anyway. He grabbed the gun by the handle, holding on to the rock with one hand. He aimed toward the flashlight above him. But the flashlight wasn't aimed at him. It was shining on the floating, flailing Pryor.

Wychovski fell backward. His head hit a jutting rock. Hurt. But the water, the cold water was worst of all.

"Can you get to him, Dave?" someone called frantically.

"I'm trying."

Pryor was floating on his back, bobbing in the black waves. I can float, he thought, looking at the flashlight. Float out to some little sailboat, climb on, get away.

He floated farther away. Pain gone cold.

"Can't reach him."

"Shit. He's floating out. Call it in."

No one was trying to reach Wychovski. There were no lights on him.

Footsteps. Wychovski looked up. On the rocks above him, Wychovski could see people in a line looking down at Pryor as he floated farther and farther from the shore into the blackness. Wychovski looked for the moon and stars. They weren't there.

Maybe the anniversary hit hadn't been such a good idea.

He closed his eyes and thought that he had never fired his Glock, never fired any gun. It was a damned good gun.

Wychovski crawled along the rocks, half in half out of the water.

He looked back. There was no sign or sound of Pryor.